Amelda felt all thun... ...ge from her father and started ... ...ngs. She felt her cheeks burning wh... ...reached the small jeweller's box. She look... ...d the table with shining eyes, aching to see what was inside and yet holding back the wonderful moment just as long as she could.

'Come on, open it up before he rings,' Llewellyn told her.

'All right!' She took a deep breath then flipped open the lid. For a second her disappointment was like a physical blow. There was no ring. Her fingers trembled as she lifted a gold key from its velvet bed. Tears blurred her eyes so much that she couldn't read the words on the tiny slip of paper rolled up alongside it.

Unable to speak, she passed it over to Llewellyn, who read out: '"This is the key to Morfa Cottage, Betws-y-Coed. Michael."'

AMELDA

The Heart of the Dragon: Book Two

Marion Harris

SPHERE BOOKS LIMITED

A *Sphere* Book

First published in Great Britain 1989 by
Sphere Books Ltd
This edition first published by Sphere Books 1995

Copyright © 1989 Marion Harris

The moral right of the author has been asserted.

Printed in England by Clays Ltd, St Ives plc

ISBN 0 7474 0042 3

Sphere Books
A Division of
Macdonald & Co (Publishers)
Brettenham House
Lancaster Place
London WC2E 7EN

To Keith, Jill and Hayley

1

'Come along now, just one more push, Mrs Vaughan, and it will all be over. Steady . . . steady . . . relax now!'

'Is the baby all right?' Nesta gasped as a thin, shrill cry rent the air. Drenched in sweat and utterly exhausted, she tried to raise herself up on one elbow.

'Just relax. Your daughter is perfect,' the Staff Nurse assured her.

'You did say "daughter" . . . you are quite sure it is a little girl?' Nesta asked anxiously.

'Check for yourself!' The nurse settled the small naked body in her arms. 'Did you want a boy?'

'Oh, no! I've got a boy, Llewellyn. He's fifteen months old. He's lovely, but I've always longed for a little girl,' Nesta said wistfully.

'Well, you've got one now, a little beauty,' the nurse told her as she took the baby from Nesta and placed it on the scales. 'And she weighs in at six and a half pounds. Have you decided what you are going to call her?'

'Amelda. It's a Welsh name.'

Amelda, Amelda! The name sang in Nesta's ears like a melody. She closed her eyes, overcome by emotion. Silently she vowed that this little girl would be cherished and sheltered, surrounded by love. Through Amelda she would relive the childhood she herself had been denied. She would give Amelda all the things she had longed for, and in doing so free herself from the grip of the past.

Amelda! she sighed contentedly, imagining the joy on Gwilym's face when he learned their dreams had come true and Llewellyn now had a little sister.

'Dear little Amelda,' she whispered, stretching out a

1

hand to the crib beside her bed, and letting her fingers trace the outline of the sleeping baby, 'your life will be so very different from mine!'

Not that all her memories were sad ones, she reflected. The early years, when she had lived with her grandparents, had been filled with love and laughter. Best of all had been when her tall, handsome, sailor father came on leave. Those brief interludes had been packed with excitement, highlighted by outings together when the entire world took on a golden magic.

Then, overnight, her life had changed.

She turned her head restlessly on the pillow, trying to forget the next ten years. She sometimes wondered if it had all been a bad dream . . . or happened to someone else. Life, as she knew it now, had really started at the end of the war when she had been discharged from the ATS on compassionate grounds so that she could look after her father.

Idwal Cottage was so small that from a hundred yards away it simply looked like a large rock jutting out from the side of the mountain path. The stone-flagged kitchen was little more than a scullery. A steep, twisting staircase, from one corner of the living room, led up to the two small bedrooms. The view from the tiny windows, though, was breathtaking and one which Nesta never tired of gazing at.

Ever since she had received her Aunt Wynne's letter to say that her father's treatment for TB was completed and he was being discharged from the sanatorium, Nesta had felt that her luck had changed for the better.

Getting her discharge from the Forces on compassionate grounds had been far easier than she had imagined. True the war was over, but everyone said it would be several months at least before even the ATS could hope to be demobbed.

And when Wynne had told Nesta that there was a cottage near them that she and her father could rent, she had felt dazed with happiness even before she had seen it.

With Wynne's help, she turned the cold empty shell into a cosy home in next to no time. Wynne lent her rugs and curtains. They bought second-hand furniture and although none of it matched it didn't seem to matter. When the two armchairs were drawn up to the roaring fire it was home and she and her father spent an idyllic autumn, just enjoying each other's company.

Nesta knew she ought to get a job but felt unable to take such a step until she had news about Gwilym. She had gone on writing to him regularly, all through the weeks after the D-Day attack, and then afterwards when his squadron had been reassigned to fight the Japanese over Malaya. When she heard that he had been shot down and taken prisoner, she still continued to write. And though she had not heard a single word in reply, she was sure he was still alive.

Once she had phoned his home in Liverpool but his parents hadn't heard from him either.

'You will let me know if you get any news,' Nesta begged as she told Gwilym's mother her new address.

Sara Vaughan's reply had been non-committal and Nesta sensed that Gwilym's mother still hadn't forgiven her for postponing the wedding and upsetting all their plans.

She had tried so hard to explain that she felt duty-bound to go to her cousin Chris Jenkins when he was dying and asking for her. Out of all her cousins, he had been the only one who had befriended her after her grandparents had died and she had been forced to make her home with his family in Pontypridd – the only one who hadn't considered her a nuisance and a misfit.

Chris had died almost as soon as she had reached his

bedside and she had turned straight round and come back to Liverpool, believing there would still be time for her and Gwilym to be married before his leave ended.

Looking back, she supposed it was the shock of finding he had already been called for the D-Day invasion, together with the news that her father had been taken into hospital with TB, that had decided her to give up her job in the Land Army and join the ATS. If by completely changing her lifestyle she had thought she could put Gwilym from her thoughts she had been completely mistaken – her remorse at having messed up their wedding day haunted her.

All the time she was in the ATS, moving around from one busy army camp to the next, she longed for the tranquillity of North Wales. For her, nothing could ever replace the grandeur of the mountains and the beauty of the countryside, and the magnificence of the scenery seemed to be enhanced when at last she and her father were able to live there together.

It had been the longest, coldest winter on record and late February before there were tangible signs that spring really was on its way. When the snowdrops pushed up through the frosted bank that rose steeply behind Idwal cottage and the yellow starlike flowers of winter jasmine bravely faced the sharp winds that whistled round the porch, her hopes rose.

As she came home from the village, laden with shopping, Nesta had sensed something was wrong. The cottage had such a deserted air. Even the spiral of smoke from the chimney was a mere thread, as if the fire had been banked down. Yet, when she had set out to do the shopping, she had left it roaring away so that her father could benefit from its warmth as he sat at the table writing letters.

She stopped, resting the two heavy shopping bags on the ground and breathing deeply in an attempt to quell the rapid thumping of her heart. She made an attractive picture: a tall, slim young woman, muffled up against the bitter cold day, her thick dark hair just showing beneath the ear-hugging, red woollen hat, her straight dark brows drawn together in a puzzled frown.

'Da,' she called, as she pushed open the cottage door and stumbled inside with her load.

There was no reply, only an empty, echoing silence. Leaving her shopping just inside the door, Nesta went to the foot of the stairs and called again. Then she saw the note lying on the table.

Anger and frustration mingled as she picked it up.

For a moment she felt too incensed to read it. Her father, going out on such a bitterly cold day the moment her back was turned, might undo all the months of careful nursing he had had since he had come home from the sanatorium. She sighed. She had sensed he was growing restless. Four months of being virtually a prisoner. The roads, so blocked by snowdrifts that sometimes even the postman could not get through, had cut them off from almost everyone. Only Aunt Wynne and Uncle Huw had struggled up the lane each day, even though fresh falls of snow had often made it a treacherous trip.

She knew her father had been longing for the weather to improve so that he could lead a more active life, but to venture out in this, she thought angrily, straightening out the note, was sheer madness on his part.

GONE TO CHESTER.
EXPECT ME HOME BY SIX TONIGHT.

Rhys

What on earth could he be doing in Chester, she wondered as she took off her outdoor clothes. She glanced across the room at the small clock on the dresser. She had been gone

5

for over two hours. Well, there was nothing she could do about it now, she thought resignedly, except have a hot meal waiting for his return.

It was dark and Nesta had already closed the curtains when she heard her father's key in the door. The savoury smell of the rabbit stew wafted through the house, and the table was laid in readiness for their meal. She was about to reproach him for going out in such weather when she became aware that he was not alone.

For a moment she could only gape in disbelief.

The thin, gaunt figure standing a few paces behind him looked more like a ghost than a man. The broad shoulders were bowed, the face almost skeletal with sunken cheeks. The once thick wavy hair was cropped to the scalp. Only the eyes, as green and brilliant as emeralds, were unmistakable.

As they ate, Nesta couldn't take her eyes off Gwilym. Could this thin, emaciated man be the happy laughing young airman she had almost married?

Without his overcoat he looked even thinner. His jacket and trousers hung on his bony frame, his shirt stood away from his scrawny neck as though it was several sizes too large. But it was his face which shocked her most of all. The skin stretched so tautly across the prominent cheek bones was parchment yellow. The only colour in his gaunt face was the vivid green of his eyes which burned feverishly bright, sunk deep into their sockets.

She was conscious of the nervous jerkiness of his hands. He seemed as if he was constantly on edge. Her gaze kept wandering to the close-cropped skull. The skin showed like arid ground beneath a stubble of corn. Down his left cheek was a long gash as though he had been struck or cut, and a shiver went through her at the thought of what he must have been through.

Afterwards, Gwilym told them about his time in the prison camp. The Japanese interrogators had shown no mercy. They had started with minor punishments. Denying their captors water, then food, then sleep.

Day upon day of interrogation followed. They were not allowed to sleep. The guards changed shifts, he told them, but the interrogation of the prisoners went on until they collapsed from exhaustion.

He spread out his thin bony hands to show them his nails, ragged and paper thin now, where once they had been almond shaped, smooth, shiny and strong. Pulling out their nails had been just one more minor torture inflicted when they refused to tell what their captors wanted to hear.

It was Rhys who asked about the scar on his cheek.

'Oh, that!' Gwilym's hand went up to finger the long jagged groove, as he gave a bitter laugh. 'They did that with a whip. I was slow in answering,' he shrugged dismissively, 'not very surprising after thirty-six hours of non-stop questioning.'

'It looks deep,' Rhys said, eyeing it speculatively.

'It was!' Again his fingers moved down his cheek. 'It turned septic and took months to heal. Perhaps I should grow a beard to hide it,' he said wryly, raising a questioning eyebrow in Nesta's direction.

Her heart ached. She felt too choked to answer.

At the end of the meal, she asked: 'Did you get my letters? I wrote every week.'

'Letters! I guessed some of them were from you.'

'So they arrived.'

'Yes!' his teeth bit down on his thin bloodless lips. He laughed harshly, the bitter sound of a man who had known the ultimate depths of frustration. 'Yes, they arrived. We were shown them . . . from a distance.'

'You mean they weren't given to you!'

'That was part of the torture. The promise that we could have them if we would tell them what they wanted to know.'

'But once you had been a prisoner for any length of time how could you know anything that was of any importance?' Rhys asked, frowning.

'They seemed to expect it. Some of the men fabricated tales, told them what they thought they wanted to know. When their stories were checked out and the Japs found that they were lying, they killed them.'

'They what?'

'Not quickly and clearly, you understand. They left them chained up out in the compound in the burning sun, without food and water, for days on end until they went mad from thirst. After that they were usually too weak to bother, even when the guards placed bowls of food and water out in the yard for them. Of course,' he added, his mouth twisting cynically, 'the bowls were always just out of their reach, on other side of a fence carrying an electric current so that when they stretched over it they received a shock.'

When the meal was over, Rhys said he felt tired and was going to his room. Nesta was immediately concerned.

'You shouldn't have gone out, not on a bitterly cold day like this,' she admonished. Then she stopped, as she realised that it was simply an excuse to leave her and Gwilym alone.

After the door closed behind Rhys, Gwilym rose from the table and stood in front of the fire. Slowly, Nesta walked across the room towards him.

For a moment he held both her hands, his vivid green eyes studying her hungrily. She felt self-conscious in her plain brown tweed skirt and red polo-necked jumper. If she had known her father was bringing him home she would have dressed up, worn her new pink woollen dress, with the white lace collar, that she was saving for just such a special occasion.

Her heart thudded against her rib-cage when, with a groan, Gwilym pulled her towards him. As she felt his arms tightening around her, the years of waiting rolled away. A feeling of joyous expectation replaced the aching void she had known for so long.

She reached up to stroke his face, tracing the lines left by pain and suffering, lingering on the cruel scar. As her hands moved higher, her finger tips rasped as they moved over his shorn scalp.

He pulled her closer, crushing her body fiercely against his own. Then his mouth found hers, in a deep, tender kiss that left her burning with need.

His hands were gentle but eager as they began to peel away her clothes, his breathing became rapid as his lips caressed her bare flesh and his desire mounted.

In front of the glowing cottage fire, they whispered their pledges to each other as their long separation was finally bridged.

2

Nesta was watching out of the bedroom window when Gwilym's car pulled up outside Idwal Cottage. As he stepped out and stood there for a moment, bareheaded, looking up at her and waving, her heart skittered with happiness. He looked such a picture of health that it was hard to believe that only three months ago he had been practically scalped and nothing but skin and bone. Now, his broad shoulders filled his brown tweed sports jacket, his face no longer looked drawn and gaunt and the haunted look had gone from his brown eyes. His hair, though still quite short, was thick and wavy, glinting gold in the sunlight.

Nesta took a quick peek in the mirror to check she was still looking her best and smiled happily at her reflection. Knowing that Gwilym was coming she had washed and set her hair so that it swept forward onto her cheeks, a dark gleaming frame to her oval face. She had also added a faint hint of colour to her cheeks, which seemed to make her dark eyes larger and more shining, she reflected with satisfaction.

Her fingers crossed for luck, she sped down the cottage stairs to greet Gwilym.

'Well?' she asked eagerly the moment he had kissed her. 'What news?'

'Which do you want to hear first?' he teased. 'The Good or the Bad?'

'Have the *Echo* given you back your job as a reporter?' she asked anxiously.

'No! They said it would be much too arduous, but . . .'

'Go on,' she urged, sensing from the glint in his green

eyes that in spite of his serious face there was some good news to come.

'They offered me the job of Assistant Features Editor on the *Post*. It's a tremendous step up!'

'Oh Gwilym!' Her relief brought tears to her brown eyes.

'There's just one proviso,' he added sternly. 'They said it was really a job for a married man.'

'So what did you tell them?' she asked, biting her lower lip to stop from laughing.

'I said I thought that could probably be arranged. What do you think?'

'Are you proposing . . . again?'

Gwilym didn't bother to reply. He swept her into his arms and her heart raced with happiness as he hugged her until they were both breathless.

'I start a week next Monday,' he told her as they went indoors to tell her father their news. 'I know it's going to be a bit of a rush, but, he tapped his pocket significantly, I haven't wasted any time; I've got a special licence.'

'You mean we should get married *before* you start work?' Nesta gasped.

'It might be difficult to fit it in afterwards. Gwilym can hardly ask for time off the moment he starts the job,' Rhys opined. 'Any idea about where you are going to live?'

'That's all fixed up,' Gwilym assured him. 'I've managed to rent a furnished flat in New Brighton. It's not too far to travel each day. I can take the ferry across to Liverpool and walk from the Pier Head to the *Post* offices.'

'Sounds fine!'

'Hold it a minute, you two,' Nesta said heatedly. 'Who said I was going to leave here? You are not fit to look after yourself yet, Da!' she added lamely, her brown gaze scanning his sparse frame and pallid face. He still looked like a man who had been desperately ill.

'I can manage all right. I've done so for years . . . and

without the comfort of a home of my own,' he told her bluntly. 'As it is, I have everything I need here, and Wynne is only a hundred yards down the road. She'll be popping in and out by the minute, you can be sure of that. I probably won't get a moment's peace.'

'We're not going to be all that far away, Nesta,' Gwilym reassured her. 'The flat does have two bedrooms so your father can come and stay any time he likes.'

'A stroke of luck, managing to rent a place, I would say,' Rhys agreed. 'Take no notice, Gwilym. It's too much for her to take in all at once. A job, proposal and a new home all in one breath . . .'

The next few days proved as hectic as any Nesta had ever known.

Her anxiety about leaving her father to fend for himself seemed to magnify itself after she went to bed at night. For what seemed to be hours, she would toss and turn, worrying about whether or not she was doing the right thing.

If only she could have talked the problem through with Gwilym it would have been so much easier, but whenever she brought the subject up he simply dismissed it with a shrug of his broad shoulders.

'He's already told you he can take care of himself. He's probably looking forward to being on his own.'

'But he's still a semi-invalid. He needs proper meals and . . .'

'And Huw and Wynne will see that he gets them. You can't spend the rest of your life playing nursemaid . . . or feeling guilty.'

Although he had said it in a light, teasing voice, Nesta caught the undercurrent of warning in Gwilym's tone. She felt her colour rising, remembering the harshness of his voice the last time he had used the same expression, when she had postponed their wedding so that she could go to her cousin Chris's bedside.

She couldn't call off the ceremony a second time.

As it was, Mr and Mrs Vaughan seemed sceptical about Gwilym marrying her. They refused to be involved in any of the arrangements, although they did agree to attend. The wedding was to be held at the Chester registry office and Gwilym had booked a meal for them all at the Crown Hotel afterwards. He and Nesta were to stay on at the hotel overnight and then, next day, move into their flat.

Nesta was not at all sure that she would like living in the centre of a town again. After she had moved from Cardiff to the splendid isolation of North Wales, she had vowed she never wanted to live anywhere else.

Now she tried to convince herself that the flat at the top of a three-storey Victorian house was a compromise. The windows at the front looked down onto the promenade and New Brighton pier. Directly opposite, on the other side of the Mersey, was Liverpool, its waterfront dominating the skyline. And away to the left, there were dark purple smudges on the horizon which Gwilym assured her were the Welsh mountains.

The flat had two bedrooms, a fair-sized, comfortably furnished living room and the smallest kitchen she had ever seen, but, by way of compensation, it had a gleaming new gas stove. The novelty of not having to cope with the eccentricities of a temperamental open range filled her with delight.

'I won't know what to do with myself all day, with no fires to stoke up,' she told Gwilym.

'Cooking, cleaning, and queuing at the shops for our rations, will keep you busy,' he laughed.

She had only a few days to shop for her wedding dress, and the right hat to wear with it. A superstitious streak prevented her from wearing the blue suit Wynne and Huw had bought her as a wedding outfit for the ceremony that should have taken place two years earlier. This time she chose a flowered dress and wore a short

13

cream linen jacket over it. Her cream hat was trimmed with a full-blown rose and she carried a posy of pink rosebuds.

Huw, Wynne and Rhys travelled with Nesta in the hired car, but from the stilted conversation during the long drive they might as well have all been strangers.

Huw, sitting in front with the driver, fingered his unaccustomed tight collar, turning his head from side to side uncomfortably.

Wynne sat immediately behind him, bolt upright as if afraid of creasing her neat grey suit, the feather on her white hat crushed against the roof of the car.

Only Rhys Evans seemed relaxed and enjoying the view as they motored towards Chester. His dark suit emphasised his pallor, but there was natural colour in his cheeks, not the scarlet flush of the consumptive.

Nesta's conflicting loyalty to her father and her love for Gwilym tore her apart. And Gwilym refused to discuss it.

'We've been over this before,' he reminded her when she tried to confide in him. 'It's that damn Catholic upbringing of yours. Nothing I say will make any difference. You have to sort it out with yourself. Your problem is that you have an over-active conscience. I wonder you don't want us to be married in a Catholic church. In their eyes you'll be "living in sin" if you get married in a registry office,' he reminded her.

'I haven't been a practising Catholic since I was a child, and you know it,' she defended hotly.

'You might have given up going to Mass, and all the rest of it, but your conscience hasn't,' he laughed. 'Unless you take yourself in hand you are going to be guilt-ridden for the rest of your life,' he scolded.

She knew he was right. The thought that perhaps if she regarded marrying Gwilym as some sort of duty the feeling would go away, brought a half-smile to her lips.

Gwilym's parents arrived at the registry office just minutes after they did. Goronwy Vaughan had put on a lot of weight since Nesta had last seen him and his portly figure seemed to be bursting out of his dark mohair suit. She noticed, too, that his hair was now almost silver. His grey eyes, though, were still just as sharp and hard as she remembered.

Gwilym's mother, on the other hand, looked even younger than she had last time they met. She was wearing an elegant 'New Look' dress, in pale turquoise blue that almost matched her sea-blue eyes, under a hip-length honey-coloured Ranch Mink fur coat. Her light green hair was swept up in a mass of carefully arranged curls. Her heavy make-up was flawless and in her cream, high-heeled shoes she looked extremely elegant.

Despite Nesta's initial forebodings, the ceremony went smoothly and by the time they were all sitting down to their meal everyone seemed to be in a happy, relaxed mood. Any ill-will that Sara and Goronwy Vaughan may have harboured from the previous encounter was quickly drowned in champagne.

After the usual toasts, Rhys insisted that they should fill their glasses once more.

'To your future happiness and a fresh start in life,' he proclaimed, raising his glass towards Nesta and Gwilym. 'Most of us regard the saying "this is the first day of the rest of your life" as rather trite, but in this instance I think we will all agree, it has very real significance.' His gaze fastened on Nesta and she felt it was as if he was hypnotising her, willing her into discarding the past and starting anew.

She felt strength flow into her, dispelling her last lingering doubts, as Gwilym's hand tightened over hers, and she knew he whole-heartedly condoned her father's sentiments. With a tremendous physical effort she transferred her gaze from her father to her new husband. It was like severing an invisible chain. Once free of the dark hypnotic hold the tenseness lessened, her muscles relaxed, and the guilt ebbed away. She looked up at Gwilym as his arm encircled her waist and felt a surge of happiness as she saw her reflection mirrored in the clear green depths of his eyes.

Her father was right; it was going to be a completely different life. Silently she vowed there would be no more remorse or feelings of guilt, no hankering back to the past. Gwilym would be her new strength and in no way would she fail him.

As the small party broke up, Goronwy and Sara Vaughan to return to their opulent home outside Liverpool, Huw, Wynne and her father to their cottages in North Wales, Nesta stood with her arm linked through Gwilym's, in happy anticipation of the final culmination of her wedding day.

The large bedroom was well appointed, but she barely noticed the deep pile golden carpet or the gold velvet curtains that contrasted so delightfully with the powder blue, quilted satin bedspread. All she was conscious of was that at long last she and Gwilym were man and wife.

They clung together, murmuring each other's names and meaningless words of endearment. Then, as their fleeting kisses became more and more impassioned their craving for deeper fulfilment became stronger. With deft, eager fingers, Gwilym unfastened her dress, easing it from her shoulders until it slithered down over the gossamer fine nylon slip she wore beneath it, and lay in a heap around her ankles. His mouth still covering hers, he lifted her bodily and carried her across to the bed. Tenderly he removed the rest of her clothes, saluting each newly exposed area with his lips.

'You are truly beautiful, my darling,' he whispered huskily as he peeled away the frothy nylon.

16

Swiftly, and without ceremony, he shed his own clothes, his eyes never leaving her. Then he was on the bed beside her, his hands stroking the contours of her smooth body, his burning lips moving slowly down the curve of her throat to the well-formed pouting breasts. As he took the pertly prominent tips between his lips, Nesta felt her stomach tighten with expectancy. Sharp stabs of pleasure coursed through her as his hand gently but firmly slipped between her thighs. Desire flooded through her as she arched towards him and of her own volition her own hand began exploring the length and breadth of his body. She caught her breath sharply as her exploring fingers touched the series of weals on his back and buttocks, permanent reminders of the beatings he had endured in the Japanese POW camp.

The memory was fleeting and was forgotten as they found fulfilment in their urgent need for each other; only the present mattered.

Their bodies united, consolidating into a rhythm that brought wave after wave of pleasure flowing between them. Exhausted and spent, utterly fulfilled, they slept, cradled together, limbs entwined, his head pillowed against the softness of her breasts.

Nesta settled into her new way of life very quickly. There was always something happening so she had no time to feel lonely.

From their living-room windows she could look out over the wide promenade, usually packed with holiday-makers now that it was summer, and watch the busy stream of ships being tugged up and down the Mersey as they put into dock in Liverpool or Birkenhead, or set sail for unknown destinations. The ten-minute bus and ferry service to anywhere in Wallasey, Birkenhead or Liverpool meant she was able to explore her new surroundings at will.

To her great surprise, she found she loved to wander

round the shops. Even though most things were still in short supply, or rationed, or too expensive for her to buy, the colours, the textures and the scents and smells, together with the sight of other people buying, transported her into another world. She soaked up the atmosphere as greedily as a child with a bag of sweets.

Occasionally, when she felt homesick for North Wales, she would lean out of the window, looking longingly towards the purple shapes etched against the skyline, and imagine she was back there in the heart of the mountains.

She had no idea Gwilym knew of this, not until he brought her home a pair of second-hand binoculars.

'If you walk to the end of the promenade on a clear day, you should be able to pick out the sheep on the mountainside with these,' he teased.

They had lived in the flat for over a year before Wynne came to stay. Nesta gave her a guided tour of Liverpool's fashionable Bond Street and Lord Street with all the enthusiasm of a convert. As they moved from one store to the next, Nesta smiled indulgently when Wynne stopped to stare in dismay at the gaping holes and mounds of rubble, evidence of war-time bombing, that still pockmarked the city. She had grown so used to such sights that they no longer registered as she rushed eagerly from one Aladdin's cave to the next.

'Whew! you've changed, cariad,' Wynne puffed, as she collapsed into an armchair after they had returned from window-shopping in Liverpool.

'What do you mean?' Nesta frowned as she poured her aunt a cup of tea.

'You used to say you hated towns. You never moved more than a hundred yards away from the cottage when you were in North Wales.'

'I did! After I left Blodwyn Thomas's farm and went to work for Parry Jones I used to drive miles and miles.'

'Yes, but not sightseeing. You never once went to Caernarvon or Harlech or Conway to see the castles, or even to the shops in Bangor or Llandudno.'

'Probably because it was so difficult to get to any of those places. I could hardly use Parry Jones's van for a shopping trips, now could I?'

'No, I suppose not,' Wynne admitted. 'Still, I do think you should come and stay with us so that I can show you these places. All you've seen of North Wales are the mountains.'

'That's the memory that is most dear to me. It's what comes into my mind whenever I think of you and my Da,' Nesta said quietly.

'You're not still worrying about him, I hope,' Wynne said sharply. 'He is well able to take care of himself, cariad. Don't forget he was once a sailor and they can always look after themselves. Anyway,' she went on in a softer tone, 'I keep an eye on him and Huw walks up to see him most evenings when he's taking the dog for a walk so you've no cause to worry.'

'Do you think he's lonely without me?'

'Not him! He's taken up with the Plaid Cymru movement again. He spends all his time reading, or writing letters, or going off to meetings.'

'I wish he'd come and stay with us. I've asked him several times, but he always says he is too busy and can't manage to get away. I'm sure he could if he really wanted to come and see me.'

'Leave the invitation open. He'll get round to it in his own time. Of course,' she added persuasively, 'you could always come on a visit to me. Kill two birds with one stone that way. I know you and Gwilym have visited him, but it would be nice if you could stay for a few days, especially if you could persuade Gwilym to let you have the car.'

'What do you mean?'

'You and me could go sightseeing to all the places I've been telling you about. And you would have a chance to see your Da without his feeling you were checking up on him! There's no hurry,' she added hastily as she saw a frown knit Nesta's dark brows. 'Think it over.'

'No, it's a great idea, but it will have to be soon, within the next four or five weeks.'

'Oh? Why is that, then?' Wynne's deep-set blue eyes looked perplexed.

'After that, Gwilym probably wouldn't think it was safe for me to go gadding on my own.'

'You mean . . .' Wynne left the rest of her sentence unfinished, but the delight on her round plump face as she seized Nesta's hand spoke volumes.

'That's right!'

'When?'

'Next February.'

'Oh, Nesta!' Wynne Morgan hugged her enthusiastically. 'I'm so pleased! I bet Gwilym is delighted.'

'I haven't told him yet,' Nesta laughed, her dark eyes sparkling. 'You are the first to know.' She patted her stomach. 'I wanted to be quite, quite sure.'

3

Llewellyn Vaughan was born just before eight o'clock in the morning on 26th February.

It had been a long, arduous delivery. What Nesta had thought to be labour pains when she had asked Gwilym to drive her to the maternity hospital just as dawn was breaking had proved to be mere twinges compared with what she suffered as the day wore on.

When Gwilym came to visit her that evening she was too worn out even to talk to him. She longed to sleep, to die, anything to escape from the excruciating waves of pain that engulfed her every few minutes until she lost count of time and of her surroundings.

Llewellyn's first lusty cry brought her out of the anaesthetic twilight and back to reality. Even her disappointment that it was not the daughter she longed for couldn't dim her feeling of accomplishment as she cradled
him in her arms.

He was a beautiful, chubby baby with well-formed limbs, plump rosy cheeks, dark eyebrows and a crop of dark hair. By the time Gwilym arrived at her bedside, she was starry-eyed, the pain of the past twenty-four hours forgotten.

Sara and Goronwy Vaughan showered Llewellyn with presents.

'We'll have to move to a bigger flat if you bring him any more toys,' Nesta laughed when they arrived with an enormous rocking-horse that was much too large to go into his bedroom.

'I've been meaning to talk to you about that,' Goronwy
told them. 'Don't you think it's time you moved into a

house so that the boy can sleep out of doors in his pram in the daytime now the weather is getting warmer? And he will soon need a garden to run around in,' he blundered on. 'You can't keep a young lad penned up in a flat all the time, you know.'

'I take him to the park each day,' Nesta defended.

'I'm sure you do, my dear,' Goronwy agreed expansively, patting her arm, 'but he needs his own space. And you'd like to have a garden to sit out in, now, wouldn't you? Somewhere to hang out your washing. I'm sure you get plenty these days!'

'We do have a communal back yard. I usually dry the nappies out there . . .'

'That's not the same as having your own garden, believe me.'

'Goronwy is right, Nesta,' Sara agreed eagerly. 'There are some delightful bungalows near us and we thought . . .' her voice trailed away as she looked towards her husband for support.

Nesta tried to control her rising anger as she saw the gleam of interest on Gwilym's face. Couldn't he see what would happen if they listened to his parents and moved to Liverpool? Goronwy and Sara would always be dropping in and she certainly didn't want that.

She intended bringing Llewellyn up in her own way, without daily interference from grandparents. At least as things stood now they had to phone to say they were coming.

'I don't think we could afford property near you,' Gwilym prevaricated.

'No need to let that put you off; I can help out, you know,' his father told him.

'Thanks all the same, but I would sooner leave it for a while. Rumour has it that I will be promoted to Features Editor in about three months time when Bill Johnson leaves. That means a pay rise and then we'll start looking for something to buy.'

Nesta breathed a sigh of relief. She was quite happy in their flat and enjoyed her independence. If they decided to buy a house she would prefer to stay in the Wirral, certainly not move across to Liverpool.

Goronwy and Sara Vaughan were not easily deterred. They constantly came up with tempting offers to try to entice Gwilym to live nearer to them.

Gwilym finally settled the matter by saying he had found the very house for them, just a few miles away in Wallasey and persuaded Nesta that they should at least go and look at it.

The modern detached house on St Hilary's Hill, overlooking sandhills and the wide sweep of the Mersey estuary where it met the Irish Sea, took Nesta's breath away.

'It's absolutely wonderful,' she breathed ecstatically as she moved from the lounge, with its enormous bay with built-in window seats, to the dining room that also looked out over the sea. The back door of the large, airy kitchen opened onto a paved yard and a small walled garden.

'Oh, Gwilym, it's absolutely perfect!' Nesta breathed.

'You haven't even looked upstairs yet,' Gwilym grinned, delighted by her pleasure.

The three bedrooms were airy, and all of them large enough to take a double bed as well as other pieces of bedroom furniture. There was a separate bathroom and toilet and, on the landing, an enormous airing cupboard.

Gwilym took her into the main bedroom last of all. As he led her across to the huge bay window Nesta gave a gasp of pure joy. It not only looked out over the sandhills and the sea but away in the distance she could even see the Welsh hills.

Nesta stood in wrapt silence absorbing every detail.

'Isn't it amazing how much nearer North Wales seems, yet it is only a matter of three miles from our flat to here'

Gwilym murmured softly as he stood beside her, his hand resting on her shoulder.

'It's incredible! I feel that I could almost reach out and touch those mountains,' Nesta sighed. 'Do you think that is the Snowdon range?'

'You had better bring your binoculars along tomorrow and check it out before we decide to take the house,' Gwilym teased.

'Can we really afford to buy it?' Nesta's brown eyes widened excitedly.

'Well, now that I have been made Features Editor, I am sure we can. My new appointment does carry a healthy pay rise.'

'Gwilym, you mean you have really been promoted! I thought you were just saying that to stall your father.'

'No.' He grabbed her round the waist and waltzed her around the empty room, their feet clattering over the bare boards. 'Just think of the fun you are going to have furnishing this place. Imagine it, a real home of our own at last! We can invite friends in and make as much noise as we like. We have our own garden, somewhere to park the car, and plenty of space for Llewellyn when he starts to run about. So do we buy it?'

'How could I say anything else but "yes",' Nesta grinned.

Planning their move to the new house took most of the summer. Nesta found that having to take the baby along when she went shopping was restrictive, but she refused to let Sara look after him for more than the occasional afternoon.

The first time Wynne came on a visit after they moved to St Hilary's Hill she was overawed by Nesta's new home.

'It's fantastic, cariad. That view! And such lovely rooms. And so near the shops,' she sighed enviously.

'Come on, now. You know you wouldn't swop places,'

Nesta laughed. 'Three days here and you'd be pining for your mountains. You are just like my Da!'

Wynne didn't smile. Her plump face became anxious as she asked: 'How much have you told your Da about this place, Nesta?'

'Not a lot. I thought I'd leave it as a surprise for when he comes to visit us. Why?'

'He's not going to like it . . . all this opulence.'

'Rubbish!'

'Not it's not, Nesta. You seem to forget that he's a socialist at heart, you know. He doesn't approve of people having too much luxury.'

'This isn't luxury!' Nesta exclaimed, her eyebrows raised in astonishment. 'You've seen the home Gwilym's parents have.'

Wynne's lips tightened, but she said nothing.

'Has my Da ever criticised them . . . or their home? He has been there, has he ever commented on it?' Nesta persisted.

'No. But, then, he wouldn't . . . not to me.'

Although they didn't discuss it further, the implied criticism worried Nesta. She knew the house was a little beyond their means and suspected that Goronwy's 'little bit of help' had, in fact, been quite substantial. Since there was nothing she could do about it she had conveniently put it out of her mind.

In much the same way, Nesta had accepted Sara's generous help towards furnishing their new home. It had come as a godsend!

She knew she had overspent on their bedroom, but she had wanted it to be outstanding.

And it was.

The oyster velvet curtains and matching silk bedspread, the cream, pink and green flowered Axminster carpet had made the perfect setting for the fumed-oak bedroom suite and massive four-poster bed.

'We'll have to live up here until we can afford to furnish the lounge,' she remarked ruefully when she took Sara up to see it. 'I've already used up all our furniture dockets.'

'There are ways of getting more,' Sara told her archly. 'My daily-help's daughter, Maria, has just got married, but she won't be using her allocation because she has married a GI and is going back to America.'

'You mean she might be willing to sell them?' Nesta's velvet brown eyes widened, then her face clouded as she added, 'Gwilym wouldn't agree to us doing that and, anyway, we can't afford to.'

'Look, I want a new three-piece suite,' Sara told her conspiratorially, 'and I had thought of buying the dockets from Maria.' She sighed effectively. 'The problem is trying to convince Goronwy that our present suite is worn out since we only bought it at the beginning of the war. We renewed everything then as a sort of insurance in case things were in short supply for a few years.' She stopped, her face brightening. 'If I gave our lounge suite to you and Gwilym . . .'

'Do you mean the cream leather one!' Nesta gasped.

'That's right . . . OK?'

'I don't know what to say . . .'

'Just say "yes" and you'll be doing me a favour,' Sara assured her.

'I'll have to ask Gwilym . . . but, yes, yes, yes!'

Nesta's voice trailed off as, starry-eyed, she began planning how the room would look. The huge cream, three-seater Chesterfield settee, with its matching armchairs, would look very impressive and completely furnish the lounge. She couldn't believe her luck. She hoped Gwilym wouldn't object.

'I don't mind if you don't,' he told her, accepting the situation with a shrug of his broad shoulders. 'We can always buy new when I get my *next* pay rise.'

Sara immediately arranged for the suite to be delivered

26

and when it arrived Nesta found she had also sent along the matching side tables and the glowing red, washed-Chinese carpet on which everything had stood.

Nesta had written to her father, telling him all about their new home, and had extended an open invitation for him to visit them whenever he felt like it, but he had neither written nor phoned. Remembering Wynne's warning that he wouldn't approve of her opulent lifestyle, Nesta grew uneasy whenever she thought about him.

Then, in mid-October, Rhys came to see them.

He arrived without any warning around mid-morning on a glorious autumn day. Nesta had just fed and dressed Llewellyn and wheeled the pram out onto the paved terrace outside the kitchen window so that he could sleep while she did her chores.

'Are you going to ask me in or do I have to pay an entrance fee?' Rhys asked, his dark eyes glinting with amusement as he saw the amazement on Nesta's face.

'Da . . . oh, Da, is it really you?' she gasped as she hugged him. He looked so fit and well that she felt bursting with happiness.

She took him at once to see the baby.

Llewellyn stared up at his grandfather, wide-eyed and solemn and Nesta held her breath, aware of how like each other they were. The shape of the nose and jawline, the colour of the eyes and the thick dark hair were almost identical. Yet when the baby's face creased into a wide gurgling smile it was Gwilym's mouth and dimpled cheeks she could see.

'Can I pick him up?'

'Of course!' Smiling, she undid Llewellyn's pram harness and drew him out from his nest of covers.

'Bring him indoors, Da. I'll make you a hot drink. You must be famished after your journey. How did you get here?'

'Bus, train, bus again and then Shanks's pony. Rather

a stiff climb up here from Wallasey village, isn't it? You must find it so when you are pushing a pram.'

'Keeps me fit,' she laughed.

She took the baby from her father after she had poured out the tea. 'Sit down and drink that. I'll just put Llewellyn back in his pram again.'

The baby seemed reluctant to settle and cried noisily.

'Upset his routine, have I?' Rhys apologised.

'Never mind. We'll take our tea through to the other room, then we won't hear him,' Nesta said as she placed her father's cup and her own on a tray and led the way.

'Good heavens!' His exclamation of surprise startled her and she looked round anxiously.

'Has Gwilym had a windfall, or something?' Rhys asked in amazement, standing stock still in the doorway.

'He did have a pay rise when he was made Features Editor,' Nesta said defensively, not sure whether he was expressing pleasure or dismay.

'Not enough to pay for all this, not with the mortgage he must have had to take on,' he said, frowning darkly. 'Are you up to your ears in hire purchase? The truth, now.'

'Of course we're not,' she defended hotly.

He didn't answer but as his gaze levelled with hers she added almost defiantly, 'Everything in here is second-hand. Throw-outs from Gwilym's parents.'

As Rhys stroked his beard with his long fingers she wished the floor would open and swallow her from his penetrating stare.

She knew what he must be thinking, and resented being placed in a situation which let all her old feelings of guilt float to the surface and spoil the occasion for her.

'There's nothing wrong in having things second-hand. We can always replace them when we have the money to do so,' she said defensively.

He still said nothing, just sipped at his tea, his dark eyes

28

studying every detail of the magnificent room. Nesta held her breath, holding back her tears as he put down his cup and moved to the window and stood there staring out.

'Those purple shapes in the distance are the Welsh mountains, or so I'm told,' she gabbled nervously. 'I like to think it's the Snowdon range . . .' her voice trailed off. 'Come and see the rest of the house,' she invited.

As he followed her out into the hall she had to fight back the urge to turn and fling herself into his arms and beg forgiveness. Clenching her fists until her nails dug into the soft flesh of her palms, she led the way upstairs.

Almost defiantly she displayed the splendours of the main bedroom and the pretty blue and white nursery that was Llewellyn's. By the time they came to the spare bedroom she felt drained. She wanted him to approve. It mattered so much to her that he was proud of what she had achieved.

'We haven't had time to do anything to this room yet,' she muttered, pushing open the door to reveal the room bare of everything except a single bed and a chest of drawers.

'This will suit me fine,' Rhys murmured, as he walked in and stood looking round.

'You mean you are staying with us?' She felt a rush of joy, of excitement, of relief.

'Just for a couple of nights, if that is convenient.'

'Of course it is! It won't take a minute to make up the bed,' she prattled excitedly. 'I'll bring up a chair and put down some rugs and make it really comfortable for you in here . . .'

'No, Nesta!' Rhys held up a hand. 'Stop fussing. I would much sooner you left the room exactly as it is. Just make up the bed and it will do me fine.'

4

Nesta found that having Rhys under the same roof seemed to blight their lives.

Normally when Gwilym came home at night they would spend an hour happily playing with the baby and bathing him. Then, after they had put Llewellyn to bed they would sit down to a leisurely meal in their own good time.

Now the routine was completely disorganised. Anxious to prove to her father what a good wife and mother she was, Nesta became over zealous. The baby sensed her tension and, as if aware of a larger audience, seemed to go out of his way to be difficult.

Gwilym maintained the reason that Llewellyn refused to settle after they put him down in his cot at night was because he was cutting teeth, but in her heart Nesta knew that it was partly her fault. Instead of a leisurely bath and playtime she tried to rush things so that she would have more time to prepare an elaborate meal.

She wasn't sure why she was doing this, since both Gwilym and her father enjoyed simple dishes, soups and stews and home made pies, as long as they were properly cooked.

The underlying tension even undermined the affection between her and Gwilym. When they went to bed she felt uneasy when he began to cuddle her, afraid to make love in case her father might hear them.

'He is a man of the world, and he surely doesn't think we found Llewellyn under a gooseberry bush?' Gwilym snapped, hurt by her rejection.

Burying her face in the pillow, Nesta cried herself to

sleep, wishing her father would go home.

Next day, ashamed of her feelings, she organised a dinner party. As well as Gwilym's parents she invited Beryl and Simon Peterson, a married couple who had lived in the flat below them in New Brighton, and Ralph Hendrix, the political editor from the *Post*, who had become a close friend of Gwilym's since his promotion.

As the eight of them sat down over the meal she had spent most of the day preparing, Nesta felt more relaxed than she had for days. Llewellyn was sound asleep, everything from the simple melon starter and roast lamb and two vegetables main course to the home-made apple pie that followed had been well received. The wine Goronwy had brought along had induced a mellow mood and as she carried the coffee through the lounge she felt it had been a perfect evening.

She had even changed her opinion about Ralph Hendrix. On the two previous occasions when she had met him she had considered him arrogant and self-opinionated. Tonight, though, she had found him erudite and witty and had actually enjoyed his dry sense of humour.

He was a tall thin man, handsome in a dark saturnine way, with a wide cruel mouth and a hawkish nose under beetling dark brows which contrasted strangely with his dove-grey eyes.

She knew he was quite some years older than Gwilym, but she was surprised to learn from the conversation around the dinner table that he was more or less the same age as her mother-in-law. They even had friends in common, a fact which seemed to win him a lot of attention from Sara.

As she set the tray down, Ralph jumped up from his armchair to help Gwilym arrange the leather-topped side tables so that everyone had one within reach, then cleverly changed his seat so that he was sitting next to Sara who had draped herself attractively on the upholstered window seat, the full, mid-calf skirt of her 'New Look' black dress fanned out in a semi-circle.

'Come to enjoy the view?' she asked with a provocative smile.

Ralph paused for a moment, staring out at the star-spangled vista, then his chiselled lips quirked into a half-smile as he blatantly studied Sara. 'I almost think it was better from where I was sitting before,' he said meaningfully.

'Then perhaps you would like to change places with me,' Rhys Evans said, standing up and walking over to the window, leaving Ralph no choice but to vacate his seat, which he did with a mocking bow towards Sara.

Nesta saw the shadow of annoyance that darkened her father-in-law's face and quickly tried to cover the awkward pause that followed. She was acutely aware of the tension in the room and that all eyes were on her father, Ralph and Sara.

In the same moment, she remembered that there was a fifteen-year gap between Goronwy and Sara. And tonight it really did show. Goronwy looked grey and shrunken and, despite his podgy cheeks and hands, there was a network of wrinkles around his mouth and eyes. He was a gnome of a man when compared with Ralph Hendrix, or even with her father.

'You can see the purplish outlines of the Welsh mountains from here on a clear day,' she said to break the awkward silence. 'I like to believe it's the Snowdon range.'

'You lived there, didn't you, Nesta, at one time?' Beryl asked.

'During the war I worked there. I was in the Land Army,' Nesta grinned.

'We had a summer cottage just outside Mold when Gwilym was small,' Sara murmured. 'I quite liked it. In those days the Welsh people were so friendly,' her sea-blue eyes fluttered at Rhys as she spoke and Nesta

32

cringed, embarrassed at the way she was openly flirting with him.

'Vaughan is a Welsh name isn't it?' Beryl Peterson asked.

'Yes. My father owned a slate quarry near Bethesda,' Goronwy told her. 'Of course, that was a long long time ago.'

'Before the peasants revolted, you mean!' Ralph Hendrix murmured derisively, crossing his long legs and studying the toes of his elegant shoes.

Nesta saw her father's lips tighten. She looked helplessly at Gwilym, willing him to intervene.

'Nesta and I met at a Plaid Cymru meeting in Dolgellau,' Gwilym said pointedly, a warning in his green eyes as he glanced directly at Ralph.

'Of course, you were a reporter before you went into the Air Force,' Ralph murmured. 'Ah well, I suppose you can be forgiven if it was in the line of duty!'

Nesta saw the dull flush creeping over her father's face and prayed he would ignore Ralph's taunts.

'That means Llewellyn has Welsh blood on both sides,' Simon Peterson observed with interest. 'You'll have to make sure he learns to speak Welsh, Nesta. That's the real proof of your ancestry. So many of these so-called patriots can't understand a word of their own language, except what Plaid Cymru means, of course.'

'Plaid Cymru! Most of them are just Reds waving the Welsh flag, don't you agree, Gwilym?' Ralph said contemptuously.

'Socialist, Nationalist, what does the label matter as long as their heart is in the right place and they have their country's interest at heart?' Gwilym hedged uneasily.

'But do they?' Ralph Hendrix pulled himself into an upright position and glanced round obliquely, his pale grey eyes gleaming malevolently. 'Most of them have a dog-in-the-manger attitude. They oppose anything and everything that smacks of English interference, even when it is intended to benefit them. Let an Englishman take over one of their coal mines or slate quarries and they go on strike. Let someone from England buy one of their cottages or farms and they immediately set fire to it and hound him out. Bible-thumping fanatics most of them.'

'I would have thought that a man in your job would have been more discerning and less biased,' Rhys Evans commented blandly.

'Probably it's because of my job, knowing the background details, many of which are never printed, that I am not easily hoodwinked.'

'Preferring to hoodwink the public at large so that you can print a good story,' Rhys argued in a dangerously soft voice.

'Not at all! Take the stories that circulate about this chap they call the Dragon . . .'

'Would anyone like some more coffee?' Desperate to stop what was becoming a highly volatile topic, and not sure whether Ralph was deliberately goading her father or not, Nesta interrogated each of her guests in turn, but none of them took the slightest notice of her interruption. All eyes and ears were fixed on the two protagonists. Rhys Evans' hooded gaze was locked with the arrogant stare of Ralph Hendrix. A thin, supercilious smile twisted Hendrix's wide mouth; his light grey eyes were coldly challenging. Only the lacing and interlacing of his bony fingers gave any clue to the emotions behind his barbed comments.

As political editor of the *Post* he must surely know her father was the Dragon, Nesta thought, aghast as she saw the flush deepen over her father's prominent cheek bones and saw his slate-grey eyes harden. She knew from the timbre of his voice that he was barely controlling the fury which Ralph Hendrix's taunts and comments had aroused in him.

At the same time she was also aware of the excitement on Sara Vaughan's face, her blue eyes gleaming like shards of glass, her lips parted, the tip of her tongue nervously licking the edge of her top lip as the two men parried words.

It's almost as if she feels they are fighting for her favours, Nesta thought. Bewildered, she turned to speak to Gwilym, only to be startled by the cold anger in his green eyes, and was shocked to realise that it was directed at her father.

Miserably, she blamed herself for the confrontation. She should never have given the party. It had been stupid to invite people who by their very wealth and status were directly opposed to her father in their views.

As she tried desperately to think of some way of cooling things and bringing the evening to an end the discussion grew more heated. She completely lost the thread of the argument. All she realised was that Ralph Hendrix and her father were hurling insults at each other while Gwilym, his father and Simon Peterson were desperately trying to pacify them both. Sara, smiling enigmatically, first at Ralph and then at Rhys, seemed to be egging the two of them on to express even wilder taunts and accusations.

Above the pandemonium Nesta suddenly heard Llewellyn crying.

'Now look what you've all done,' she yelled tearfully. 'You've woken my baby!'

The hysteria in her voice as she ran from the room, restored a semblance of order. By the time she came back downstairs, after settling Llewellyn, the room was empty except for Gwilym who was stacking the empty glasses and coffee cups onto a tray.

'Have they all gone?' she asked in a subdued voice.

'Yes!'

'I didn't hear my Da come upstairs.'

'Beryl and Simon took him to the station.'

35

'At this time of night!'

'There will be a train to Chester.'

'And how is he going to get home from there?' she demanded, her eyes blazing.

'How should I know?'

'You don't even care!'

'Frankly, no!' Gwilym agreed. 'I owe a lot to Ralph Hendrix and for your father to be so downright rude to him in *my* house . . .'

'Your house? Don't you mean *our* house?'

'All right, then, our house,' Gwilym agreed testily, 'although since *my* father paid for it I feel that it is mine.'

'Your father did what?' White-faced and trembling, Nesta stared in disbelief at Gwilym. 'You told me you were taking out a mortgage in our joint names . . .'

'That was what I intended to do,' Gwilym agreed. 'Then Dad said it was senseless for us to scrimp trying to pay a mortgage when he had money doing nothing.'

'But you didn't bother telling me?'

'No. I should have done, I suppose, but you were so involved in furnishing and decorating . . .'

'That it didn't seem important. What an excuse!'

'Come on, don't let us start quarrelling; there's been enough of that here tonight.' Tenderly, he placed an arm around her shoulder and with his free hand tilted her chin until their lips met in a long, deep kiss.

'Let's leave clearing up until tomorrow,' he whispered, propelling her towards the stairs.

For a moment Nesta resisted, struggling against her own inner anger. Then the magic of the chemistry between them overcame all other feelings. As Gwilym's arm went round her waist she felt her pulses throb, her resistance crumble. Overwhelmed by her love for him, she sighed and leaned against him as they made their way upstairs to their bedroom.

***

36

Nesta stayed at home the next day expecting to hear from her father. By mid-afternoon, when she could stand the suspense no longer, she phoned Wynne.

'He only got back about an hour ago,' her aunt told her. 'He looked rather worn out. Has he been living it up while he's been at your place?'

They talked a while longer, until Nesta said she must go because the baby was crying.

'I'll let your Da know you phoned. Any message for him?'

'No! Don't tell him I've been in touch with you. He'll only think I was checking on him and you know how he resents it.'

Even though she knew her father was safe it did little to allay her feelings. She could understand the feud between her father and Ralph Hendrix since they were both political animals, but she still couldn't forget the way her father had responded to Sara's coquettishness. She felt affronted that it had happened in her house and realised, not for the first time, how little she really knew about him.

When Gwilym arrived home she tried to discuss it with him but he simply shrugged it off.

'Stop making a drama out of it,' he told her. 'It's just Mum's way. They'd all had quite a lot to drink, remember.'

'I know that, but she was openly flirting with both my Da and Ralph Hendrix . . .'

'Rubbish!'

'Well, she was certainly behaving in a very friendly fashion towards Ralph, seeing that she had met him for the very first time.'

'You're forgetting they have background connections,' Gwilym reminded her. 'They must have practically grown up together. They certainly have a lot of friends in common.'

'How old is Ralph, then?'

'Forty-seven or forty-eight . . . about Mum's age. They're both about the same age as your father,' he added.

'I'll never get used to the age difference between your parents,' Nesta sighed. 'And last night he really did look old.'

'Yes. His doctor has advised him to retire. His heart's not too good.'

'Is that why he was looking so grey last night. I thought it was because he was upset at the way your Mum was behaving.'

'No, I don't think it bothers him. It's all quite harmless . . .'

'Is it? We nearly had a fight on our hands last night!'

'Nonsense! That's just Ralph's quirky sense of humour. You don't want to take any of what he said to heart. He knows quite well that your father is the Dragon.'

'You mean he was trying to show off in front of your mother,' Nesta snapped. 'Out to prove what a clever chap he was. Very impressive! I hope you don't intend modelling yourself on him now that you are on the Editorial Board.'

Without giving Gwilym a chance to reply or defend himself, Nesta flounced out of the room. She felt seething with indignation, not sure which was worse, her father being taunted by Ralph Hendrix or teased by Sara Vaughan.

Inwardly she knew she was behaving quite irrationally. The real reason she felt so tetchy was the fact that Goronwy Vaughan had paid for their house. She knew she should be feeling grateful, relieved that they didn't have the burden of a mortgage to contend with, but somehow she wasn't. The very fact that it had all been done without Gwilym even bothering to mention it to her, rankled. He might be the wage earner but marriage was supposed to be a partnership.

38

No wonder Gwilym hadn't hit the roof when she had overspent on decorating and furnishing, she thought resentfully. What did an overdraft matter when you had no mortgage to worry about? She had a good mind to go out and spend, spend, spend and see what he would do about that. The only trouble was, she thought crossly, she would have to get his signature if she bought anything on hire purchase and, if he refused after she had ordered the goods, she would feel so ridiculous.

She walked round her new home, trying to find some major flaw so that she could insist they moved, but even in her super-critical mood she had to admit it was ideal for them in every way.

Slowly, sanity returned. St Hilary's Hill was one of the finest sites in Wallasey. Where else could she look out of the window, whether she was upstairs or down, and see her beloved Wales and dream she was back amongst the mountains?

And she had another reason for wanting to stay there. She hadn't said anything to Gwilym yet, but she was pretty certain that she was pregnant again . . . and this time she was quite positive that it would be the daughter she still longed for so much.

5

___

And now it was May and she had given birth to her longed-for daughter. As she held the new baby in her arms for the first time she felt an overwhelming sense of fulfilment.

Amelda was the exact opposite of Llewellyn. She had a halo of wispy fair hair and a doll-like face with big eyes, long lashes, a rosebud mouth and shining pink cheeks.

As she cradled Amelda in her arms, Nesta mentally counted her blessings. She now had everything her heart desired: a handsome, loving husband, a son of fifteen months whom they both adored, and a truly beautiful home. She was reunited with her father and her close friendship with Wynne amd Huw was an added bonus.

She was even on good terms with Gwilym's parents. She had made it clear right from the start that she had no intention of letting them dictate how she was to bring up her children, and they had accepted this quite amicably.

Things were so amenable between them that she had happily accepted Sara and Goronwy's offer to look after Llewellyn when she was in hospital having Amelda.

Gwilym had thought it an excellent idea because it left him free to visit Nesta in hospital. It also proved an unexpected treat for Llewellyn although he was such a bundle of energy that his grandparents soon found they had taken on more than they had anticipated.

From the very first day she brought Amelda home, Nesta found she had her hands full. Llewellyn was delighted by his new sister. He was very protective towards her and showed no sign of jealousy at all. He was always eager to help Nesta when she was feeding, bathing, changing or dressing Amelda. And, right from the very start, Amelda seemed to respond to Llewellyn in a special way that delighted Nesta.

As the months went by Amelda proved to be a contented baby, never happier than when Llewellyn was playing with her or when she could watch him from her pram or high-chair. With her golden curls and delicate features she looked like a beautiful doll and everyone commented on the unusual colour of her eyes.

'They're like purple pansies,' Goronwy remarked as he cradled his little granddaughter in his arms. 'She's going to grow up to be a real beauty.'

Once Amelda reached the toddling stage, she and Llewellyn were even more inseparable. He was so good with her, sharing all his favourite toys, including her in everything he did, that Nesta grew concerned in case she became spoilt.

'He gives in to Amelda's demands much too readily,' she told Gwilym as they watched through the window as the two children played together in the garden. 'Just look at that! The moment he gets on his tricycle she wants to ride it, then the moment he climbs on the swing she pulls him off so that she can go on it. And he lets her!'

'Don't worry about it,' Gwilym laughed. 'It's much better than having them fighting and squabbling the entire time. You ask anyone who has children of that age and you'll soon realise just how lucky you are.'

Nesta had to admit he was right. As she watched the two children having a rough and tumble with Gwilym, or when she wheeled them both to the park to feed the ducks, or play on the swings, she often felt that life was almost too good to be true – as if the sun was always shining on her.

She was so cocooned and contented that she scarcely noticed what was happening on the periphery of her own busy life.

41

She knew Goronwy was not too well, but when Sara phoned to say he had had a stroke and was in hospital, Nesta felt shaken to the core.

Since his retirement he had not come to see them as often because he found the journey rather a strain. He no longer enjoyed driving, and the alternative, a journey by train or by bus and ferry, was very tiring.

Instead, whenever Gwilym had a weekend off, they took the children to see him. Usually this was about once a fortnight and Nesta felt guilty about not making the effort to visit them more often.

The weeks that followed the news of Goronwy's stroke were worrying for all of them. Each evening, after he had finished work on the *Post*, Gwilym would collect his mother and take her to the hospital. Afterwards he would drive her back home again.

'Wouldn't it be much easier on us all if your mother came back here after you've been to visit your father? She could stay the night and you could take her back to Liverpool in the morning, on your way to the office,' Nesta suggested.

But Sara wouldn't agree to this. For over three weeks Gwilym made the long detour each evening, arriving home too tired to enjoy the cooked meal Nesta had waiting for him. Llewellyn and Amelda were in bed and asleep so Gwilym only saw them for a few minutes each morning before he left for the office.

It was a great relief to Nesta when Gwilym told her that they were discharging his father from the hospital.

'He's completely lost the use of his legs, though, so he will have to use a wheel-chair to get about. I don't know how my mother will manage,' Gwilym frowned worriedly.

Sara couldn't cope. Every day, or so it seemed to Nesta, she was on the phone to Gwilym, asking him to come over because his father needed attention. She was incapable of lifting him and even had difficulty in assisting him from the bedroom to the bathroom on her own.

As the weeks passed, the situation worsened as Goronwy showed very few signs of improvement. There were some days when he was too ill to get out of bed at all.

They had long family discussions about what ought to be done for the best. Gwilym wanted his parents to move into a bungalow, preferably somewhere in Wallasey, so that he and Nesta could be close by to give a hand whenever necessary. Sara was adamant that she intended to stay where she was in her own home in Liverpool.

'All my friends are here. I can't possibly move over to the other side of the river; I would be completely isolated,' she exclaimed in wide-eyed dismay.

'You'd have us living nearby. You wouldn't be lonely,' Gwilym assured her.

'It's out of the question,' she snapped, her face set.

'Why don't you think it over,' Nesta begged. 'You don't have to decide right away.'

'If you haven't the time to come and help your father then I shall have to think about getting a nurse for him,' she told Gwilym when he tried to persuade her to reconsider their suggestion about moving to Wallasey.

Gwilym was quite hurt by her attitude, especially when his mother told him, just a few days later, and without any further discussion, that she had arranged for a nurse to come in twice a day so there was no need for him to visit them after work each day.

Nesta said nothing. Secretly, she was greatly relieved by Sara's decision. After a few weeks, even Gwilym had to admit that with the help of the nurse his mother was now coping surprisingly well.

When Goronwy's health deteriorated still further, they all agreed that a live-in nurse was necessary.

He was now not only permanently confined to his wheel-chair but his speech had become impaired and he found it impossible to communicate unless he wrote things down. Within a very short time, he found even this was difficult. His writing was so spidery that everyone found it hard to decipher what he had written, and this caused him even greater frustration.

Sara accepted the situation with great fortitude. Then, as the nurse took on more and more responsibility, Sara started to lead a life of her own. She began visiting St Hilary's Hill, ostensibly to see Llewellyn and Amelda, but Nesta soon realised that Sara's visits invariably coincided with a surprise visit from Ralph Hendrix. And since Ralph was returning to Liverpool, and his car was outside, it seemed only sensible that they should leave together rather than Sara make her own way home. Knowing how sick Goronwy was, Nesta wasn't sure whether it was the deception or the actual affair which angered her most.

When she mentioned her suspicions to Gwilym he merely shrugged and from the look on his face she wondered if he had known all along and actually approved!

She tried to tell herself that what her mother-in-law did was none of her business either. After all, Ralph Hendrix was a family friend and it would seem strange if he didn't offer her a lift.

So Nesta kept her own counsel.

And it worked, except on the few occasions when both Sara and Ralph called and her own father also happened to be visiting St Hilary's Hill at the same time.

When this happened, it angered Nesta to see how Sara would flirt with him, mesmerising him, with her sea-blue eyes so that he gave her his undivided attention. Sara even encouraged him to talk about Plaid Cymru and listened with rapt attention.

Nesta sensed that it annoyed Ralph Hendrix when Sara did this, and she wondered if she was deliberately trying to provoke him and make him jealous. Usually he would walk out of the room as if he could stand it no longer. Often he would seek out the children, seeming to prefer their company.

When they were in the garden, Nesta would watch from the kitchen window. It always surprised her how well both Llewellyn and Amelda responded to Ralph. She always found him supercilious and cynical and, although she sometimes enjoyed his barbed wit, it often unnerved her when it was directed at her father.

With the children he was a different person.

Amelda was enchanted by him. Her big violet eyes would glow like amethysts as she smiled up at him, clinging to his hand. She would sit gazing into his eyes enthralled as he told her a story, her rosebud mouth slightly parted as she listened intently to his every word.

He treated Llewellyn as an equal and they would have long, serious discussions about the collection of snails, spiders and stick insects so dear to Llewellyn's heart.

Nesta often thought it was a waste that Ralph wasn't married with a family of his own. Her attempts to pair him off with any of her unmarried girl-friends had never met with any success.

He had always seen through her ruse and his thin sensual lips would curl derisively when she made the introductions and his pale grey eyes would meet hers obliquely, implying that he knew what she was trying to do. Then he would deliberately charm the girl, so that by the end of the evening she would be utterly captivated by him but not at all sure about his intentions.

In the end, Nesta had given up trying. There were so many other things happening of much greater importance, such as looking after her two small children and watching them develop into happy, sturdy, children.

Amelda seemed to crawl and walk much earlier than Llewellyn, although she was nowhere near as quick as him when it came to talking. Possibly this was because she didn't need to make herself understood, as he had done. Amelda had only to point at something and Llewellyn was there to get it for her. She delighted in dropping toys from her pram or high chair for the sheer pleasure of watching him run and pick them up.

She was quite fearless. Nesta would often hold her breath as Amelda clambered down steps and stairs or ran headlong down the garden path in pursuit of Llewellyn.

They both loved animals, and remembering how much she had always wanted a pet of her own, Nesta had let them each have a kitten and promised that when they were older they could have a dog.

'Why can't we have one now?' Llewellyn wanted to know.

'Because I have enough to do looking after both of you,' Nesta told him.

'A dog has to be taken for a walk every day and it has to be on a lead. When Amelda is old enough to go for long walks then we'll have a dog,' Gwilym promised.

Nesta had felt quite sad when it was time for Llewellyn to start school. She had to struggle to keep back her tears as she watched his dark-haired little figure dressed in new grey shorts and grey jumper, shoulders squared, striding across the playground. She felt as if she was deserting him. He had refused to kiss or be kissed and only his scowling frown showed just how nervous he was of what lay ahead. There was a lump in her throat as she turned away from the school gates and wheeled Amelda to the shops. It was a milestone in her life as well as his.

She knew he could cope. He was a bright, intelligent little boy who thoroughly enjoyed books and learning and he had been counting the days to when he would start school.

She was confident he would soon settle down and make friends. He had Gwilym's easy-going approach to people, even though at times he was as thoughtful and introspective as her own father.

Whenever Rhys came to stay, Llewellyn dogged his footsteps, eager to listen to folk tales and anecdotes about Wales. Watching them together, Nesta remembered her own early childhood, when she had been not much older than Llewellyn, and how her father had regaled her with the same stories whenever he came on shore leave.

From a very early age Llewellyn developed a love of Wales, especially the mountains, and longed for their holidays when they stayed at Rhys's cottage in the shadow of Moelwyn.

Wynne and Huw Morgan also looked forward to these visits. Their own son, Trevor, had married a London girl who preferred a career to a family so they had come to look on Llewellyn and Amelda almost as their own grandchildren.

They were both now in their fifties. Wynne, who had put on weight, suffered a great deal with her feet and legs, and found walking very difficult.

Huw was much fitter and would take the two children for long, rambling walks, telling them the name of every flower and bird they saw on the way. He would let them paddle at the sandy edge of the wide blue lakes that were hidden away in secret cwms, or fish with rod and worm in the crystal-clear streams as they flowed over rocks and boulders on their way down to the sea.

Most of all they enjoyed being taken to see new lambs, or to watch the sheep being dipped or sheared, depending on the time of year. For Llewellyn and Amelda, these were magic moments they never forgot. Long after the holiday was over they would remember something they had seen or done while on holiday and relive it all over again.

Wynne would teach them games they had never heard of before, or take them to visit neighbours where they

47

would be the centre of attention. They would be treated to newly made bakestones, bara brith, or some other Welsh speciality.

On rainy days, they loved sorting through her button box, or going through the albums of old pictures and postcards she would bring out to amuse them. She would tell them about what it had been like when she was just a little girl and laugh with them as they looked at the pictures.

The holidays were never long enough for them to explore the countless treasures that Wynne and Huw had saved for them. Each curio was accompanied by a special anecdote, many of which Nesta was sure were pure figments of Wynne and Huw's imagination, specially dreamed up for the children.

Nesta enjoyed these visits to North Wales as much as the children did. When Gwilym's holiday was over she would stay on for an extra week or even longer, just to enjoy the tranquillity the mountains offered.

She felt closer to Wynne and Huw than she did to anyone, even her father. Perhaps it was because they had befriended her when she had first arrived in Wales and had been rejected by her grandparents, she thought with affection. They had also given her a home when she had worked as a Land Army girl, and she had been able to count on their support ever since.

Wynne was the nearest she ever came to the mother she had never known. She found herself confiding in her as they did the housework or prepared vegetables and cooked a meal. By using Wynne as a sounding board, she found she could put things which had been troubling her into their right perspective.

She told her how worried she was about her Da and his politics, and about the rivalry between him and Ralph Hendrix and how Sara was playing one off against the other.

Even though Wynne didn't offer any advice, just having a sympathetic ear to unburden herself to did wonders for Nesta's peace of mind.

By the time she returned home again to St Hilary's Hill, Nesta always felt relaxed and refreshed. It was as though she had left her troubles behind her in North Wales and was ready to cope with anything life might offer.

6

Even though he had been ill for several years, Goronwy's death came as a shock, particularly to Nesta.

He had deteriorated so gradually that those who saw him regularly were hardly aware of how ill he had become. Ever since he had lost the ability to speak clearly he had stayed shut away in his own room, shunning the company of everyone other than Gwilym and Sara, and very occasionally, Nesta. He had grown very tetchy and had told them not to bring Llewellyn and Amelda up to see him as he couldn't stand their chatter and the noise they made.

At the time, Nesta had been quite upset. Then, on one of his better days, Goronwy had scrawled a note to her explaining his reasons. He explained he was so self-conscious about his appearance that he found it embarrassing for them to see him, since they were too young to understand the reason. Also, his speech impediment made it impossible for him to talk to them.

Nesta had been deeply touched when she read it and thanked him with tears in her eyes for his concern.

She wished she could do more for him. Although he was well-cared for physically, she sensed he was very lonely. Whenever they went to visit, she would sit by his bedside chatting away about what the children had been doing, and any other news she thought he might find interesting, even though he could not respond. She sensed from the pressure of his hand as she held it between her own that he understood what she was telling him.

Often when they called, Sara would not be there. As Goronwy's health deteriorated, her social life had seemed to become more and more hectic. She rarely seemed to be at home. Whenever Nesta phoned to enquire about Goronwy it was usually the nurse who answered. And there was always an edge of censure in her voice as she stated that Mrs Vaughan was out.

Sara had not been at home on the night Goronwy had died.

It had been just after midnight when the nurse had phoned to tell Gwilym what had happened. She had apologised for disturbing him, but said that she thought that someone in the family should know as soon as possible. He had gone across to Liverpool immediately.

His mother had still not returned from the theatre when he got there, yet Gwilym sprang to her defence when Nesta had expressed surprise when he told her this.

'How could Mother possibly know that this was the night he would die?' Gwilym growled angrily. 'The doctor said he could have gone at any time. Anyway, the nurse was there. She hadn't gone out and left him on his own!'

Throughout the funeral service Sara, looking slim and fragile in her close-fitting black suit and wide-brimmed black hat, leaned heavily on Gwilym's arm. As the coffin was brought into the church, and again when the vicar eulogised over Goronwy Vaughan's many attributes, Sara dabbed at her eyes with a wispy, lace-edged handkerchief, her shoulders shaking as she tried to contain her emotion.

As they gathered round the newly dug grave in the cemetery, shivering as a keen east wind chased heavy rain clouds across the sullen sky, Nesta found herself thinking not about the aged man they were burying but about the future of the widow he had left behind.

Although Sara was in her mid-fifties, she had an elegant attractiveness that drew men, like bees to a honeypot. Nesta was sure that it was out of concern for Sara, and not because of Goronwy, that her own father was there at the graveside. She studied him. Rhys, too, was now in his mid-fifties, a lean spare man, his eyes still dark and piercing, his high cheek bones giving his face an aesthetic look, together with its heavy dark beard and dark brows. He was standing shoulder to shoulder with Ralph Hendrix whose handsome, clean-shaven face was set like granite, his wide mouth a hard line, his grey eyes hooded.

As the minister droned on, Nesta thought about the feud that still smouldered between Ralph and her father. Whenever they met their horns locked. They used politics as a weapon, words as bullets, in their struggle to impress Sara.

Aware of her power over both of them, Sara would flutter her lashes, widen her sea-blue eyes and smile provocatively, first at one and then the other.

Nesta felt positive that although Sara listened to each of them with rapt attention, she was quite unable to comprehend their arguments. She didn't think Sara was really interested in doing so, either. For her the thrill lay in arousing the emotions of the two men, playing them as if they were fish on the end of a line. When she tired of her little game she walked away . . . until the next time she felt the need to boost her own ego.

Ralph's barbed comments about Plaid Cymru, his oblique references to the Dragon, although he knew quite well that it was the name by which her father was known in the Plaid Cymru movement, kept their feud actively alive.

'They are just like two small boys squabbling in a play-ground,' she had said angrily to Gwilym, after a visit from Ralph and Sara while her father had been staying at St Hilary's Hill.

'Just ignore them. They're not doing any harm,' Gwilym laughed.

'It's the atmosphere when they are here together,' she had protested. 'Anyway, I don't like to hear my father being slated by Ralph Hendrix.'

'He gets a lot worse when he faces a public meeting,' Gwilym reminded her.

That was very true, she reflected. Her father's gift of oratory made him a ready target for hecklers. Invariably, some sort of fracas would ensue, and often someone got hurt. Next day there would be glaring headlines in the national dailies about the Dragon.

Nesta hated the publicity.

As she walked Amelda and Llewellyn to school, or went shopping, she was sure people were nudging each other and talking about her. Gwilym assured her she was imagining it since it was unlikely that anyone outside their family knew who her father was.

'Rubbish!' she'd retorted angrily as Gwilym tried to placate her. 'His picture was in the paper and even Llewellyn recognised him. He even got involved in a fight in the school playground because some of the other boys were taunting him about it.'

'Well, what can we do?' Gwilym asked wearily. 'You wouldn't want to tell your father not to come here any more.'

'No, but you could have a quiet word with your friend, Ralph Hendrix,' she told him, her dark eyes blazing.

'About what?'

'If he stopped writing such scurrilous things about my Da it might help,' Nesta told him spiritedly. 'He only does it to impress your mother and to try and turn her against him.'

She had listened in stony silence as Gwilym had pointed out that even though it might seem like a personal vendetta, the *Post* was simply reporting a news item, the same as all the other newspapers were doing.

For several days afterwards there had been a rift between

53

them. Finally, they resolved not to talk about Rhys's political activities since it was a subject they would never be able to agree on because of their divided loyalties, Nesta's to her father, Gwilym's to his newspaper.

After the funeral, Nesta stood silently watching as Sara accepted the condolences of family, friends and neighbours. Black suited Sara, and although she had toned down her make-up she still looked more like an actress playing a part than a grief-stricken widow, Nesta reflected. The tears were there; from time to time, Sara dabbed at her brilliant blue eyes with a dainty, lace-edged handkerchief. And the occasional husky catch in Sara's voice brought murmurs of sympathy.

As she stood on her own, sipping a glass of port, Nesta found herself wondering how her father-in-law's death would affect her and Gwilym. Sara could hardly go on living in such a huge house now that she was on her own. The upkeep must be enormous, Nesta mused. The resident nurse would go, of course, but Sara would still need her daily woman and the gardener who came three mornings a week.

She refused to contemplate Sara moving in with them. Having people to stay always seemed to create tension between Gwilym and herself. Much as she loved her father, she was always relieved when his visit was over. She could never relax with someone else in the house. She always felt self-conscious, cringing away if Gwilym even put an arm around her.

'It's like living in a monastery when your father's staying here,' Gwilym always teased, whenever Rhys came for a few days.

And remembering this Nesta knew it would be disastrous for their own happiness if Sara moved in with them, even if it was only on a temporary basis.

She had worked hard to make her marriage successful and to provide a warm, loving background for Llewellyn

54

and Amelda. Remembering her own childhood, after her grandparents had died and she had lived with relatives who resented her presence, she had been determined that homelife for her children would be something special.

And it was a happy home in every way. She always made sure she had time to play with Llewellyn and Amelda, take them to the park and welcome their own little friends to tea. The only real bone of contention there had ever been in her marriage was over her father and the embarrassment of his outspoken affiliation with Plaid Cymru.

For months they would neither see Rhys nor hear from him and then suddenly, like a bomb exploding, he was headline news. Usually it was the result of something he had said at a meeting that aroused indignation from a political opponent. And invariably it was something reporters seized on and built up to relieve an otherwise mundane event.

Then his remarks, and often his picture, would be front page news, especially in the *Post*. Gwilym would arrive home with a copy, grim faced, his green eyes emerald chips under a scowling brow. He would fling the paper down on the table, stabbing at the offending article with his forefinger. Then, even before she had a chance to read the report, his fury would erupt and their truce forgotten as he gave vent to his feelings.

'Why does he have to go on fighting a lost cause?' Gwilym would exclaim, running his hand through his hair in exasperation.

'It's not a lost cause to him,' Nesta would point out. 'And he is right. Unless people are concerned about what happens, Wales will be devastated. Mines and quarries have already scarred the countryside, the mountains are cloaked in firs so that most of the indigenous plants and trees have been destroyed. And why? Just so that some entrepreneur from England can make a profit!'

Knowing her argument was well-founded only seemed to incite Gwilym's anger.

'How do you think I feel when people I work with ridicule the Dragon. They all know who he really is . . . and our relationship!'

'And you are ashamed to admit it?'

'No!' Gwilym sighed and hugged her close. 'But I wish he wasn't always hitting the headlines the way he does.'

The last time it had happened, some few weeks earlier, Gwilym had threatened to ban Rhys from coming to the house.

'You mean the only way I can meet my Da, and he can see his grandchildren, is if we go to visit him?' Nesta asked balefully.

'I wasn't suggesting that, either,' Gwilym snapped.

'You mean . . .' Nesta's velvet brown eyes became glassy as she stared in disbelief. 'You mean stop seeing him?'

'I don't know what I mean!' Gwilym thrust his hands through his thick wavy hair as though desperately trying to brush the problem away. 'It might be best, though, if you didn't invite him here . . . for a while at any rate . . . and that you went to see him on your own. You said yourself that Llewellyn was getting into fights at school because . . .'

'So I did!' Nesta admitted scathingly, 'and if I remember rightly you just laughed it off, so why the change of heart? Has Ralph been getting at you?'

'No, it's just that Llewellyn believes implicitly everything your father tells him. If we don't watch out he's going to end up just as fanatical as Rhys about Welsh politics.'

'And, of course, you wouldn't like that?' Nesta said frostily.

'No, I certainly would not! Llewellyn's got his way to make in the world and he'll never get anywhere with a

Plaid Cymru label tied round his neck.'

'It depends where he wants to go,' she retorted icily. 'Not everyone wants to be a True Blue Tory, like your father.'

And now the True Blue Tory was dead and the staunch Plaid Cymru supporter was paying his last respects to a man whose views had been so directly opposed to his own, Nesta thought wryly.

Wynne, Huw and Rhys were the first to take their leave of Sara. They had a long train journey back to North Wales and were anxious to be on their way. One by one, the rest of the mourners departed, but it was early evening before Sara, Nesta and Gwilym were finally alone.

'I feel absolutely exhausted,' Sara exclaimed as she sipped off her high-heeled, black shoes and collapsed onto the settee. 'I need a cup of tea. Gwilym, go and ask Mrs Mottram to make some before she starts clearing up.'

'Would you like Gwilym and me to stay here tonight?' Nesta suggested as she sipped her tea.

'No, I shall be perfectly all right.'

'You can't stay here on your own, Mother. Come on back with us,' Gwilym persisted.

'You are being very kind and thoughtful, darling,' she told him with a tremulous smile, 'but I really would prefer to stay here . . . in my own home . . . with my precious memories.'

Her decision worried Gwilym. He was reluctant to leave, and could talk of nothing else as they drove home. The moment they were indoors he phoned to make sure his mother hadn't changed her mind. He let it ring for at least five minutes, but there was no answer.

'She has probably taken a couple of sleeping tablets and gone to bed,' Nesta yawned.

'There's an extension phone by the side of the bed,' he said worriedly.

'Perhaps she switched it off so that she wouldn't be disturbed. She must have been exhausted. I know I am! Come on,' she linked her arm through his. 'Let's make the most of the fact that Llewellyn and Amelda are staying with the Petersons and have an undisturbed night ourselves.'

When Gwilym insisted on phoning again, Nesta went on up to bed. She was almost asleep when he finally gave up trying and came upstairs.

He was just leaving for the office next morning when the phone rang.

'It's for you . . . it's your mother,' Nesta said handing him the receiver. 'She sounds awfully odd!'

'What did she want? Is anything wrong?' Nesta asked worriedly as Gwilym slammed down the receiver.

'I think she is out of her mind,' Gwilym said exasperatedly. 'She was phoning from London . . . she says she will be staying there for a few days and then going either to Spain or Portugal.'

'On her own!'

'No, that's the devil of it.' He paused, rubbing his hand over his chin, his green eyes perplexed as his gaze met Nesta's. 'She says she is going with Ralph Hendrix.'

7

'Nesta, have you seen this?'

The crash as Gwilym's hand came down on the kitchen table set the dishes rattling.

Llewellyn and Amelda, who were also having their breakfast, looked up quickly as their father stabbed at the newspaper in front of him. Llewellyn's dark brows creased in a heavy frown, Amelda pushed her fair hair back from her face as she twisted her head sideways so that she could read the headline her father was pointing at.

'Granda Rhys playing the field,' she quipped saucily as she spotted the photograph.

Gwilym scowled in her direction but ignored her comment. He passed the newspaper to Nesta who read the headline and caption in silence, then gave a cursory glance at the picture of two long-limbed girls wearing wide sashes emblazoned 'Plaid Cymru 1966' who stood on either side of her father.

'Just an election publicity stunt,' she murmured non-committally as she handed the newspaper back.

'Exactly!' Gwilym looked affronted. 'Yet when I asked him to let me do an in-depth profile, a serious comment about his beliefs and aims, he turned me down flat!'

'He probably didn't trust you,' Nesta told him as she buttered a slice of toast. 'I expect he was afraid that Ralph Hendrix would get his pen to it and twist what was written.'

'Utter rubbish!' Impatiently, Gwilym pushed his plate of bacon and eggs away and stood up.

'Aren't you going to finish your breakfast?'

'You expect me to eat with this hanging over my head?

Can you imagine what will be said at the editorial meeting this morning? This,' he jabbed angrily at the paper, 'makes me look a complete fool. They'll think I either couldn't be bothered or else that I didn't want to run a piece on him for family reasons. They certainly won't believe he refused to talk to me!'

'You should have let Llewellyn write the article,' Amelda said pertly, 'he can persuade Granda to do just about anything he wants him to.'

'Don't talk rot, Amelda,' Llewellyn muttered, colouring violently and scowling at his sister.

'He takes more notice of you than he does of me!' she protested mildly.

'That is probably because I listen to what he has to say and talk to him about things that interest him,' Llewellyn told her loftily. 'All you do is gossip about what you do at school, or with those silly friends of yours. Or about pop records. He isn't interested in the Beatles and . . .'

'Shut up, both of you; this is a serious matter,' Gwilym barked. 'Did you know your father would be speaking at the Camarthen by-election in support of Gwynfor Evans?' he asked Nesta sharply.

'Not specifically, but it stands to reason that he would be there to support the Plaid Cymru candidate, doesn't it?'

'Then why wouldn't he agree to letting me do a write-up? It would have been first-class publicity for the party and for him.'

'Don't ask me! I haven't seen him for weeks. Wynne said he might as well rent Idwal Cottage out for all the time he spends there.'

'It certainly makes me look a fool when the national papers can manage to get a quote from him and I can't,' Gwilym rumbled on.

'Perhaps if you were a little more sympathetic towards him he would be more co-operative,' Nesta told him tartly. 'You don't exactly go out of your way to make him welcome. And it's not all that long ago that you tried to ban me from seeing him.'

'Utter rubbish!'

'No, it is not. You said you didn't want the children's minds filled with Welsh nonsense. And you've said more than once that Llewellyn was hardly likely to get anywhere if he had a Plaid Cymru label tied round his neck.'

'You are dreaming it!'

'Oh, no, I'm not. Didn't your father say that, Llewellyn?'

'Leave me out of your arguments!' White-faced, his dark eyes blazing, Llewellyn made for the door. 'I'm sick to death of hearing you two squabbling about Granda and going on about what he does. Why can't you leave him alone. What he says makes sense . . .'

The rest of Llewellyn's remarks were drowned as he slammed the door noisily behind him. Nesta sighed as she heard him running up the stairs and then the sound of his bedroom door crashing shut.

'He seems to be getting more and more touchy every day,' she said worriedly. It sometimes seemed unbelievable to her that such happy-go-lucky children had become such difficult to handle teenagers.

'Take no notice, he's worrying about his A Level results,' Amelda said airily, helping herself to marmalade.

'Why should he be worried?' Nesta asked sharply, her dark eyes puzzled. 'He always comes top in class exams.'

'They had to do an essay on one of the most important problems facing the world in 1966. He did his on "The Fate of the Welsh Language" and now . . .'

'He did what!' Gwilym's roar cut short what Amelda was saying. 'The bloody fool . . .'

'Why? What's wrong with that for a subject?' Nesta looked from one to the other bewildered. 'It's relevant, isn't it?'

'It is also a topic that the government are trying to play down,' Gwilym groaned. 'The very last subject to choose for A Levels if he wanted to impress the examiners!'

'I still don't understand,' Nesta looked at him perplexed.

'Surely you've read in the papers that they are saying that the future of Wales depends on the Welsh language being recognised equally with English. They've taken Tynged yr Iaith 'Fate of the Language' as their rallying cry! They've even had it printed on banners and wave them outside the university buildings and at public meetings. Its given Welsh-speaking students a "cause" and they're being egged on by fanatics like your father and Saunders Lewis.'

'And they believe that every person is of equal value, regardless of sex or age and that they have the right to control their own lives,' Amelda added, flicking her long hair back over her shoulders with a challenging gesture.

'And what is that supposed to mean?' Gwilym demanded.

'That Llewellyn is entitled to his opinion. And if he thinks what Granda is doing is right then he should be able to say so without having you shout him down,' she said defiantly, her violet eyes smouldering.

'And what about you?'

'Nothing to do with me what Llewellyn does,' she shrugged, looking down at her plate.

'I'm asking what your opinion is, Amelda. Do you think your grandfather is fighting for the right cause?'

'Of course!' She giggled nervously. 'You didn't think I went on that campaign with Granda and Llewellyn, when they painted out road signs that were in English, just for kicks did you?'

'I see!' Gwilym straightened his tie. 'So we have a Welsh outpost in this house, do we? Perhaps you'd like England to be under the control of a Welsh parliament . . .'

62

'That's the whole point of their argument, isn't it?' Amelda said quickly. 'The English wouldn't like it if they were under Welsh rule so why should the Welsh people have to put up with being ruled by the English. The present bunch of MPs either don't know what is best for Wales or don't care.'

'By the sound of it your grandfather has brain-washed you as well as Llewellyn,' Gwilym said disapprovingly. 'Well, I haven't time for all that nonsense this morning,' he added looking at his watch. 'You'd better go and get ready or you are going to be late for school.'

'That's the trouble with you, Daddy,' Amelda said angrily, 'you treat me like a child and won't listen to me.'

'That's quite enough, Amelda.'

'You won't listen to anybody else's opinion,' Amelda blundered on, ignoring her mother's warning glance. 'Just because you are a journalist and read all the press handouts, you think you know it all. Granda feels these things deep inside him and he knows whether they are good or bad because he loves Wales and only wants what is right for the people living there. That's why he is working so hard to see that Gwynfor Evans is returned as MP for Camarthen. He knows he is a man who can be trusted to support the right policies when he gets there. He's not trying to get into Parliament for the glory of it or to make a name for himself but to protect Wales for future generations.'

'Spare me the lecture, Amelda!'

'There you go again . . .' her cheeks flushed, her violet eyes bright with tears of frustration, Amelda pushed back her chair and ran from the room.

'Now you've upset her as well,' Nesta sighed as she began to stack the breakfast dishes.

'Let's hope the natives are more friendly at the office,' Gwilym muttered as he picked up his brief-case and made for the door. 'I doubt it though . . . not after they've seen that one of the nationals has actually managed to get an interview with the Dragon.'

Llewellyn waited until he heard his father's car drive away then he crept stealthily down the stairs. He paused half-way, smiling to himself as he heard the clatter of dishes coming from the kitchen as his mother cleared away the breakfast and washed up.

As quiet as any burglar he let himself out by the front door, swung his heavy duffle-bag over one shoulder and loped away towards the bus stop.

He didn't breathe freely until he reached Liverpool's Lime Street station and had bought a train ticket to Cardiff. As he settled into a corner seat, just as the train was pulling out, he wondered how long it would be before they discovered he was missing and came looking for him.

Not that they would stand much chance of finding him, he thought smugly as he relaxed and stretched out his long legs. There must be thousands of eighteen-year-olds dressed in blue denim jeans and black leather jackets wandering about, killing time while they waited for their examination results, or looking for work now that.the school year had ended.

He felt guilty about not saying goodbye to Amelda and his mother, but he couldn't take the risk since they were sure to tell his father what he was up to. He hoped they wouldn't get all weepy and upset when they discovered he was missing.

He hadn't even taken Granda Rhys into his confidence. He knew that would be the first check-point his father would make and he didn't want to put his grandfather into the position of having to lie or refuse to say what he knew.

He studied the three people travelling in the carriage

with him and wondered if any of them would remember him should they ever be asked. He decided not. The man with the brief-case was far too absorbed in the papers he kept taking out and reading. The middle-aged woman was engrossed in her knitting and the other man, a railway workman judging by his blue serge uniform, was using the journey as a chance to catch up with some sleep.

I will only be in Cardiff a day or two, Llewellyn thought complacently. Once he'd signed on a boat the world would be his oyster, and no one could trace him. He studied his reflection in the glass as the train shot into the darkness of a tunnel and decided he was not all that outstanding. His face looked long and lean with high cheekbones, his mouth just a straight line. In fact, the only really noticeable features were his dark eyes, heavy eyebrows and his thick, dark hair.

When he reached Cardiff, Llewellyn took a bus from Central Station to the Pier Head. He wandered around for a while and then asked a workman painting some railings the way to the docks office.

'What exactly are you looking for, boyo?'

'A job . . . on a boat. I want to sign on.' He felt himself colouring up as he spoke.

'I see!' The man pushed his cap back and scratched his head thoughtfully. 'Not a lot of openings, like. Not unless you are skilled at something, I mean?' He looked questioningly at Llewellyn then shook his head thoughtfully. 'Probably the best thing you can do is go along to Britannia Road, to the port manager's office. They just might have something to offer you. Better still,' he added as an afterthought, his face brightening, 'nip into the Minerva Café. Alice, the woman who runs it, keeps her ear to the ground. She'll know what boats are due to sail . . . and if they need any deck hands.'

The moment he pushed open the door of the café, and the smell of hot food wafted across the room, Llewellyn realised how hungry he was and that he hadn't eaten since breakfast. He ordered a hot pie and chips from the woman behind the counter and took them across to a corner seat.

'Are you Alice?' he asked as she came to clear the table next to where he was sitting.

'No . . . I only work here. What do you want with Alice?'

'I was told to ask for her.'

'I'll tell her. Come over to the counter when you're ready,' the woman told him as she picked up a pile of dishes and walked away.

When he had finished his meal, she took him through into a living room at the back of the café. It was small but cosy and cluttered with ornaments and pictures.

'You wanted to see me?'

The woman sitting there in a high-back armchair was stout and heavily made up. Her dyed hair was piled high on her head and she wore a tight-fitting, high-necked black dress.

'A man outside told me to ask for you,' Llewellyn said nervously.

'Well, what do you want to know?' She lowered the paper she was reading and looked at him enquiringly.

'I . . . I'm looking for a job. I . . . want to go to sea.'

'Just left school, have you?'

For a moment he thought of lying, but her shrewd green stare unnerved him and he could only nod.

'Running away?'

'No . . . of course not!' he blustered. Then, as he saw the gleam of amusement in the green eyes he gave a slight shrug of his shoulders and nodded.

'Why don't you sit down and tell me about it? I may be able to help . . . but not with a job on a boat. There's not many of those these days. Anyway,' she frowned, 'you don't look the type to be running away to sea. Bit old for that, aren't you?'

66

'I'm eighteen,' he said flatly. 'I'm waiting for my exam results to see if I've got a place at university or not.'

'And you are worried in case you haven't,' she said thoughtfully as she studied him. 'Where have you come from?'

'Up north . . . Wallasey. It's part of Merseyside.'

'So why come to Cardiff? Aren't there any boats sailing from Liverpool or Birkenhead? Or was that too near home, and it would be too easy for your folks to find you?'

'No, I had other reasons. My grandfather used to sail from Cardiff.'

She stared at him again for a long moment, frowning in a slightly puzzled way.

'Have you anywhere to sleep tonight?'

'No . . . I thought I'd get taken on right away and be able to sleep on the boat . . .'

'You are a green horn!' Alice laughed derisively. 'You expected to just walk onto a ship and get signed on. What about union cards?'

'Union cards . . . I don't know anything about those. I just thought you could work your passage . . .'

'You're living in the past, son. No good thinking you can do the same as your grandfather did. When he was your age you could even stowaway if you were really desperate to go to sea. Pick 'em up in one port, drop 'em off in another and no questions asked. It's not like that today. You'll have to register at the shipping office so that they can issue all the necessary papers and even when you've done that you will have to wait until there is a vacancy.'

'I'd better go and register, then,' Llewellyn said, standing up.

'You've left it too late to do that today. They close at four o'clock.'

'Oh!' Llewellyn ran his hand through his thick hair in a

gesture of despair. 'Do you know where I can get a room for the night?' he asked. 'I can't afford hotel prices.'

'You can stay here . . . I have a spare bedroom,' she told him. 'I'm probably out of my mind suggesting it, but you do remind me of someone. Now,' she stood up, 'take yourself off and have a look at Cardiff. Be back here by nine o'clock, no later. You can have some supper here in the café before you turn in. Off with you, then.'

When he started to thank her she gave him a push towards the door. 'Go on with you, before I change my mind,' she said briskly.

8

Alice was waiting in the open doorway when Llewellyn reached the café.

'I'm not late, am I?' he asked breathlessly.

'No, it's only five minutes to nine,' she told him, looking at her watch. 'I was just enjoying the evening air since there are no customers. Its been a glorious day and by the look of that red glow in the sky it will be fine again tomorrow. I'll lock up now that you are back.'

Llewellyn waited as she fixed a steel mesh grid over the glass portion of the door and then rammed the locks on the top and bottom of the door securely into position.

'Can't afford to take chances,' she said as she led the way to the room at the back of the café. 'Rough area, this; always has been. Quieter now than it was in the old days, of course, because there aren't as many boats sailing from here. Most of them berth at Southampton nowadays.'

As he followed her formidable figure through into the sitting room behind the café, Llewellyn thought it was highly unlikely that anyone would try to break in if they knew they had to face her.

He judged her to be at least sixty. She was almost as tall as he was, twice his weight and massively built. She looked muscular, not fat. She wore her hennaed hair piled up in an elaborate arrangement of coils and curls that added to her height. Her face was plump and so heavily made up that it was impossible to tell whether she was wrinkled or not. Her green eyes were as bright and sharp as those of a woman half her age, and her voice was crisp and decisive.

'Sit down, then; your supper is ready. This should fill you up.' She placed a steaming plate of sausages, mash and beans on the table in front of him.

After she had taken away his empty plate, Alice returned with coffee, biscuits and cheese and sat down facing him.

'Come on,' she invited, 'help yourself and tell me a bit about yourself. Is it the first time you've been to Cardiff?'

'Yes, but I've heard a lot about it. My mother was born here. She worked at the City Hall after she left school. I went to have a look at it and she's quite right: it is a magnificent building, in a wonderful setting. I would have liked to go inside Cardiff Castle but they were closing when I got there.'

'And you say your name is Vaughan?' Alice asked, smiling at his enthusiasm, but following her own train of thought.

'Her name was Evans before she married.'

'Evans?' A look of disbelief widened Alice Roberts' green eyes.

'The name probably sounds familiar because there has been a lot in the newspapers about my grandfather, Rhys Evans, lately,' Llewellyn told her.

'You mean the Dragon?'

'That's right!' Llewellyn's dark eyes glowed proudly. 'He's been making the headlines with his speeches in the Camarthen by-election. He's a staunch Plaid Cymru supporter.'

'And he's living on Merseyside?'

'Oh, no. He lives near Blaenau Ffestiniog. He has a cottage there tucked way at the foot of Moelwyn Mawr. It's absolute heaven,' Llewellyn said enthusiastically. 'Have you ever been to North Wales?'

'Never . . . and I don't speak Welsh either. Do you?'

'No,' Llewellyn admitted, colouring up, 'none of my

family speaks Welsh, not even my grandfather. But I intend to learn. That's why I've applied for Bangor or Aberystwyth.'

'What's wrong with Cardiff University, then?'

'They don't seem to have the same feel for the language here in South Wales as they do in the North,' Llewellyn said shaking his head. 'Mind you,' he grinned, 'after going to have a look at it this afternoon I might change my mind. It's a very handsome building.'

'If you take yourself off to sea then you won't be going to any university at all,' Alice reminded him sharply.

'That's true!' His face clouded. 'Perhaps I should have thought it through more carefully. I suppose if I do get a place at university I will be living away from home anyway.'

'Well, I certainly think you should sleep on it,' Alice told him as she began to stack the dishes. 'It's a pity to throw away the chance of a good education.'

After Llewellyn had gone to bed, Alice Roberts took a pile of newspaper cuttings from the sideboard drawer and sat looking through them. Many were yellow with age, all were reports about the fiery political speaker known as the Dragon.

It was almost midnight when the phone rang.

Nesta jumped up to answer it then paused, looking questioningly at Gwilym.

'You go,' her voice was barely a whisper. She held her breath as he picked up the receiver and spoke into it, trying to reassure herself that everything was going to be all right and that it would be news of Llewellyn.

'I shouldn't worry,' the policeman had told Nesta when she had reported him missing. 'Lads of that age often take off without a word to their families. He'll be back.'

'But can't you look for him?' she asked.

'It's too soon to say he's missing, I'm afraid,' he'd told

her. 'And he is over eighteen. If he'd been a child, now . . .'

'But he hasn't left school yet!'

She had gone over the conversation with the policeman a dozen times in her mind during the three hours since she had reported Llewellyn missing.

She blamed herself and she blamed Gwilym. They should have understood the strain Llewellyn was under, waiting for his examination results. He wanted to go to university, he wanted them all to be proud of him, especially his grandfather. It was almost like reliving her own longing to go to university. Not being able to afford to do so had seemed calamitous at the time.

Gwilym probably didn't attach the same importance to it all because he had had such a different background. An only child, he'd never had to prove himself. His parents had had paid for his education. And he had always known that if he wasn't happy in the career he'd chosen then there was always a safe niche waiting for him in his father's firm.

'There's a woman on the line, says she wants to speak to you. She wouldn't give her name but says she's speaking from Cardiff . . . and that it has something to do with Llewellyn,' Gwilym called out, breaking her train of thought.

As she took the receiver from him, Gwilym waited anxiously. His frown deepened as her face grew more and more puzzled and the disbelief in her voice grew stronger.

'Well . . . what did she want?' he asked impatiently as Nesta replaced the receiver.

'It was about Llewellyn . . .' Her voice choked and she began to cry, deep lung-bursting sobs that left her trembling.

Gwilym led her across to the settee and sat there, cradling her in his arms until she calmed down. Then he poured them both a stiff whisky.

'I'm as worried as you are, you know, but drink this before you tell me what she said,' he told her.

'I'm sorry!' She caught at his hand, resting her cheek against it.

'Well?' He brought his drink over to the settee and sat beside her, an arm around her shoulder.

'Llewellyn's quite safe. He's in Cardiff, and at the moment he's in bed and sound asleep . . .' She hesitated and looked sideways at Gwilym. 'Now don't get angry. He wanted to go to sea . . . like his grandfather.'

She felt Gwilym's arm tighten, and saw his mouth set into a grim line as he waited for her to finish.

'It's such a coincidence . . . I still can't believe it,' she murmured, wiping the tears from her eyes. 'Someone told him to go to this café as the woman who ran it would know what boats were due to sail and if any of them needed deck hands. While Llewellyn was having his supper, she talked to him, to try and find out where he was from and why he was running away from home. She said she thought there was something vaguely familiar about him. When he told her that his grandfather was Rhys Evans, she realised who he was. After he'd gone to sleep she got his name and address from the label on his duffle-bag and phoned us.'

'So why ask for you? Why couldn't she have told me all this?' Gwilym said irritably.

'That's the incredible coincidence! She knew me when I was a little girl! She used to be a friend of my mother's. It was through her that my mother and father met. In those days, her family ran a pub near the docks. Then they moved away and we all lost touch with each other. Alice hasn't seen my Da for years and years, not since long before the war. She's seen his picture in the newspapers several times and thought it was the same Rhys Evans.'

'She never got in touch with him?'

'No. She said she didn't think there was any point in

reviving such old memories. I was only about seven the last time she saw me . . .' Nesta's voice drifted off as she recalled those far off days. One of her most vivid memories was when she had been about fifteen, and she had gone to Tiger Bay to try and find Alice Roberts in the hope that she might be able to tell her where her father was.

'Well, what about Llewellyn? Are we going to leave him there or collect him?' Gwilym asked looking at his watch.

'He's safe until tomorrow. Alice has given me her phone number so I will ring her and let her know what we've decided to do.'

'What I don't understand,' Gwilym frowned, 'is why he went to Cardiff.'

'Perhaps he needed to get right away from all of us,' Nesta said thoughtfully. 'Maybe it would do him good if we left him where he was . . . for a few days at any rate. Alice will keep an eye on him, now she knows who he is. And when he finds it's not so easy as he thought to get a job on a boat, then he may come back home of his own accord.'

'The theory is all right, but what if you are wrong and he does manage to get on a boat? The damn thing might have sailed and we mightn't be able to reach him. It could even end up that he loses his university place.'

'No,' Nesta said quietly confident. 'I'm sure he wants that place far too much to let it slip through his fingers. Let's go to bed. We can sort it all out in the morning.'

'You've got more faith in him than I have,' Gwilym told her huffily. 'I thought you would want me to get the car out and drive down to Cardiff overnight so that we could drag him back to the nest.'

'I can think of much better things to do overnight,' she told him, sliding an arm around his waist as they moved towards the stairs.

'Everything seems to have changed! It wasn't a bit like this the last time I was here,' Nesta exclaimed as she and Amelda walked out of Cardiff General Station into the heat of a bright July day.

'Daddy said we were to get a taxi from the station,' Amelda reminded her. 'Come on, the rank is this way.'

By the time they pulled up outside the Minerva Café Nesta felt dazed and bewildered by all the new buildings and the many changes that had taken place since she had lived in Cardiff.

'It was over twenty years ago, Mum!' Amelda reminded her. 'I imagine a lot of the people you knew are dead and gone. This Alice Roberts must be an old woman now so I don't suppose she will recognise you, either.'

The warmth of Alice Roberts' welcome took their breath away. When she released Nesta from her bearlike hug she turned to Amelda and the sparkle of joy in her vivid green eyes turned to one of incredulity.

'Eleanor, oh, my dearest Eleanor,' she gasped as she took both of Amelda's slim hands between her large ones and stared into Amelda's upturned face as if she was seeing a ghost.

'It's Amelda . . . her name is Amelda, not Eleanor,' Nesta corrected her.

'You should have named her Eleanor . . . after your own mother,' Alice pronounced. 'She's the spitting image of her. I've never seen such a likeness. You must have noticed it!'

'How could I?' Nesta murmured bewildered. 'I never knew Mother.'

'Oh, I know that, but you must have seen a picture at some time. Rhys had one of Eleanor, surely?'

I do have an old snapshot of her with Da, but it's so faded I can't really see what she looked like. I don't think Da has any others, though. When I kept house for him there wasn't a single picture in the whole of the place.'

'But hasn't Rhys ever commented on the likeness?'

'Never!'

'He couldn't help but notice it,' Alice said in a puzzled voice, her eyes never leaving Amelda. 'You've got her slender figure, and the same shape face and colouring. And those eyes! I've never seen anyone else with eyes of that soft shade of violet. They're like amethysts . . . it's quite incredible!' Alice murmured. 'Even your hair is the same colour as Eleanor's was. I remember how I used to envy the way it curled over her forehead in soft little tendrils, just like yours does. A shade or two lighter, perhaps, than I remember.'

'Were you a friend of my grandmother's?' Amelda asked.

'Oh, yes! We grew up side by side, as close as sisters until she married. Then, just a year after that when your mother was born, dear Eleanor died.' Alice sighed and dabbed at her eyes. 'Meeting you brings it all back to mind. Just as seeing your brother reminded me so vividly of Rhys Evans when he was a young man.'

'Yes, Llewellyn does look like Granda.'

'He's the spit and image of Rhys when I first knew him. And he has your grandfather's spirit. All fire and high falutin' talk. Idealists, both of them! Out to set the world on fire, or put it to rights. I've followed your grandfather's goings-on in the newspapers for years now. All this carry-on with Plaid Cymru! I was pretty sure it was the Rhys Evans I once knew, and who had married my best friend all those years ago. Mind you, that beard makes him look different from the clean-shaven young sailor he once was. When that brother of yours walked in here and I found out just who he was, then I knew for certain that I was right. It was like meeting the young Rhys Evans all over again.'

'Where is Llewellyn now?' Amelda asked.

'I've put him to work repairing the lock on the back door, but he should be finished by now.' She smiled broadly. 'Why don't you go and find him? He wants to show you the Civic Centre here in Cardiff, and the university. I think he'd quite like to go to university here . . . that is if he's managed to get through his exams,' she added as she bustled Amelda towards the back of the café.

'Now, while the two of them are doing that, Nesta, you and me can go through to my sitting room and have a cup of tea and catch up with each other's news.'

9

'I've managed to get two extra press tickets for the Investiture so you can ask your father to come to Caernarvon with us if you wish, Nesta.'

'What about Llewellyn and Amelda? It's such an important historical event they might like the chance to be there. I can watch it on TV if you want to take them,' Nesta suggested.

'They didn't seem all that interested about coming with us when I mentioned it when they were here at Easter,' Gwilym reminded her. 'What was it Llewellyn described us as? "Golden oldies of a past generation!"'

'He was only joking!' Nesta defended quickly, remembering how incensed Gwilym had been at the time by Llewellyn's rather tactless remark.

Since he had been at university, Llewellyn had become both supercilious and disparaging, she thought unhappily. It seemed hard to believe that less than three years ago, when he had tried to run away to sea, he had been so nervous and unsure of himself. Now he was always ready to censure them and their lifestyle in a depreciating way that could be most hurtful.

It was all part of growing up, she supposed, but was thankful that Amelda was less brash. She was still quick to criticise or ridicule, but she managed to do it more gently and without malice, and her accompanying smile always seemed to take the sting out of her words.

'Was he?' Gwilym's green eyes levelled with hers. 'I know I'm going grey, but I sometimes think he considers us even older than your father. At least Rhys thinks along the same lines as him politically.'

78

'I'm wondering how my Da is going to react at the Investiture,' Nesta said worriedly.

'He won't make a scene, I hope.'

'Keep your fingers crossed,' Nesta sighed. 'I don't think he knows whether to be pleased because Prince Charles is being given the title Prince of Wales or against the whole idea.'

'He probably thinks it should be a direct descendant of Owain Glyndwr receiving the honour,' Gwilym grinned. 'Mind you, from the research I've been doing for the ten-page feature we are running I think they've managed to trace Prince Charles back to Llewellyn the Great so that should keep everyone happy, your father and our Llewellyn included.'

'I'll phone my Da tonight and let him know about the tickets,' Nesta promised. 'Are we going to pick him up on our way there?'

'No, it's better if we all start out from here. There's going to be a tremendous television and press coverage so we'll have to be in our places early.'

'I wonder what the weather will be like?'

'Sweltering hot, and with a thunderstorm to liven things up, probably, seeing it is lst July.'

'I'd better tell him to bring a raincoat, just in case.'

'Do that. I'm not sure if our seats will be under cover or not and if it does rain you can't dash for shelter.'

Rhys was far more pleased by the idea of going to the Investiture than Nesta had thought he would be.

'You're sure it isn't going to be too much for you, Da?' she enquired anxiously. 'All the crowds and so on . . . Caernarvon will be packed solid.'

'Crowds!' he told her scornfully. 'Compared to an Eisteddfod gathering or one of the Plaid Cymru conventions, it will be a picnic. The trouble with you, girl, is that you sit at home too much. It will be an eye-opener for you.'

79

In that Rhys was right.

Caernarvon was jammed with people from all over Britain as well as overseas visitors. And the town was gay with bunting and flags flying from every rooftop and pole.

'Good thing we brought a picnic with us; we'd never manage to get served anywhere with this crowd,' Nesta said as they prepared to eat their lunch, sitting in the car park.

'You'd better ration the coffee to one cup each. Once you are in your seat I think you may find it is impossible to move,' Gwilym reminded her.

'How long does the Investiture take?'

'About an hour but everyone will have to be in their places at least an hour before the ceremony is due to start.'

'And you may not be able to leave right away afterwards,' Rhys added.

'When its all over, the best thing, then, is for you and Rhys to make your way back here and wait for me in the car,' Gwilym told her.

'You mean you aren't going to sit with us?' Nesta asked, her brown eyes widening in astonishment, her voice sharp with disappointment.

'For me it's work, not pleasure,' Gwilym reminded her. 'I have to phone through my copy while the event is going on if it is to make the afternoon editions.'

'Thank goodness you are here to chaperone me, Da,' Nesta said pointedly, turning to Rhys with a wide smile.

'You think there's going to be trouble then, do you?' he asked gravely, his dark eyes gleaming.

'Well, no . . . leastways, I hope not,' she said, uncertain of whether or not he was teasing her.

'You could be right, of course. There might well be Plaid Cymru uprising against Prince Charles. Why should the greatest accolade in Wales be given to a man who is not Welsh? Tell me that?'

'The monarch of England's eldest son has always inherited the title,' Nesta said quickly.

'Only since 1301 when Edward I pledged his newly born son to the people of Wales and proclaimed him Prince of Wales. And he tricked them by telling them that the child couldn't speak English. Are we going to be tricked again today and told that this prince can speak Welsh?'

'He will have learned enough to make the necessary responses, perhaps a speech, even,' Gwilym assured them.

'Which is flagrant trickery,' Rhys proclaimed angrily. 'It would be far better if they admitted he hasn't the tongue . . .'

'Stop it, Da. You're getting yourself all worked up. You can't speak Welsh either, but you are one of the staunchest defenders of Wales for the Welsh that I know. So why shouldn't Prince Charles feel just as impassioned about Wales as you do?'

'The last Prince of Wales did,' Gwilym reminded them. 'It made headline news the way he used to visit the south Wales miners . . .'

'And a lot of good it did him or them,' Rhys roared. 'Ministers didn't approve of him going down the mines, or travelling round the Valleys and seeing for himself the conditions and squalor of the people who lived there. They proclaimed him king but they never crowned him Edward VIII. King for a matter of a few weeks and then forced to abdicate.'

'Look, I want to enjoy my day out so not another word about politics, Welsh or otherwise,' Nesta scolded.

'Right, a truce it is,' Rhys agreed. 'I won't even wave the flag I've brought with me if it's going to upset you.'

Grinning, he pulled a miniature flag from his inside pocket and unfurled it. The Welsh dragon, blood red on its white and green backing, was flanked by the words Plaid Cymru.

Nesta found the ceremony sheer magic.

From where they were sitting they looked directly down onto the huge round dais of blue slate that contrasted sharply with the verdant green grass of the Inner Ward of the castle. The Queen, Prince Philip and Prince Charles were seated in the centre of the dais beneath a transparent canopy that had been specially contrived so that the entire ceremony could be a television spectacular.

And in a great circle around them, flanked by the Welsh Guards, resplendent in their colourful uniforms, were the choirs, the bands, courtiers and members of the government. There were lords resplendent in red and ermine, judges in gowns and wigs, and the heads of the armed forces in their magnificent gold-braided uniforms. Representatives of other nations, their national dress vying with VIPs' morning dress and the colourful dresses and stunning hats of their ladies, sat in tiered rows against the grey stone backcloth of the castle walls.

When Prince Charles, resplendent in his purple velvet cloak with its white ermine cape, knelt before the Queen to pay homage to her, Nesta felt tears of emotion prick her eyes. And a lump came into her throat as the Queen placed the crown on Charles' head, proclaiming him Prince of Wales and Earl of Chester.

She felt proud to have a son of about the same age.

'If we get separated, Da, remember to make for the car park,' she reminded Rhys when the ceremony ended and people began to surge towards the exit.

'Perhaps it would be best if we stayed in our seats for a few minutes until things have quietened down,' Rhys suggested.

As they sat back, watching the surge of people streaming past them towards the exit, Nesta heard someone call out to Rhys. She looked up in surprise as a woman in a smart black and white linen suit pushed her way towards them and hugged Rhys enthusiastically.

'Sara!' Nesta gasped, staring at her mother-in-law in amazement.

'Surprise, surprise.' Nesta turned quickly as Ralph Hendrix's mocking tones sounded above the cacophony of noise.

'Isn't this exciting!' Sara exclaimed, straightening her black and white straw hat as she sank down in the vacant chair next to Rhys. 'I was sure you would be here somewhere. I knew you wouldn't be able to resist such a spectacle even if you didn't approve,' she teased.

'I thought you were in Spain! When did you get back to England?' Nesta asked bemused.

'Ralph wanted to come over for the Investiture so of course I just had to come with him,' Sara explained. 'We weren't too sure when we would get away so we thought we'd contact you after it was all over. We're staying on in London for about a week.'

'Isn't Gwilym here?' Ralph frowned.

'He has just gone to phone his copy through. We were waiting for the crowds to thin down a bit before making our way back to the car to meet him. Have you got time to come back to the car or do you have a train to catch?'

'We've all the time in the world. We're staying overnight at the Royal here in Caernarvon. Why don't you all come back there with us and have dinner?' Ralph invited.

'Give us a chance to catch up with each other's news,' Sara agreed, laying a hand on Rhys's arm.

'Well, that sounds very nice,' Nesta agreed. 'Gwilym will certainly want to see you,' she added smiling at Sara. 'Are you coming to stay with us for a few days.'

'Sorry, darling, it is quite out of the question,' Sara told her quickly. 'Ralph has business in London and I must do some shopping. The Costa del Sol is a wonderful place to live, but the shops in Almeria aren't quite up to Harrod's

83

standard. My wardrobe is sadly in need of replenishing!'

It was almost three in the morning by the time they had taken Rhys home and then driven back to Liverpool, yet Nesta felt very wide awake. Meeting up with Sara and Ralph had been so unexpected and had added an additional piquancy to the outing.

It was the first time she had seen her mother-in-law since Goronwy had died and Sara had gone to live in Spain with Ralph Hendrix.

The fact that she must be almost seventy seemed unbelievable. In the flowing blue-flowered silk dress she had changed into for dinner she could easily have been taken for mid-fifties. Her hair which should by now have been grey, was a very discreet blonde and her make-up was so carefully applied over her golden tan that she looked quite radiant.

'Maybe it's because she's happy at last,' Gwilym commented when she remarked on it to him as they were undressing for bed.

'You mean she wasn't happy when she was married to your father?' she asked in surprise.

'I don't imagine it was much fun,' he said with a shrug. 'He was fifteen years older than her, you know. And he was a stickler for etiquette and always doing all the right things. He was pretty stingy and always kept her short of money even though we had a wonderful home. We never once went on a holiday abroad, you know. Mother always longed for the sun but he said he did enough travelling the world in the way of business and his idea of a holiday was a week at Port St Mary in the Isle of Man, where he could play golf everyday.'

'Couldn't she have taken you away somewhere?'

'God, no! He knew he couldn't trust her out of his sight. She would flirt with just about anything in trousers.'

'Gwilym!'

'It's a fact and you know it. Look how she dallied with your father and Ralph when we were first married. Mind, Ralph was just as bad as she was. They deserve each other.'

'You mean you don't think that Ralph and your mother are happy together? I thought they seemed perfectly well suited.'

'They probably are. Anyway,' Gwilym grinned as he settled himself in bed, 'if they're not then it's better that they should be making each other unhappy rather than two other people. And at least they both seem to enjoy the kind of life they are leading. Being in a rut, living a normal sort of life, must have been a terrible disappointment to my mother. I think when she married Dad she was expecting him to take her globetrotting, but of course he had no intention of doing that. And after I was born he had every excuse not to. I think she probably hated me because I kept her tied down.'

'But she had a wonderful home and they entertained a lot and she had all the clothes she wanted.'

'All chosen by him . . . even their friends! Flirting became her chief pastime because she was so bored. When I was in my teens and old enough to understand what was happening I never took any of my friends home because she always made a play for them and I felt such a damn fool.'

'That's how she met Ralph, of course,' Nesta agreed thoughtfully, 'through you bringing him home when she was visiting us.'

'By then it didn't worry me,' Gwilym said with a dismissive shrug. 'Anyway, I felt Ralph was old enough to take care of himself. He's always been a philanderer and it was better that he played the game with her than with *my* wife.'

'Would you have minded if he had?' she asked as she

slipped into bed beside him.

'Well, now, what do you think?' Gwilym's green eyes narrowed as he raised himself on one elbow and stared down at Nesta.

'I don't know.' Slowly she stretched her arms up to encircle his neck and draw his face down towards her own.

'If she'd responded like this then I would have minded very much,' Gwilym told her with a low chuckle as he teased her eager mouth with his tongue and lips.

She felt his strong smooth hands moving over her skin, following the line of her body to the curve of her waist and on to the swell of her hips. With a sigh of pleasure, she arched towards him, her palms moving down his broad, muscled back to draw him even closer.

Their deep need of each other was as vibrant as it had ever been. In their moments of passion, she forgot that she was now a middle-aged mother with two children at university, or that Gwilym was a respected senior editor on the *Post*.

Enfolded in each other's embrace, their flesh united, they were young and carefree once more, conscious only of the delights they could bring each other. Neither was aware that the slim litheness of youth had gone for ever, only of the raw excitement of enjoying each other's caresses, of the exquisite sensual satisfaction they were still capable of giving, and taking, as their passion reached its peak.

Tomorrow, with its work, family and problems wa another day, tonight was theirs, to delight in each other' sexuality and then to drift into sleep, limbs still entwined Nesta's head resting on Gwilym's chest.

10

'Politics, politics, politics, that's all we ever talk about in this house,' Nesta exclaimed angrily, her brown eyes blazing, as she pushed back her chair from the table and stormed out into the kitchen.

While she waited for the coffee to finish percolating she could hear the drone of voices from the dining room where Gwilym, Rhys and Llewellyn were arguing over the latest battle being fought by Plaid Cymru against the British Government's insistence that English, not Welsh, should be the main language in schools throughout Wales.

Frankly, she thought, as she heated up some milk, she couldn't have cared less about such a topic if it hadn't been for Amelda. She had only a few more months at Aberystwyth University before she sat her finals, and instead of spending her time studying she had been taking part in demonstrations that had ended in scuffles with the police. Several young people had ended up being forcibly dragged away to spend the night in prison and to appear before the magistrates next day. And because they refused to converse with these officials in English, some had ended up with seven-day sentences.

Nesta could see the sense of the argument, but it irked her that her father supported the cause quite so strongly since he didn't speak Welsh himself. It wouldn't be so bad, she thought, if he didn't involve Llewellyn and Amelda.

By the time she went back into the room, however, the subject had changed to that of land reclamation, the latest campaign being fought by her father.

As she handed him a cup of coffee, Nesta felt depressed by the enthusiasm he put into his beliefs. What did a frail, grey-haired old man in his seventies think he could achieve? she wondered.

He was egged on by that other patriarch, Saunders Lewis, of course, she thought angrily. Both of them should be sitting back and enjoying their old age, not draining their energy by battling against the cleverest men in London. Saunders Lewis must be almost eighty and yet he was still playing an active part in the fight to have the 500,000 acres of Welsh countryside still retained by the War Office released back to the people of Wales.

The matter had become such top line news that she and Gwilym had been forced to cut short their long-planned trip to Spain to see his mother and Ralph. Gwilym had suggested she might like to stay on for another week, but secretly she had been relieved to get back home. Ten days with Sara was quite long enough, she decided.

It was only a little over a year since they had seen her, when she and Ralph had come to England for the Prince of Wales investiture, but Sara had changed dramatically.

'What the hell's happened to mother?' Gwilym had exclaimed when they had gone up to their room to freshen up after their arrival at the penthouse flat in Almeria. 'She looks terrible and her voice is so slurred. Do you think she's hitting the bottle?'

'I'm sure it's more serious than that,' Nesta told him. 'I think she's had a stroke. One side of her mouth seems to be all twisted.'

'A stroke, at her age?'

'She is seventy. And she has lived it up these last few years.'

'No,' Gwilym dismissed the unpleasant suggestion. 'It's probably too much drink and too much sun,' he said, as he changed into a clean shirt. 'Come on, they'll think we are talking about them if we stay up here much longer.'

During their visit, however, it became more and more obvious that Nesta's surmise was the right one. Sara had not only lost the clarity of her speech but she was extremely forgetful and frequently very unsteady on her feet.

Like countless other exiles from Britain who had made their home on the Costa del Sol, Ralph was enjoying a very full and active life. It worried Nesta that he seemed to be quite oblivious of what was happening to Sara as she struggled to keep pace with his hectic social life.

'Why don't you rest more?' she told her mother-in-law. 'This heat is quite killing. I feel exhausted so I am sure you must feel the same.'

'And leave Ralph to flutter on his own?' Sara parried, patting her bleached hair. 'I'd lose him within a week!'

'Sara! Things aren't that bad between you, are they?'

'I'm old, Nesta. I know I've had my fling, but I'm not prepared to give in yet.'

'Ralph's the same age as you . . . more or less!'

'In years . . . yes. But he's worn better than I have. Men do, you know. Goronwy was in his late thirties when I married him, but you would never have known it. He was as virile as any of the lads of my own age. He burned himself out, mind you, trying to keep up with me. Now, Ralph has turned the tables on me.' Her thin, vividly rouged lips twisted in a bitter smile. 'I know, now, how Goronwy must have felt when he saw me flirting with men half his age.'

'You mean . . .'

'I mean that whenever Ralph can slip away from me he has a fling. Orgies with nubile young girls half his age. All these "men only" trips he goes on are for one thing only. He and his bunch of male cronies have it made. They're all desperately striving to recapture their youth, of course.'

'Are you sure, Sara?'

'Oh, yes. Most of the other women don't care. After

89

twenty or thirty years of marriage they're fed up with their partner, anyway. And if you want company there are plenty of handsome young Spaniards willing to be your escort . . . for a price.'

'Oh, Sara . . . you don't . . .'

'Don't what?' Sara's wrinkled face screwed up into a bitter laugh. 'Pay for it? No, I can't bear to look in my bathroom mirror these days so I certainly couldn't bring myself to strip off in front of a younger man and see the derision, or worse still the revulsion, in his eyes. My days are numbered, anyway, Nesta. I haven't told Ralph yet, but I've seen a doctor and it's the Big C. Six months at the most, he says. Don't say anything to Gwilym . . . not yet, anyway.'

Nesta had done as Sara had asked, and respected her confidence, but the knowledge was a burden that soured her holiday in Almeria. She had the uneasy feeling that she ought tell Gwilym so that they could be doing something to make the last few months of Sara's life more happy.

Her heart ached that Sara should end her days so desperately unhappy. She had never trusted Ralph Hendrix, not since Gwilym had first brought him to St Hilary's Hill over twenty years earlier. She still didn't like him and regarded his treatment of Sara as despicable.

The worry about Sara haunted Nesta. Gwilym had not been very close to Sara, especially since she had married Ralph and moved to Spain, but, for all that, she was his mother and the news of her illness would undoubtedly distress him.

The secret spoiled Christmas for Nesta.

As Gwilym carved the turkey and she handed out the loaded plates to Llewellyn, Amelda, her own father, Huw and Wynne Morgan, she felt guilty that her family was there but none of his. Perhaps this is the moment to tell him, she thought wildly, then pushed it from her mind. How could she introduce such a note of gloom to what was supposed to be a festive family occasion?

Replete with Christmas pudding, they settled into comfortable armchairs in front of the log fire to open their presents. Soon the floor was littered with discarded Christmas wrappings by each person's chair.

'That's the lot,' Gwilym announced as he felt along the base of the tree. 'No, hang on, one more.' He picked up a small package. 'It's for you, Amelda!' He frowned as he handed it towards her. 'That looks like my mother's writing . . .'

'It is. I put it there. She sent it to me and asked me to give it to Amelda,' Rhys said gruffly.

A shiver of apprehension snaked down Nesta's spine as she watched Amelda eagerly tear the wrappings away. Inside was a small box and as she opened it Amelda gave a breathless squeal of excitement.

'Look!' She held it out for inspection. Inside, gleaming against its nest of black velvet, was a ring set with a single square emerald.

'That's Mother's ring,' Gwilym exclaimed, as Amelda drew it out and slipped it on her finger. 'It's her most precious possession, so what is she doing sending it to you? When I was small she used to tell me the story of how Dad brought it back from a mine in Kimberley.'

That night Nesta told Gwilym about Sara.

'She must think she is pretty near the end and that is why she sent her ring to Amelda,' he said sadly. 'Perhaps we should go and see them again. As soon as things are back to normal after Christmas. I'll take some time off.'

Although he had every intention of going to Spain, work intervened. Early in January there were rumblings of discontent from the miners which eventually developed into a full-scale stoppage. Gwilym, who was now the Deputy Editor on the *Post*, found that so many of his reporters were away ill that he was not only having to take charge but even undertake coverage himself on occasion. When he left the house early in the morning, Nesta was never sure whether he would be home again at six o'clock that evening or not until midnight.

When Ralph phoned to say that Sara was dying and asking for Gwilym, she didn't even know how to contact him.

'Can you come, then . . . and leave a message for him to follow?' Ralph asked. 'You'll have to be quick. She . . . she took an overdose . . . some tablets the doctor gave her to ease the pain . . . You knew she had cancer?'

The moment she replaced the receiver, Nesta felt a wave of panic. She phoned through to the *Post* but no one could help her. They had no idea where Gwilym could be reached or when he would return.

'He's covering the miners' strike so he is out visiting as many sites as he can, you see, Mrs Vaughan,' Sonia Best, his secretary, explained. 'I'll phone around and see if I can locate him and if I do manage to get in touch with him I'll ask him to call you.'

'No, don't worry,' Nesta told her. 'I've been called away, but I'll leave a note for him.'

As she packed a suitcase, Nesta found the thought of travelling to Spain on her own quite daunting. She decided to ask her father to go with her. When she phoned him there was no reply. She rang Wynne who told her he had gone to a Plaid Cymru meeting. 'It's something to do with this miners' strike. I have no idea when he will be home again,' Wynne told her.

Sitting down on the stairs, her head in her hands, Nesta tried to work out what she must do. In the past they had gone to Spain overland, but since Gwilym had the car that was impossible. Anyway, to drive that distance on her own in mid-winter was out of the question. She would have to fly, she decided. She wasn't sure whether she could get a direct flight from Liverpool or Manchester, or whether she would have to go to London Heathrow. With trembling fingers she phoned a travel agent.

She noted down the times and details and agreed she could be ready in an hour if they sent a car to take her to Speke airport. It wasn't until he said, 'And you won't forget your passport Mrs Vaughan, will you,' that her nerves went to pieces.

'Passport? I haven't got one!' she said frantically.

'I thought you said you had visited Almeria before?' he said patiently.

'Oh, I have. We used my husband's passport.'

'Ah! You mean you haven't one of your own. Well, I think it will be all right if you bring his . . .'

'But I haven't got it . . . he carries it with him.'

'I see!'

She felt her breathing grow noisy, each intake hurt her chest like a knife tearing through it. Her pulse was hammering and cold runnels of sweat were trickling from under her bra.

'Are you still there, Mrs Vaughan? Right, just leave the matter with me for the moment, and I'll see what I can do . . . I'll phone you back.'

While she waited, Nesta switched on the radio, anything to deaden the oppressive silence. As she did so the music programme faded and an announcer broke in with a news flash.

'The miners' strike has been made official. It is estimated that some 280,000 men are now out and . . .'

With a cry of anger she switched it off. It was all their fault that Gwilym wasn't at home when he was needed, that she didn't have a passport to go to Sara, that her father was caught up in Plaid Cymru affairs.

When the phone shrilled she snatched it up expecting it to be the travel agent. Instead it was Ralph Hendrix.

'Sara died ten minutes ago,' he told her. 'Glad I'm in time to save you and Gwilym making a wasted journey. I'll let you know the funeral details . . . just in case you want to come.'

Long after she replaced the receiver Sara could hear his cold precise tones ringing through her head. He had sounded so relieved that Sara was dead. She wondered if it was because Sara was now out of pain . . . or because it left him free.

Nesta wept for a long time.

She knew it wasn't because of Sara's death; they had never been that close. It was for herself. She was almost fifty and the futility of her life filled her with despair.

Gwilym was so immersed in his work. He expected to become Editor when Don Jones retired in April. Theoretically, it meant more regular hours, but the responsibility would be so much greater. Everything would rest on his decision so he would be more wrapped up with his job than ever. She would find herself caught up in the extended social scene: dinners, press parties, official openings and banquets. If she didn't make the effort to go to them, then Gwilym would just make excuses for her absence and manage quite well without her.

That left only her father. And, although he was into his seventies, his enthusiasm and involvement in Plaid Cymru was as great as ever.

He didn't need her . . . no one really needed her, she thought bitterly.

If I disappeared off the face of the earth tomorrow they'd all grieve for a few days and then forget me, she thought bitterly. I'm not even a person in my own right. I haven't even got my own passport. I'm just one of Gwilym's appendages!

And unless I pull myself together and do something

with my life I'm going to end up like Sara, worn out and discarded, she thought miserably.

She closed her eyes, picturing Gwilym as others must see him. For a moment she could only see the handsome broad-shouldered, slim-hipped man she had married, his head of thick, wavy, fair hair standing out above the crowds because he was so tall. It still did, although it was now flecked with grey and the slim figure had become rather fuller. His deep-set, green eyes were still as bright as ever and he had lost none of his charm.

She wondered how younger women, like Sonia Best, his secretary, saw him. Somehow she didn't think they would regard him as a kindly, father figure, not for many years yet.

Her sudden awareness of his masculinity sent her to the mirror, to stare critically at her own reflection. Sara had fought to the very end to stay glamorous – she never even tried. Her dark hair was streaked with grey and she wore it pulled back in a French pleat in much the same style as she had worn it for years. She had put on weight and she looked plain and dowdy. Respectable, middle-aged and middle-class. Neat and nice. But was that what Gwilym wanted in a wife?

How did Llewellyn and Amelda see her, she wondered.

'She's probably ashamed to admit I'm her mother,' Nesta muttered, grimacing at her reflection. 'I really must take more time and trouble with how I look!'

She rarely bothered to put on any make-up these days. Her face was shiny, her eyebrows needed tidying up and the beige sweater she was wearing made her look washed-out and sallow. It was no wonder Amelda had hardly any time for her!

She remembered the promise she had made to herself when Amelda was tiny, Amelda with her halo of pretty fair hair, her Dresden-doll looks and her warm happy nature. She had been determined then that she would be like

95

a sister to her, the sort of mother she had longed to have when she was growing up.

The years had flown by. Amelda would be leaving university in the summer and within no time at all she, too, would be independent, just like Llewellyn, Nesta thought, and panic welled up inside her as she wondered if she had left it too late.

11

'The Llechwydd Slate Quarries have won The Festival of Wales Tourism Award, so I'm going to Blaenau Ffestiniog next week, to attend the presentation. Do you want to come along with me, Nesta?'

'That sounds a nice idea. We'll be able to pop in and see my Da and Huw and Wynne'

'Do you mean, stay with them for a few days?'

'I'd like to . . .' The excitement in Nesta's velvet brown eyes faded as she saw Gwilym frown. 'It will a be very fleeting visit otherwise,' she argued.

'I tell you what,' he leaned forward and took one of her hands, holding it between both of his, 'I will have to get back to the office, but why don't you stay on for a few days? I could come and collect you at the weekend.'

'Yes, I would quite enjoy that. I haven't seen my Da for ages. We really ought to visit him more often, or have him here to stay. He is getting on, you know. And so are Huw and Wynne, if it comes to that.' She sighed. 'There is something so depressing about everyone getting old.'

'Including us?' Gwilym grinned.

'I'm not joking!' She reached up and stroked his face. 'We are getting on, you know. You will be fifty-two next birthday.'

'That is the prime of life . . . for a man,' he told her teasingly.

She bit her lip and said nothing. She was remembering Sara's comments on the subject the last time they had been in Almeria. They had haunted her ever since and, given the slightest encouragement, they floated to the surface of her mind like some insidious weed, reminding her of the resigned bitterness in Sara's voice, the haunted sadness in her ravaged face.

She phoned her father several times over the next few days to find out if it was convenient for her to stay at Idwal Cottage, but there was never any reply.

'Off on one of his Plaid Cymru ventures, I suppose,' she grumbled to Gwilym.

'Why don't you ring your aunt and see if she has a key to your father's cottage,' he suggested.

'No, I haven't a key and Rhys won't be back until the weekend, but you can stay here with us,' Wynne told her. 'Be lovely to have you. It's ages since we had the chance of a good long chat.'

Blaenau Ffestiniog had changed. The town abounded with gift shops and the streets were full of people, strangers bemused by the blue-greyness of their surroundings, just as she had been when she had first arrived there from Cardiff over twenty-five years earlier. The slate mines had become sight-seeing attractions. Trains that had once hauled trucks of slate now carried tourists through the underground caverns.

Sleeping in her old room at Wynne's cottage took Nesta back to wartime days when she had been in the Land Army. She quickly found herself reliving the past as she swopped anecdotes with Wynne and visited some of the places where she had worked.

The sheer beauty of the surrounding countryside, the awesome mountains, the spectacular waterfalls, and the tranquil cwms, enthralled her as much as ever. The picturesque setting of Beddgelert and the grandeur of Snowdon, still delighted her the most.

Gwyndy Farm, where she had first worked as a Land Army girl, was no longer a rambling conglomeration of sheds and stables. It had been spruced up and modernised and was now a holiday riding centre.

'A young couple from London made all the changes,'

Wynne told her. 'They bought it after Blodwyn Thomas died. People round about were shocked when they got rid of all the sheep and cattle; it's always been a mixed dairy farm, see. Anyway, they built all the new stabling, and what they call an Indoor School where they can hold gymkhanas, and they've never looked back. In the summer they are booked up with holiday-makers. You see them out on the mountain roads, a dozen horses at a time. They seem to enjoy it, though it wouldn't be my idea of a holiday, I can tell you.'

'And what about Parry Jones, who owned the dairy farm where I worked after I left Gwyndy Farm?'

'He's dead as well. His wife sold out and went to live in Llandudno.'

'It's so sad to think of them gone forever,' Nesta said softly.

'That's the way of it,' Wynne sighed. 'One by one the old folk disappear. Me and Huw will be next, mark my words.'

'Oh, come, don't be so morbid!' Nesta exclaimed.

'It's the nature of things! My Huw will be seventy-five next birthday and I'm only three years behind him. We could pop off at any time. Hope it's a nice quick heart attack, not something where you linger for months a burden to everyone.'

'And how is my Da?' Nesta asked, wondering whether or not Wynne was leading up to bad news.

'Oh, he's all right. Very chirpy and as independent as ever. He won't let me inside his place . . . and I know for why,' she added, her lips tightening. 'I've peeped in through the windows and a right old mess it is in. He never does any cleaning, you see. Always away at some meeting or the other.'

'I do hope he gets back before Gwilym comes to collect me on Sunday,' Nesta frowned.

'So do I. He'll have to let you in and then perhaps you

99

can have a word with him about the state of the place. He might take some notice of you.'

'Is it *that* bad?'

'We'll walk up there and you can see for yourself,' Wynne told her.

It was a lovely clear day as they set off up the stony track to Idwal Cottage. In the distance Nesta could see sheep dotted about on the side of the mountain, their occasional plaintive bleat the only sound that shattered the heavy stillness. There was an atmosphere of peace, as tangible as though Moelwyn shielded them from the rest of the world. And since it was all her father held dear and had ever wanted, she wondered why he couldn't settle down and enjoy it. What restlessness sent him scurrying from one end of Wales to the other, working so feverishly for Plaid Cymru?

'Just look at the state of this garden,' Wynne exclaimed as they opened the low white gate. 'It's only the size of a pocket handkerchief; you would think he could keep it tidy.' She sighed. 'Huw would look after it, but Rhys would jump down our throats if he touched it. Independent old devil!'

'I wish we had a key,' Nesta murmured. 'The curtains could do with taking down and washing, let alone anything else.'

As they walked round the side of the cottage she peered in through the kitchen window and gasped in dismay. 'He's gone away and left the sink full of dirty dishes,' she exclaimed.

'Yes, I can well believe it,' Wynne agreed, her lips tightening disapprovingly. 'And the bed unmade, if I know Rhys. And a pile of dirty clothes lying around. Now you see what I mean! If he'd leave his key with me then I could straighten the place up for him so that it was clean and tidy when he came home again.'

'What does he do about his washing?'

'Does it himself, of course. He always says a sailor can wash and iron better than any woman. I wish he'd prove it,' she added bitingly.

It was Saturday morning before her father arrived home. He was pleasantly surprised to find her there and made her very welcome.

'How about letting me tidy up for you,' she suggested. 'I'm aching to do something,' she added. 'Wynne won't let me lift a finger and I'm not used to sitting around doing nothing all day.'

'Don't come that nonsense with me, girl,' Rhys chortled. 'Wynne's been telling you that I live like an old tramp, now, hasn't she?'

'She is very worried about you,' Nesta told him sharply.

'Well, she's got no cause to be. I can look after myself. When I can't then I shall just walk off into the mists that swirl around Cader Idris or the Eyrie and disappear just as Owain Glyndwr did,' he told her, his dark eyes gleaming fanatically.

'And have the Mountain Rescue teams risking their necks looking for you, I suppose,' Nesta snapped, her brown eyes blazing. 'Well, don't think you will become a legend like he did; you'll just be another accident statistic,' she added sarcastically.

'They won't come looking for me because no one will miss me, providing that busybody sister of mine doesn't raise a hue and cry,' he retorted grimly.

Nesta did what she could to make the cottage clean and homely. It saddened her to find he had so few comforts and she longed to be able to throw out his worn armchair and replace it with a new one, put bright rugs down on the floors and brighten the rooms with new curtains. But he would have none of it. Without asking, she restocked his cupboards with a plentiful supply of tinned meats, soups, vegetables and puddings.

101

'I don't think you ought to be here on your own, Rhys,' Gwilym told him when he came to collect Nesta.

'Yes, why don't you came and stay with us for a while?' Nesta added eagerly. 'We've plenty of room. Anyway . . . I'm lonely,' she confessed.

'What about all these dinner parties and glamorous functions you go to Gwilym? Don't those keep her busy?' Rhys asked, pointedly.

'There are plenty of long days in between,' Nesta laughed.

'Then fill them, girl! There's so much needing to be done and not nearly enough people to do it. You've got the time to spare and you can afford to give your services.'

'You're not suggesting she should work for Plaid Cymru, I hope?' Gwilym said quickly.

'Why not? There's worse things than that she could support.' He looked hard at his son-in-law. 'Not the right politics for your image, is that it? You don't want your chances of promotion to the Editor's seat to be blighted.'

'Something like that,' Gwilym agreed.

'Well, leave it to Llewellyn. Very dedicated, he is. He'll make headline news, you know, when the Welsh Language Act goes through Parliament. He's one of the leading supporters. Good speaker, he is too. His education hasn't been wasted. Very proud of him, I am.'

'You shouldn't encourage him,' Gwilym said angrily. 'He's young, he's got his way to make in life and . . .'

'He won't get far with a Plaid Cymru label tied round his neck,' Rhys mocked. 'You've said it before, boyo! I suppose there's something to be said for you that you stick to your principles. Well, I stick to mine. Wales for the Welsh, that is what Plaid Cymru is all about.'

'You are entitled to your viewpoint, Rhys, but don't drag Llewellyn into the mire with you. Do you understand?' Gwilym rasped.

'It's a great pity that Llewellyn wasn't born in Wales,' Rhys went on, unabashed by Gwilym's outburst. 'Mind you, Saunders Lewis wasn't born in Wales either. The funny thing is, you know,' he went on his dark eyes gleaming, 'Saunders Lewis was also born in Wallasey, and look what he has done for the movement.'

'And you think Llewellyn is following in his shoes?'

'No doubt about it! Perhaps you should come along and hear Llewellyn speak at Conway next week. It will be a splendid occasion for him.'

'He's giving a talk . . . about Plaid Cymru?'

'He's speaking in support of the Welsh Language Act. He has organised a demonstration at his school and afterwards they are planning on marching to the town hall. You should both come. It would be an eye-opener for you and make a wonderful front page story for the *Post*!'

They drove back to Liverpool in deep silence. From the set of his jaw, Nesta knew Gwilym was angry about what he had just heard. He had not been pleased when Llewellyn had insisted on becoming a teacher.

'With your qualifications you should go for something in the City,' he had argued when Llewellyn had told him of his decision.

'Big business doesn't hold any appeal for me,' Llewellyn told him.

'Big money might, though,' Gwilym reminded him. 'You'll never earn a decent salary teaching.'

'I want job satisfaction.'

'Then what about research? Plenty of openings in Liverpool, Birkenhead or Port Sunlight . . .'

'Later, perhaps. First, though, I want to teach,' Llewellyn had maintained doggedly, his dark eyes hardening, his lips clamping tightly together as he struggled to keep his voice even.

But Gwilym was not so readily appeased.

'If communicating with people is what you want, then

what about journalism? With your qualifications you could get a top job in Fleet Street in next to no time. Make your voice heard, have your work read by millions.'

'I haven't anything to say that is important, not yet,' Llewellyn told him mildly.

'You would soon find something; that is if you have any talent.'

'Journalism isn't my scene,' Llewellyn told him quietly. 'Someday I will write, but when I do it will be about things that need saying, not just stringing words together to fill up a few columns, cause a sensation, or titillate the man in the street.'

Gwilym hadn't answered, but a dark flush of anger had crept up from his collar as the barbed criticism sank in.

It had been the beginning of a rift between the two of them and one which, because there was no way she could stop it, Nesta had preferred to ignore. Now, she suspected, her father's remarks about Llewellyn's activities had opened up the sore afresh and would widen the rift.

Men! she thought angrily. Why did they have to be so bigoted? Her father had devoted his life to Plaid Cymru, and now Llewellyn was about to put his career in jeopardy in his fight to establish the importance of Welsh language. Yet, as far as she knew, he couldn't even speak Welsh!

Even Gwilym was ready to put his work on the *Post* before his family, she reflected bitterly, remembering how he had been too busy to go out to Almeria when his mother was dying.

In many ways she envied them this tremendous commitment, this inner drive that consumed them, that made men so much more resilient than women. Her father still felt that he was needed, that there was work he must do, and it kept him fulfilled.

Even Gwilym started each morning planning what he

intended to achieve that day, important things that could affect other people's lives.

And all I have to look forward to is washing the dishes, making the beds and shopping, Nesta thought despondently as they reached home. She couldn't go on like this. Visiting North Wales had revived too many memories, dragging her back into the past. What she needed now was something to show her the way ahead and stop her feeling so completely useless.

Perhaps I should go to London to see Amelda, she thought, as she undressed for bed. We could go shopping, take in some shows, do some sightseeing. We could even go to the British museum and the Victoria and Albert and the art galleries, she thought, her spirits lifting. She'd mention it to Gwilym. It would be something to look forward to . . . she could be the one to start making plans.

12

'You are becoming a regular gadabout, aren't you?' Gwilym teased when Nesta mentioned that she was thinking of going to London for a week.

'You can come along as well, if you like,' she invited, smiling.

'You know you are quite safe in saying that, the way things are in the office at the moment,' he grinned. 'Leave it for another month, or so, until everyone is back from their summer holidays . . .'

'I don't want to wait that long. I've made my mind up; I want to go now,' Nesta told him decisively, her mouth tightening.

'Oh? What's the rush?'

'Life's slipping by and I feel left out of things. I suppose I'm becoming more and more bored with being just a housewife.'

'Surely you can find something to do locally, without going to London to look for it?' he said in a puzzled voice.

'I'm not going there to look for something to do,' she said exasperatedly. 'I just thought it would make a change and be an opportunity to see Amelda.'

'A chance to check up on her you mean, don't you?' Gwilym parried. 'It's high time you let her stand on her own feet,' he added sharply. 'She's only been away from home for a couple of months. Give her time to settle down.'

'We've only her word for it that this flat where she is living is suitable,' Nesta said worriedly. 'She would say it was even if it was a slum. You know what she is like when she wants her own way.'

'It can't be too bad, since the address is in Chelsea,' Gwilym argued.

'I'll decide that when I've seen it for myself,' Nesta told him balefully.

'She's sharing with two other girls, remember, so she probably won't be able to put you up,' Gwilym warned.

'I've already phoned her to say I was planning a trip to London and she said they have a spare bedroom.'

'You're lucky! You might have found it difficult to get a hotel. London's always packed out with overseas visitors.'

Nesta knew Gwilym was trying to deter her from going, but she stubbornly refused to listen. She had made up her mind and nothing was going to stop her.

She had been worried ever since Amelda had said she was planning to share a flat in London with Cindy Forester and Penny Payne, two girls she had been friendly with when she was at university. The flat belonged to Cindy Forester's parents who had gone abroad for two years.

'We are only being charged a nominal rent, just to cover running costs,' Amelda had told them, her amethyst eyes dancing excitedly. 'Isn't it a stroke of luck? Flats are like gold dust in London.'

Gwilym had agreed with her, but Nesta had not been happy about the arrangement. She had missed Amelda while she had been away at university and had been looking forward to her being back at home again. She had hoped that Amelda would find a job locally.

'Cindy says her parents would rather have us living in the flat than letting it stand empty in case of vandals or squatters. And they don't like the idea of Cindy being there all on her own because they think she would be lonely.'

'But you haven't even got a job, so how on earth are

107

you going to pay your share?' Nesta had asked. 'Are either of these other girls working?'

'Cindy isn't but Penny has a job in the library at the House of Commons.'

She knew it was silly to be as anxious as she was, since, after all, Amelda had survived three years at university. Even so, she still seemed very unworldly. She had lived in a Hall of Residence while she had been there so she'd led quite a sheltered life and Nesta was sure she was not yet ready to leave home . . . certainly not to live in London.

'Of course she'll be all right. By the time you were her age, you had served in the Land Army and in the ATS,' Gwilym pointed out, when she confided her fears to him.

'I had a very different upbringing from Amelda.' I'd had to learn to stand on my own feet,' she reminded him. 'Also, there was a war on and I had met you,' Nesta agreed ruefully, 'which goes to prove my point. Amelda's never even had a boy-friend!'

Despite all Nesta's misgivings, Gwilym still remained convinced that Amelda was doing the right thing in going to London and sharing a flat with her friends. He had even advanced her a loan to 'tide her over', as he put it, until she managed to find work.

'I'll pay you back, Dad, the moment I have a job,' Amelda promised, smiling happily as she hugged him.

The upheaval of Amelda's leaving had kept Nesta fully occupied for several weeks, but after she had actually gone the house had felt like a morgue. With Llewellyn living in Wrexham and Gwilym out all day she had time on her hands. The awful frustration of feeling useless returned and made her edgy.

Gwilym had put her bouts of depression down to her age and tried to bully her into taking up some voluntary work.

'There must be something you can do that will keep you busy and give you an interest outside the home,' he urged. 'It's pointless turning yourself grey worrying about Amelda.'

It was all very well for Gwilym to talk like that, Nesta thought, crossly. He was out and about every day, mixing with people, involved in his work on the *Post*. She was stuck at home on her own and even while she was doing her housework, she had the constant fear that Amelda might be in some sort of danger. She was so pretty, so vulnerable, so unworldly.

Even when Amelda found work as a research assistant for an American firm of investment brokers, Nesta still had misgivings. Amelda sounded over-ecstatic about the flat and her letters were too full of details about her handsome boss and luxurious office for Nesta's peace of mind.

Going to London was the only way to really set her mind at ease, Nesta thought, as she settled into the corner seat of the Euston-bound train. At least I will be able to see for myself if everything is as marvellous as Amelda claims.

Amelda met her mother at the station. As they hugged each other rapturously, Nesta felt reassured to see her looking so well, since at least that meant that she was eating properly.

The flat was even more spacious than Amelda had led her to believe from her description, and far exceeded Nesta's expectations. It was on the second floor of an imposing Regency house, within walking distance of Sloane Square.

Each of the three girls had their own en-suite bedroom and there was an elegantly furnished sitting room with massive bay windows that looked out onto a small park. There were also two other rooms, as well as a large well-equipped kitchen.

'You *have* fallen on your feet!' Nesta exclaimed admiringly after Amelda had showed her round and was helping her to unpack in the well-appointed guest-room. 'This is absolutely wonderful. I wouldn't mind living here myself.'

'Well, it's certainly better than the average bedsit,' Amelda grinned happily.

'Yes, you'll come down to earth with a bump when Cindy's parents return and you have to move out,' Nesta warned.

'I'll worry about that when the time comes,' Amelda said airily, shrugging her slim shoulders. 'So many things could have changed by then.'

'What do you mean? Isn't your job working out?' Nesta asked, quick to seize on a possible flaw in Amelda's new lifestyle.

'Oh, yes, I'm enjoying it immensely. I never thought working for a living would be such fun.'

'So you are still getting on all right with this Michael Owen? He's an American, isn't he?'

'Yes, he's from New York. But his grandparents, or great grandparents, were Welsh. They came from somewhere in the Swansea Valley, I think he said. You'd never know from his accent, mind you.'

'And am I going to have a chance to meet him?'

'You are! He's taking us out to dinner at the Hilton tonight.'

'Really!' Nesta felt quite taken aback. She had been planning to drop in casually at Amelda's office, in the hope of catching a glimpse of the man she worked for, but she certainly hadn't expected to be taken out to dinner by him.

'You needn't worry, Mum. He doesn't bite,' Amelda laughed, as she saw the surprised look on her mother's face.

'You must be on very good terms with him,' Nesta said

110

suspiciously. 'Not many bosses would do something like that.'

'Well, he's not your average British boss, is he?' Amelda grinned happily.

As they got ready for their dinner date Nesta wondered what to wear. She dithered between a rose-pink two-piece with a pleated skirt or a tailored pale blue silk dress.

'You wear whichever one you feel most comfortable in,' Amelda told her. 'Do you want me to give you a hand with your hair?'

'When it's as straight as mine is there's not a lot you can do with it except put a comb through it,' Nesta sighed.

'I can always try,' Amelda offered. 'You are getting awfully grey, you know, Mum. Why don't you colour it?'

'I don't think your father would approve,' Nesta said cautiously. 'I would probably make a mess of it and it would look awful.'

'I meant you should have it done professionally!' Amelda told her as she ran a comb through it, lifting it away from her mother's face and arranging it less formally.

'I'll think about it,' Nesta promised, combing it back into place. 'Yours is looking lovely,' she added with a fond smile as she admired the way Amelda had swept her blond hair back from her face and piled it up high on her head so that it fell in a cascade of curls. The tiny tendrils that escaped around her heart-shaped face made her violet eyes seem enormous. Her dress was almost the same colour as her eyes and Nesta wondered when she had bought it. It looked expensive. It was in a soft, shimmering silk and floated over her slim figure, just skimming her knees, and making her look very young and vulnerable.

Michael Owen proved to be every bit as interesting as Amelda had claimed. He was broad-shouldered, deep-chested and impeccably dressed in a light grey suit, crisp white shirt and a boldly patterned blue and gold silk tie. His dark brown eyes, under equally dark brows, were warm and friendly as he greeted Nesta. He radiated charm.

Throughout the evening, he was so courteous and attentive, that Nesta felt completely at ease. He was witty and entertaining and soon they were all laughing and exchanging anecdotes as though they had known each other all their lives.

'Well, what did you think of Michael?' Amelda asked, after he had dropped them off outside the flat. He had declined to come in for a nightcap because it was so late, so the two of them were enjoying the intimacy of a cup of coffee in Amelda's room.

'He is certainly very charming,' Nesta agreed. She felt pleasantly tired. The meal had been excellent, with just the right amount of wine to leave a warm relaxed glow.

'Was he like you expected?' Amelda persisted

'No. I thought he would be taller . . . and slimmer.'

'Yes, he is rather on the cuddly side,' Amelda giggled. 'Actually, he is five foot ten, but being so broad makes him look shorter than he really is.' She smothered a yawn. 'Are you ready for bed? I must be in the office early tomorrow. I'm taking the afternoon off so that we can go sightseeing.'

Although she enjoyed the rest of her visit to London, and was relieved to find Amelda's living arrangements were so comfortable, there was something about Amelda's relationship with Michael Owen that troubled Nesta.

It was the first thing she mentioned to Gwilym when he met her at Liverpool's Lime Street Station, but he refused to take her fears seriously.

'You've always pampered Amelda and worried over her unnecessarily,' he scolded. 'She's not a little Dresden doll, you know, even if she looks like one. I keep telling

112

you, Amelda can take care of herself. Just look at the way she's landed herself with this plush pad. And a job where she is being paid nearly double what Llewellyn is earning.'

'Teaching has always been poorly paid, but if it's what he wants to do then it's right for him,' Nesta defended.

'And since when has researching been a top money-earner? Why an investment company needs a researcher is beyond me.'

'Michael's firm does a lot of take-overs and she has to investigate the background of any company they are interested in. It's quite important work she is doing. Amelda must get all her facts right or they could miss out on a bargain, or even take over a company that is useless.'

'You are sure you've got it right?' Gwilym frowned. 'It sounds rather odd to me.'

'Well, it's how Michael Owen explained her job the night he took us out to dinner. He went into considerable detail, but I must admit I found it rather confusing.'

'Well, as long as Amelda understands what she's do-ing, and I'm quite sure she does, that's all that matters. I don't think either of us need worry about her any more,' Gwilym said firmly. He stared at Nesta, his brow fur-rowed as though he was puzzled.

'Is something wrong?'

'No . . . well, I don't know.' He regarded her quizz-ically. 'There's something different about you and I'm not sure what it is. You are wearing the same dress . . . but you look different.'

'Oh?' Nesta struggled to keep her face straight. 'Better . . or worse?'

'Well . . . just different. You look . . . perkier, prettier . . I don't know.' He looked confused. 'Perhaps the holi-day has cheered you up!'

'Take another look,' Nesta teased. 'I expected you to notice right away. I've had my hair coloured . . . it was Amelda's idea.'

113

13

Amelda let out a long sigh of relief as she hailed a taxi to take her back to her office in Knightsbridge. It had been wonderful having her mother to stay, but all the time she had been in London Amelda had felt as if she had been treading on broken glass. And she was pretty certain Michael had felt the same way, too.

Michael!

She settled back into the corner of the seat as the taxi nosed its way through the congestion around Shaftesbury Avenue, and gave herself up to thinking about him.

It was the first time she had ever been in love.

When she had been at school, and later, when she had gone to university, she had enjoyed the company of boys. They had always treated her as a friend and she had liked their direct, open approach to life. Until now, though, she had never been in love. But then, she thought, a smile lifting the corners of her mouth, she had never met anyone quite like Michael Owen before.

Penny had introduced them.

'He's looking for a P/A to help with research and I told him you might be interested,' Penny told her airily.

'What sort of research?' Amelda had asked, intrigued but mystified.

'Oh, I don't know. Digging into the backgrounds of British firms, or something. Anyway, I told him you had a degree in Economics and Social History and he said you sounded ideal. He wants to meet you.'

'You mean you've arranged for me to go for an interview?' Amelda exclaimed incredulously.

'Yes, I suppose I have in a way,' Penny smiled. 'I said

we'd meet him for lunch at Montalla's tomorrow.'

The news had thrown Amelda into a flap. She had washed her hair twice, tried on everything in her wardrobe and discarded it all as being unsuitable and dashed out as soon as the shops were open next morning to buy something new, only to discover that everything cost far more than she could afford. In the end she had compromised by wearing a lime-green linen suit that her mother had bought for her while she had been at university, and dressing it up with a royal blue scarf borrowed from Cindy.

'I don't know why you are making all this fuss,' Penny said, raising her eyebrows as Amelda changed from white shoes to navy ones and tipped the contents of her white handbag into a navy one, also borrowed from Cindy.

'First impressions matter,' Amelda told her, 'and I need this job. I'm broke.'

'In that case, then I'd better warn you what Michael Owen is like so that you are not put off you when you meet him.'

'You mean he's got two heads?'

'Not quite, but he can be a little over-bearing, and he has a strong American accent.'

'What's he like to look at . . . Burt Reynolds or John Wayne?'

'Gosh, neither! He's more like Burl Ives,' Penny giggled. She screwed up her eyes to concentrate better. 'He's about middle height, very broad, heavily built and barrel-chested. His hair is dark brown, brushed back and over to one side. I think it's parted on the left.' She opened her eyes and grinned at Amelda. 'He's got quite a pleasant face, warm brown eyes, a round chin, small nose and a great smile. I'm sure you'll like him,' she added with a disarming grin.

'Will he like me, though?' Amelda asked moodily. 'That's the real test since I'm the one that wants the job.'

What Penny hadn't told her, Amelda thought, as she shook hands with Michael Owen at the end of their luncheon, was his tremendous charisma. His charm was overpowering.

True, he was barrel-chested and that made him appear to be somewhat shorter than he actually was, but his very broad shoulders gave him a powerful, masculine look.

He was immaculate in his appearance, with a crisp white and blue striped shirt and a plain blue silk tie and he wore his Saville Row suit with tremendous ease. Everything about him was expensive, and signalled success, from his gold Rolex to his diamond-studded gold cuff-links and matching tie-pin. Yet he was tremendously affable and by the time their lunch ended Amelda felt completely relaxed.

All through the meal she had been aware that he was probing her about her qualifications, but he had done it in such a disarming way that she hadn't felt in the least self-conscious.

'If you are free, Amelda, why don't you come to my office tomorrow so that I can show you round and you can see for yourself if it's the sort of work that would interest you?' he invited, as they parted.

'You've got it!' Penny exclaimed jubilantly as they hailed a taxi and made their way back to the flat to let Cynthia know how they had got on.

'Do you really think so?' Amelda asked anxiously.

'Of course you have. The vibes between you both were fantastic. He wouldn't have suggested you went to see him tomorrow if he didn't want you to have the job. All you have to do now is stick out for a decent salary. He's an American, remember. He'll expect to pay good wages.'

Penny had been right. When she had arrived at the address in Knightsbridge where Michael's firm had a suite of offices, he took it for granted that she would be staying.

She had fallen under his spell so completely that even if it had meant working in a cupboard and sorting through dry-as-dust files all day, she would have taken the job just to be near him. As it was, her office was like something out of a film-set with deep-pile cream carpet, a handsome walnut desk with matching bookcases, and a profusion of green plants.

She found the work fascinating. Michael believed in finding out everything there was to know about the companies he dealt with and had perfected his technique to a fine art.

'There's only one way to ensure that people tell you everything you want to know and that is to make certain they are completely relaxed when you talk to them,' he explained to Amelda. 'Whenever possible, entertain them to drinks, or a meal, in the most pleasant surroundings you can find.' He checked his watch. 'Come on, I'll show you what I mean. I have an appointment at twelve-thirty; you can come along as well.'

When they returned to the office afterwards, he told her, 'Always check and double-check on everything they've told you before you take action of any kind.'

Amelda had done her best to follow his maxims. She had expected to be the one who had to do all the checking but she was pleasantly surprised when he regularly took her along to meetings.

'You take such a keen interest in your work that we make an excellent team,' he told her with a disarming smile, when she expressed surprise at the frequent invitations to lunch and dinner.

University, however, hadn't prepared her for Michael's sophisticated outlook on life and at first she was often startled by things he said and did.

Her limited wardrobe meant she had to use every possible device to ring the changes and appear smart for these appointments. Michael was quick to notice this and,

117

greatly to her embarrassment, suggested they went on a shopping trip.

'Just think of it as a uniform,' he joked, when she demurred. 'Come on, let's have fun!'

Michael seemed to take London over. His associates were all influential. He dealt only with the top men in business and the deals he put through involved such high finance that at first Amelda was overwhelmed, unable to comprehend the vastness of the figures they discussed.

'You'll soon get used to talking in millions,' he assured her. 'Anyway, finalising the deals isn't your problem. Just dig out the facts and make sure they are accurate. I'll handle everything else.'

His personal contacts in London were all top-drawer, too. At first she had hung back, as he mingled with TV personalities, MPs, Guards officers and members of the Royal Family. Even when they responded to his deep, gravelly voice as though they were all old friends, she had felt nervous and shy. The turning point had come when he had taken her to Smith's Lawn at Windsor to watch a polo match in which one of his business associates was playing. At the half-time break, they had joined the players in the refreshment tent. Prince Charles had been there and Michael had actually laughed and joked with him.

It was just like a dream. From that moment, Amelda knew that never again, would she feel in awe of anyone. And, with uncanny accuracy, Michael had chosen that moment to show he was interested in her as a person as well as a business colleague.

In the City, as in his leisure activities, Michael Owen achieved more in a few short months than most people did in a lifetime. He became something of a celebrity. People pointed him out wherever they went.

After the Smith's Lawn incident, Amelda even began to revel in reading about herself in the newspapers. Comments like 'the pretty young blonde seen with American

118

entrepreneur, Michael Owen' intrigued and flattered her.

She loved her new glitzy life. Dining at London's most exclusive restaurants and nightclubs, even jetting off to Paris, the South of France, or the Costs del Sol, became almost commonplace. Occasionally, though, Amelda worried in case it would all come to an end as abruptly as it had started.

She even voiced her fears to her flatmates.

'You're just digging trouble,' Cindy warned, stretching cat-like in her figure-hugging leotard. 'Just don't let him break your heart, that's all.'

'He is twelve years older than you,' Penny pointed out, as she sat painting her nails a vivid crimson.

Although Amelda listen to their counselling she knew it was too late. She was deeply in love with Michael Owen and she refused to listen to her inner conscience that kept telling her that one day, possibly quite soon, he would be going back to America.

Nothing mattered as long as Michael loved her. And she knew he did. It wasn't just the wonderful, tender things he said when they were alone, or the expensive gifts he lavished on her, which made her feel so cherished, it was the way he made love to her.

It had been a long time before she would agree to sleep with him. He had understood her reticence. The fact that she wouldn't jump into bed with him the first time he suggested it had brought a deeper quality to their relationship.

She had never slept around while she had been at university. In those days, Cindy and Penny had teased her unmercifully about her high-minded principles, but she refused to change her mind.

And once she had met Michael Owen, and became aware of how strong her feelings for him were, she was glad she had stuck to her principles.

He really was something special.

He had awakened in her deep emotions that seemed to change her personality. She became introspective, dreamy and more vulnerable. In the early days of their relationship, her anxiety to please him, or at least not cause the quick frown of annoyance that characterised his moods, dominated everything she said or did.

Being older than her, he had a different sense of values, and because he was American, his sense of humour was not the same. At first, these differences added to the piquancy of their affair, but as they grew older, Michael became impatient if she misunderstood his meaning.

In public, at any rate, he expected her to be on his wavelength at all times, cool and efficient, an extension of himself. When they were alone, however, he was a different person. Once he shed his formal suit and donned jeans and a sweater, or casual velvet cords, check shirt and anorak, his personality changed. To Amelda, these moments were precious.

She remembered vividly the first time she had agreed to spend a night at his penthouse flat. It had seemed such a tremendous commitment, as if she would be giving up her independence as well as acting against her principles.

'Stop being so two-faced,' Penny had scoffed. 'You must be lovers by now, so why not come out in the open and stay with him if you want to? If you don't he will soon find someone else who will.'

It was fear of that, as much as anything else, that had made her capitulate.

As they left an all-night party in Windsor, dawn was already a golden line on the horizon.

'If I had a spare toothbrush I'd stay the night at your place,' she murmured sleepily, cudding up to him as they drove back to London in the early hours of Sunday morning.

There had been an amused glint in his dark eyes as he'd given her a brief look before turning his attention back to the road. Twenty minutes later he had garaged his Porsche and was escorting her into the lift that would take them up to his penthouse flat.

That night they had made love for the very first time.

Next morning when she awoke and saw Michael's dark head on the pillow alongside her, she wondered why she had hesitated for so long when she loved him so much.

She had longed to confide in her mother, but had been afraid she might be shocked.

She sighed, dreamily. Michael was so totally different to anyone her parents knew that she had been surprised at how well he had got along with her mother. She couldn't help wondering, though, how her mother would have responded had she known the truth about their relationship.

14

The first thing Nesta thought about when news of the IRA bombings in London was announced on the radio was whether Amelda was safe or not.

Throughout the day, each news bulletin carried further details and when she switched on the TV the scenes of devastation filled her with horror. There was even a massive banner headline in the late edition of the *Post* that Gwilym brought home that evening.

'I've been phoning Amelda's flat all day to check if she is all right,' Nesta told him, as she served up their dinner, 'but there's no one there. I do hope she hasn't been involved in any way.'

'Why shouldn't she be OK?' Gwilym asked, looking puzzled. 'It's the Hilton Hotel that's been bombed not private houses.'

'Yes, I know, but we went to the Hilton for dinner when I stayed with her in London . . . and I have this premonition . . .'

The shrilling of the phone cut short what Nesta was going to say. As Gwilym put down his knife and fork and went out into the hall to answer it, she again felt a strange sense of foreboding.

'Who did you say? Penelope Payne . . . are you sure you've got the right number?'

'Let me speak to her . . . it's Amelda's flatmate!' Nesta grabbed the phone from Gwilym's hand, tensing herself for bad news.

'Mrs Vaughan? It's Penny . . . it's about Amelda. We've only just heard . . . they were both at the London Hilton when it was bombed. . .they're both in St James's Hospital.'

'Both?'

'Amelda and Michael . . . she was there with him.'

'At some function?'

'Well, no . . . not exactly. Michael's flat was being redecorated . . .'

Penny's voice trailed off and there was an embarrassed silence.

'Are you still there, Mrs Vaughan?'

'Yes. Yes . . . thank you for letting us know. We . . . we'll get in touch with the hospital. Thank you for phoning, Penny.'

Nesta's face was white and strained, her hand shaking as she replaced the receiver. Not only had her worst fears been realised, but the hesitation and embarrassment in Penny's voice hinted at other things and crystallised all Nesta's suspicions about Amelda's relationship with Michael Owen.

Gwilym's mouth tightened as she repeated what Penny had told her. He shook his head disbelievingly as he looked at the newspaper headline again, as if seeing it for the first time.

'I'm going to London . . . to the hospital . . . are you coming?' Nesta asked, a catch in her voice.

'What, now? It would be midnight before we got there. They wouldn't let us see her. We'll go first thing in the morning.'

'I won't be able to rest until I know how she is . . .'

'I'll phone through and find out.'

Nesta paced the floor, impatient at the delay while Gwilym contacted telephone directories. It seemed a lifetime until he was finally connected to the Ward Sister at the hospital.

'She's not seriously hurt, just shock, cuts and abrasions,' he said in a relieved voice as he replaced the receiver and came across the room and put his arm around Nesta's shoulders. 'They want to keep her in under observation for about a week . . .'

'She must be pretty bad if they're going to keep her in that long,' Nesta protested, her face serious.

'The Sister didn't seem to think so . . .'

'They never tell you anything on the phone,' Nesta said despairingly. 'It's no good, Gwilym, I won't rest until I've seen her. I'm going to pack a suitcase now and we can leave for London first thing tomorrow . . .'

'Hold on, I'm not sure I can get away from the office until I've checked my diary.'

'If you can't then I'll go on my own,' she snapped, her dark eyes hardening.

'Where will you stay? You can hardly go to the flat if Amelda's moved out. Leave it until the morning and see if you can book in at a hotel . . .'

'I could go just for the day,' Nesta said tentatively.

'Yes, why don't you do that?' Gwilym's face brightened. 'Check on how she is and if you think we ought to be there with her, then I can join you.'

Nesta spent a sleepless night. She was up, dressed and ready to leave before Gwilym was awake next morning.

As the train carried her south, she was haunted by what she might discover when she reached London. The magazines Gwilym bought for her at Lime Street station lay unopened on her lap. She couldn't concentrate on them; the implications of what Penny had told her filled her mind.

If Amelda and Michael were both staying at the Hilton because his flat was being decorated then she had to accept that Amelda was living with him.

It was as if the last piece of the jig-saw had fallen into place and she saw everything quite clearly. It had always puzzled her why Amelda was never in when she phoned the flat and Penny or Cindy would say that they would ask her to ring back. It was probably also the reason why

124

she never had time to come home for the weekend or a holiday.

She didn't want to appear prudish, but, nevertheless, she didn't approve. I suppose Amelda guessed how I would react, Nesta thought ruefully, and that is why she had never mentioned it to me.

She tried to recall exactly what Michael Owen had been like. She remembered him as a thick-set man with friendly brown eyes and a slightly gravelly voice that emphasised his American drawl. He had been extremely charming, and she had enjoyed his company, but she had been thinking of him then as Amelda's employer and not as a prospective son-in-law.

Would he ever be that? She had judged him to be in his mid-forties and she had assumed he was married, possibly with a family. He still might be for all they knew, she thought gloomily, and where did that leave Amelda?

It seemed ironic that this had happened now. When Llewellyn and Amelda had been growing up, especially when they were away at university, she had worried in case they got involved in drugs, or became hippies or drop-outs. But there had never been any hint of problems of that sort. They had both seemed to be level-headed and hard-working, and their results had certainly been gratifying.

So what had gone wrong?

It was one of the questions uppermost in Nesta's mind as she walked into the ward. Then, as she saw Amelda lying propped up in bed, her head swathed in bandages and one hand and arm bandaged, all that concerned her was how badly hurt Amelda was.

'How on earth did you know I was here, Mum?' Amelda gasped weakly.

'Penny phoned us last night. I had a premonition, though, as soon as I heard about the bombs,' Nesta told her as she bent over and gently kissed Amelda's cheek. 'Are you badly hurt, darling?'

'A gash on the forehead and some minor cuts and scratches,' Amelda smiled wanly. 'They say I'll be out in about a week. They're only keeping me here because I had concussion.'

'Why didn't *you* ask them to let us know?' Nesta chided gently.

'I hadn't got round to it. I was going to wait until they discharged me and then come home.'

'Were you? Was that the reason, or was it because you didn't want us to know that you were staying here with your boss when it happened?'

'Oh, dear, Penny told all, did she?' Amelda flushed and turned her face away as tears trickled down her cheeks onto the pillow.

'It's all right, darling.' Nesta took Amelda's hand between her own and squeezed it gently. 'Look at me. I do understand!'

'Understand, perhaps, but you don't approve,' Amelda sobbed weakly.

'I just wish that you had been the one to tell me.'

'How could I, Mum? You would only have worried about me, or tried to talk me out of living with Michael.'

'Well, it's certainly not what I would have wanted for you,' Nesta agreed. 'I suppose this is why we have seen so little of you for the past couple of years. All this talk about being too busy to come home, or of going on holiday with Penny or Cindy, was just to put my mind at rest, was it?'

'Yes, I'm afraid so,' Amelda admitted contritely. 'I just didn't want to worry you and Dad.'

'If you were so sure about how you felt, and convinced that you were doing the right thing in living together, then you should have had the courage to tell us,' Nesta told her.

'Oh, Mum!' fresh tears trickled down Amelda's cheeks and her amethyst eyes looked like pansies after a rainstorm.

'Well, since we can't turn back the clock the best thing is to forget about it . . . for the present at any rate. All I want now is to see you fully recovered. As soon as they let you out of hospital you must come home to recuperate. No nonsense about going back to work, remember.'

'I don't suppose there will be any work to go back to for a while. Michael was hurt much worse than I was. He tried to protect me and he took the full force when the masonry came crashing down. His spine is damaged.'

'Is he in this hospital as well?'

'Yes, for the moment. They are going to move him to a spinal unit later. They allowed me to visit him yesterday. He looked awful.'

'I'll go and see him presently.'

'Oh, Mum, do you think you should? You will be careful what you say . . . he has been very badly injured,' Amelda pleaded.

'I know,' Nesta told her coolly. 'I won't say anything to upset him. Afterwards, though, when you are both out of hospital, I think we should all get together and have a talk. Your father included.'

'Must we?'

'I think you both owe us an explanation, Amelda. I also think Michael Owen should tell us a bit more about his background. Is he married?'

'What?'

'He is in his thirties, Amelda. It would be highly unlikely if he didn't have a wife . . . and a family . . . back in the States.'

'Mum, I trust Michael. He would have told me if he had been married,' Amelda said confidently.

He probably knows you are too naïve and trusting to ask, thought Nesta. Aloud she said, 'Look, darling,' patting Amelda's hand consolingly, 'I didn't mean to upset you. Let's forget all about it for the moment. Getting you better and out of here is what matters. All this can be sorted out later when you are feeling better.'

Nesta sat at the bedside for a while longer until it became obvious that it was a strain for Amelda to carry on talking.

'Perhaps I should go and see Michael Owen for a little while and let you get some rest,' Nesta suggested, making Amelda's pillows more comfortable.

'I'd rather you didn't, Mum,' Amelda pleaded. 'He really is very badly hurt. It might make him worse. I only stayed with him for a few minutes and he was exhausted.'

'All right, if that's the way you want it,' Nesta agreed reluctantly.

'Why don't you go home, Mum? It was kind of you to come all this way, but there's nothing you can do for me. I'll phone and let you know when I am coming out.'

'Nonsense! I can't leave you here on your own. You have a sleep Amelda and I'll go for a walk or something and come back later.'

'No, Mum, go on home. I would rather you did . . . truly.'

Before she left, Nesta talked to the Sister in charge and was assured that it would be at least a week before Amelda was fit to leave hospital.

As the taxi taking her back to Euston passed the Hilton in Park Lane Nesta saw for herself the devastation that had been caused and a shudder went through her. It brought back memories of wartime bombing and killings and how those had dramatically changed people's lives. The far-reaching effect of such senselessness made her feel despondent. If it hadn't been for the Hilton bombings, Amelda's secret might never have been uncovered. Now, it had reared up like some ugly monster and threatened her peace of mind.

At Euston, she found a corner seat on the train and sat staring out of the carriage window, trying to concentrate on the villages and towns and open country flashing past as the train raced northwards.

Feelings of guilt were beginning to build up inside her over Amelda's behaviour. Perhaps Gwilym was right and she had been too lenient with Amelda when she had been growing up. She had been such a dainty child, enchantingly pretty with her fair hair, great violet eyes and winsome manner, that it had been hard to refuse her anything. She had, Nesta reflected with pride, been the embodiment of all she had hoped for in a daughter.

She recalled how once when she had agreed to Amelda joining a ballet class as well as a tap-dancing class Gwilym had reproached her for trying to relive her own childhood through Amelda.

'Stop pushing her! She's already learning the piano and going to Brownies and has a part in the school concert,' he'd pointed out. 'Give her some time to play with her friends when she's not at school.'

But she hadn't intended to push her.

I only wanted to make her happy, give her all the advantages I'd never had, she thought miserably. Yet, if Gwilym's right then perhaps, without knowing it, I'm the one who has made her believe she can have anything she wants from life, and that she can flaunt convention to get it.

As the train stopped at Crewe station she sat watching the couples surging about on the platform and wondered how many of them were married to their partner or just living together. As they pulled away again, Nesta studied the young couple with a baby who had boarded the train and were sitting opposite her and wondered about them. The girl wasn't wearing a wedding ring.

Perhaps I'm the one who is out of step, she thought miserably. Am I making too big an issue out of the fact that they are living together? Maybe it's me and not Amelda who has led too sheltered a life. Perhaps Gwilym is right and I ought to broaden my interests and get a job, or do some voluntary work that keeps me in touch with how people live today.

She checked the time on her watch. With any luck, she'd be at Lime Street in time to get a lift back to Walla-sey with Gwilym when he finished work.

Suddenly, more than anything else, she wanted to share her concern over Amelda with Gwilym. Talking about it, listening to his reaction, might ease the aching hurt she felt deep inside her.

15

'What do you mean, Amelda doesn't want to come here when she comes out of hospital?' Gwilym frowned. 'What is she planning to do, then?'

'She's going to stay with Alice Roberts,' Nesta told him deliberately avoiding his green stare as she spooned apple crumble into a dish and passed it across the table to him.

'Cardiff docks! That's no place to recuperate!'

'It's where she wants to be. I think it might do her good,' she added brightly. 'Amelda needs someone to talk to and Alice could be just the right person.'

'Why can't she come home?' He put down his spoon and stared at Nesta. 'She's got you.'

'No,' Nesta's brown eyes looked troubled. 'I can't talk to her about Michael Owen. Far better for her to go there. Alice will be sympathetic and unbiased, and maybe be Amelda will listen to her advice without feeling she's being preached at. No matter what I say she feels I'm getting at her . . . and she's probably right. I find her present lifestyle hard to accept.' She sighed and there was sadness in her dark eyes. 'Instead of discussing it with her in a reasonable way, I tend to fly off the handle, or start crying, and that's no good at all,' she added lamely.

'It goes against the grain to see her ruining her life like this,' Gwilym agreed worriedly. He took Nesta's hand in his and raised it to his face, resting his cheek against it. 'I still think you spoiled her when she was younger,' he sighed. 'Now she won't listen to either of us.'

'Perhaps I did.' Gently Nesta pulled her hand away and walked over to the window. 'I don't understand any of it. I tried so hard to bring both of them up to respect and appreciate true values, that it comes hard to see what they have both made of their lives. Llewellyn is as fanatical about Plaid Cymru as my Da. It seems to mean more to him than his career. Perhaps if he was married and had children, he would settle down. And now Amelda is so set on this Michael Owen that she can't, or won't, see reason no matter which of us tries to talk to her. Alice is our only hope.'

'I still can't understand why Amelda has chosen to go to her, though. She hasn't seen her for years.'

'They have kept in touch. Alice has a special soft spot for Amelda. I'll never forget that day we went to collect Llewellyn, and Alice saw Amelda for the first time. Her face lit up as if she was seeing a beautiful vision. I can still hear her voice, full of awe, saying, 'It's Eleanor come back.''

'She must have been awfully fond of your mother.'

'Oh, I am sure she was. I think, too, she held herself responsible in part for my mother's death.'

'I thought she died in childbirth . . . when you were born.'

'She did. But my mother and Alice had been close friends ever since they were children. They went around together and shared each other's secrets. It seems my mother had been pregnant the year before she was married,' Nesta sighed. 'Alice was the only one who knew about it. Because Rhys was a sailor, and they were afraid he mightn't come back, she helped my mother to get an abortion. It didn't go right, but Alice had promised never to tell anyone, so she kept quiet. Yet, if the doctors had known about the abortion when she became pregnant with me, my mother might never have died.'

'I still can't see Amelda taking any notice of a woman old enough to be her grandmother.'

'Perhaps it's for that very reason that she feels she needs

to visit Alice. Amelda may be like her grandmother in more than just looks. Perhaps she feels she can trust Alice, just like my mother did. Anyway, some things seem to be taboo between mother and daughter and this relationship of hers with Michael Owen seems to be one of them.'

'Well, I hope Alice Roberts can talk some sense into her. I hardly think it's likely, though. A woman who has spent all her life in Cardiff docks seems hardly the right person to offer advice to someone like Amelda, who is a university graduate and . . .'

'Stop being bigoted and prejudiced, Gwilym,' Nesta exclaimed sharply. 'You sound just like my Da when he is ranting on about Welsh politics.'

'I'm concerned about Amelda's future,' Gwilym said angrily. 'We know next to nothing about this Michael Owen. All this talk that his ancestors left Wales and went to America at the turn of the century doesn't mean a thing.'

'Oh come off it, Gwilym. We know that he is a highly successful businessman.'

'A fast-talking wheeler-dealer, you mean, don't you? Just because he drives a Porsche, and can afford to bed our daughter at the Hilton, doesn't make him respectable. In fact, probably the opposite,' he added gloomily.

'You haven't even met him!' Nesta exploded.

'And you have! Don't explain, I get the picture. Michael Owen turned on the American drawl and charmed you into a state of believing every word he said,' Gwilym sneered.

'I'm not going to listen to any more of this,' Nesta stated firmly. 'Amelda has decided she is going to stay with Alice for a week or so and that's all there is to it.'

Although outwardly Nesta accepted the situation, inwardly she worried. If only they knew more about Michael Owen. She had been very impressed by him. He had certainly radiated affluence, importance and authority. She could understand why Amelda thought herself to be in love with him, but Nesta couldn't forget the possibility that a man of such considerable charm might be married.

He was certainly attractive, built like an Olympic swimmer, barrel-chested and broad shouldered, with his dark brown hair, tanned, smooth skin and strong white teeth that gleamed as they clenched on a fat cigar between his full lips. She could just imagine his having a glowing wife and happy children.

He had been so cool, so self-assured and so utterly charming when they had met that Nesta had found it impossible to question him about his background. What had worried her, though, was the fact that he was at least ten years older than Amelda, possibly more.

And, although she knew that Gwilym was just as concerned as she was, she found herself defending Michael Owen whenever he criticised him. It didn't make sense.

A week later, when she could stand Gwilym's brooding silence no longer, she made her decision.

'I'm going to ring Alice Roberts and check how Amelda is,' she told him at breakfast the next morning. 'If I can persuade Amelda to come home, then how about us driving down to Cardiff to collect her? It would give you a chance to meet Alice,' she added picking up the phone before he could protest.

'Doesn't she want to come home, then?' Gwilym asked, looking up from his newspaper as Nesta replaced the receiver, a bewildered look on her face.

'She's not there.'

'Oh? Gone back to London?'

'No. She's gone to stay with my Da.'

'She's what?'

'She left Cardiff three days ago. Alice was surprised we didn't know. She said she thought Amelda had already phoned and told me.'

134

'What made her decide to go there?'

'Michael Owen has been moved to a convalescent home at Beddgelert. It's only a half an hour's walk from Idwal Cottage.'

Amelda couldn't believe her ears when Michael phoned to say he was being moved from Stoke Mandeville Spinal Unit.

'Does that mean you are better . . . or that they can't do any more for you?' she asked cautiously.

'They say I don't need any more treatment here, but I still need rest and some therapy. It may take another couple of months before my back is completely better. They offered me a choice of several places, but I remembered what you had said about the mountains and scenery in North Wales. I'm going to a place called Beddgelert. Ever heard of it?'

'Oh, Michael, how wonderful! It's quite near where my grandfather lives.'

'Great! So you can stay with him and come and see me right away.'

'Yes, I suppose I could! If he is away I have an aunt and uncle living nearby and I'm sure they would put me up for a couple of nights.'

'That's no good. I shall be in the nursing home for at least a month. Come on, I want you there.' As his gravelly voice softened, entreatingly, Amelda tried to steel herself, to shut out the memory of his liquid brown eyes gleaming persuasively beneath the dominant dark brows.

'Shouldn't I get back to London . . . to the office,' she protested half-heartedly.

'No problem. They are sending over a team from the New York office to run things until I am fully recovered.'

'But . . .'

'Look, honey, just nip round to the flat, pick up some

clothes for me, then jump in the Porsche and get yourself up here to North Wales as soon as you can. I will explain everything when I see you.'

The mid-September countryside flashed past the car windows in a shimmering golden haze as Amelda left London behind. The Porsche was as smooth as a swallow. She had only driven it once before and she felt both nervous and excited by the feel of power as the car responded to her lightest touch.

When her gaze flickered to the speedometer, and she saw it was registering over a hundred, she hastily lifted her foot from the accelerator, half expecting to hear the shrill klaxon of motorway police.

She felt dazed with happiness.

The thought of spending the coming weeks alone with Michael filled her with mind-spinning optimism. In North Wales, right away from his fast-living, jet-set friends they would have time for each other. There was so much she still wanted to know about this wonderful, sensually dominant man who seemed to exert so much power over her.

She had never indulged in casual affairs. In her early days at university they had nicknamed her the Ice Maiden and the reputation that she was aloof and frigid had stayed. It didn't worry her, since it kept the wolves at bay. Girls who might otherwise have shunned her because she was so pretty acted as bodyguards once they realised she had no intention of poaching their boyfriends.

She had never traded on her 'Dresden doll' prettiness, not until she had met Michael Owen. The moment she had walked into the restaurant, and succumbed to the power of his personality, she knew he had been the man she had dreamed of one day meeting.

His response had equalled her own.

Although he had behaved in a completely professional

manner, the combination of his American casualness and masculine magnetism created a physical response in her that until then had lain dormant.

She had tried to resist his virile charm, but she was aware of a feeling of intense euphoria that left her weak and tingling whenever she came into contact with him. His warm friendliness unsettled and excited her.

When they kissed for the first time, his full lips hot and demanding, it was no 'Ice Maiden' who responded. He had ignited a fire that glowed constantly, breaking into leaping, ecstatic flames that consumed them both.

He was her first lover.

Amelda was as inexperienced over sexual matters as she was about her new job, but she had proved to be an avid pupil under Michael Owen's tuition.

From the moment of meeting Michael, she had seemed to exist in a totally new world. Her flatmates, Penny and Cindy, had teased her unmercifully . . . until they realised that things were serious between them. Cindy, especially, was profoundly disturbed by her infatuation.

'He's much too old for you,' she warned her. 'You really know nothing about him.'

This was true, because not even Penny, who had introduced them, knew anything whatsoever about Michael's background, but Amelda had laughed derisively and ignored Cindy's warning. She had, however, tried very hard to get Michael to talk about himself, but her efforts had been abortive.

'Why waste precious time talking about me, honey?' he murmured as he crushed her to him.

And, because she needed him as desperately as a drug addict might crave a fix, she simply abandoned caution and gave herself up to the glorious sensations his hands and lips could create. She had become insatiable, responding with a vibrant urgency to his sensual touch, deaf to the insinuations about his past or warnings about her own future.

As she turned the Porsche onto the A5 at Llangollen, the reality of what she was doing suddenly hit her. She hadn't been to the office since the bombing incident because she didn't feel equal to answering a barrage of questions as to why both she and Michael were at the Hilton. Now she might have to face the same questions from her grandfather and she wondered what she should tell him. She hoped he wouldn't be shocked when he knew the truth of the situation.

'I told you on the phone, you can stay here as long as you like,' Rhys affirmed when Amelda arrived at Idwal Cottage. 'Just one thing, though, don't expect me to wait on you.'

'Thanks, Granda, and don't worry, I'll look after *you*.'

'Huh! I don't suppose you can even boil an egg,' he said scathingly.

'I'm a very good cook,' Amelda retorted. 'Ask the girls I've been sharing a flat with if you don't believe me,' she added as she saw the look of disbelief on her grandfather's face.

They stared silently at each other for a long moment, his slate-grey eyes speculative, hers questioning.

'Why don't you like me, Granda?' she asked softly.

'Like you?' His eyes became hooded.

'You treat me differently from Llewellyn. You always have, ever since we were small children, even before Llewellyn became caught up in your Plaid Cymru movement.'

'Rubbish! You're imagining it.'

'No, I am not.' A sharp edge had crept into Amelda's voice. Unshed tears made her eyes look like rain-washed purple pansies.

'Oh, Amelda!' his hand reached out and stroked her honey-gold shoulder-length hair, drawing her close until she was within the circle of his arm. He tilted her face, forcing her to look up at him. His slate-grey eyes were inscrutable as he studied her delicate features.

'What is it, Granda? Is it because I am so like Eleanor?' she asked in a gentle whisper.

For a second he looked shocked. His craggy face froze as he fixed Amelda with a leaden stare.

'Alice Roberts told me how very like Eleanor I was. She used to enjoy talking about her,' Amelda explained. 'Did you love my grandmother very much, Granda?'

'Yes!' He sighed. 'And you grow more like her each time I see you. Even as a baby, your hair, the colour of your eyes, even the shape of your face, was like my Eleanor's. Now that you are grown up you are like her in so many other ways. The way you walk, your voice, the way you smile . . .'

'And yet you never told Mum.'

'No!' He shook his head. 'What was the point? She never knew her mother! It wouldn't have meant anything at all to her, now, would it?'

'Granda, how can you say that? She has always wondered what her mother was like. It grieved her that she didn't even have a proper photograph, just a faded snapshot that she treasured so much she was afraid almost to look at it. That time we went to Cardiff, to bring Llewellyn home after he ran away, she was overjoyed when Alice Roberts told her that I was like my grandmother.'

'She never mentioned it to me!'

'Probably not. You can be very unapproachable, you know,' Amelda smiled. 'When you put on your fierce look you scare us all stiff.'

'I do?'

'Oh, come, you know you do. It's the same stern face you use at Plaid Cymru meetings when you want to browbeat the audience into agreeing with you. That

139

dark piercing look, beetling brows and your chin thrust forward so that your beard stabs the air like a baton.'

'I see! And are you afraid of me?'

'No.' Amelda looked at him speculatively. 'When I was growing up I used to feel guilty because you didn't seem to like me and I didn't know why, and I couldn't work out what I was doing wrong. As I grew older, though, I decided you just didn't like women. You were always so scathing about Aunt Wynne and the way she fussed over you. You were even off-hand with Mum. You would go months without even getting in touch with her until in the end she would be so worried that she had to phone you.'

'I've always been a loner,' Rhys told her. 'Going to sea probably made me like that. After Eleanor died I vowed I'd never again get close to any one person and get hurt like that again.'

'Except Mum?'

'Well, Nesta was different. She was part of me. When I came home from sea and found strangers in the house in Cardiff where I'd left her in the care of Eleanor's parents I almost went out of my mind. I couldn't believe they didn't know where she had gone. Day and night I walked the streets looking for Nesta. I even hung around outside the schools hoping to spot her.' He ran a hand through his thick grey hair as if the memory still confounded him. 'I couldn't even find Alice Roberts!'

'I know. She told me. Her family had moved away from the Hope and Anchor pub by then.'

'I used to have nightmares about what might have happened to Nesta. Tiger Bay was rough in those days and I was afraid she may have tried looking for me and come to some harm.'

'But you did find her again . . . here in Wales,' Amelda reminded him softly.

'Yes,' Rhys sighed. 'It was too late, though. She was

grown up by then. And she had met your father and didn't really have much time for me.'

'She's always loved you dearly . . . we all have,' Amelda told him gently.

'The bed in the spare room needs making up; you'll find sheets and blankets in the airing cupboard,' Rhys said, turning away abruptly.

'I'll see to it; don't worry,' Amelda told him, planting a light kiss on his cheek before going upstairs.

Half an hour later, when Rhys came up to see what was keeping her, he found Amelda leaning on the windowsill staring out of the wide-open cottage window, mesmerised by the view.

'Oh Granda!' she breathed, her violet eyes soft and dreamy, 'why have I never come to stay with you since I left school? This place is paradise!'

'Not in mid-winter it's not,' he told her gruffly. 'When the snow comes it blocks the lane and I can't get to the main road for weeks at a time.'

'It must look very beautiful,' Amelda murmured dreamily.

'Looks it, but it doesn't feel it unless you've taken care to stock up the larder and remembered to build up the wood pile and can stand the isolation.'

'You can.'

'To me it's home. I've lived here so long now that I plan my life around the seasons. In winter when I know I'm going to be housebound I work on my speeches. Shut away almost in solitary confinement gives me a chance to sort out my thoughts, study all the back copies of *Welsh Nation* and get the Plaid Cymru cause into the right perspective.'

'You are a deep one, Granda,' Amelda smiled. 'Dad always said you were a firebrand. I think he believes that these outbursts that make the headlines at Plaid Cymru meetings are straight from the top of your head.'

141

'Instead of which they're from the bottom of my heart. They're the result of hours, or even days, of agonising debate with myself,' he told her earnestly.

'Does it all mean so much to you?'

'Of course it does! That view you've been admiring will be completely changed if the English are left to carry on unchecked. Come back in a few years time and you'll find a rash of red brick boxes and the mountainside covered in Sitka pine. Those undulating slopes that change colour with the seasons will be just a solid mass of green. And in twenty years' time, when the pines are full grown, they'll chop them down and the scars left will be as permanent as the ones left by those who quarried the mountains.'

'Oh, Granda!'

'It's the truth, Amelda. I shan't live to see it, but you will . . . unless we can call a halt right now to what they are pleased to call progress.'

'I'd like to stay and help you, Granda.'

'You!' He gave a sharp laugh. 'You're like all the rest of the visitors. You become sentimental over the view while you are here, but once you get back to London you forget how it is being ruined by the greed of English entrepreneurs.'

'I don't want to go back to London,' Amelda told him.

Rhys gave her a dark brooding stare as if he was trying to decide whether she was serious or merely being impetuous.

'I don't think I could live there ever again . . . not after what happened,' she shuddered. 'I still dream it is happening all over again and wake up in the night, terrified.'

'That will pass with time.'

'I hope so. I still don't want to go back to London, though.'

'What about your job?'

'I'll find something else. I could always work for Plaid Cymru,' she added with a fleeting smile.

'And what is this boss of yours going to say to that? I understood he was rather special.'

'He is.' She paused and laid a hand on his arm, her voice pleading as she looked up at him, 'That is why I wanted to come and stay here when I heard Michael had been moved to a convalescent home in Beddgelert. I do so want the two of you to be friends, Granda,' she added earnestly.

16

Michael Owen was as enchanted with North Wales as Amelda had hoped he would be. Each day he seemed to grow stronger. And as they walked hand in hand through leafy lanes, or along craggy paths at the foot of Moel Hebog and Snowdon, Michael seemd to enjoy every moment of it.

By the end of the second week they were exploring further afield. The contrast between the stark, grey grandeur of the mediaeval castles, the isolated mills and waterfalls, the remote, white-washed farms tucked away in the mountains, and the popular seaside resorts intrigued and delighted him.

It had been mid-September when they had arrived and the weather had been glorious: mellow days of ever-changing colour, as trees and vegetation turned gradually from lush green to golden yellow and flaming orange, a tantalising kaleidoscope. There had been days when even the topmost peak of the Eyrie had been etched against an azure blue sky.

Now, as the mellow autumn edged towards October mists, there were colder winds, and the occasional cloud banks obscured the mountain peaks like glowering frowns. The days were shortening and the sharpness of reality was creeping back.

She stared into the distance, to where a church tower shone like a golden beacon in the autumn light, and remembered her grandfather's words about the isolation when winter snows came and they were cut off from the rest of the world. Even that would be enjoyable as long as Michael was there with her.

With each passing day, her love for Michael deepened. She felt as if she was a part of him. Even their thoughts seemed to harmonise. Blissfully they would picnic in secluded cwms, or on beaches now deserted by summer visitors, enclosed in a world of their own making.

'We're going to get caught one day,' Michael warned her as they lay locked in each other's arms in a grassy grove near Moel Hebog.

'So?' She raised herself on one elbow and tickled his face with a piece of grass.

'It might take some explaining!' He grabbed her to him, his lips making a tantalising trail up one arm and across a bare shoulder.

'Wouldn't it be wonderful if we could stay here for ever!' Amelda sighed happily, shielding her eyes from the bright autumn sunshine as she looked at him.

'You'd soon miss the London life, honey,' he told her, his mouth tightening.

'No, I wouldn't, not if you were here as well,' she told him, trailing the stem of grass across his bare chest.

Abruptly, he sat up, fastening his shirt.

'I'm due to leave the nursing home on Friday,' he told her, avoiding her eyes.

The sun seemed to disappear behind a bank of grey cloud and she found herself shivering.

'And what then?' Amelda asked, sitting back on her heels so that she could see Michael's face more clearly.

'London . . . and work, I suppose,' he answered with an imperceptible shrug.

'You mean the relief team go back to the States?'

'Sure! Leastways, I imagine that's the plan.'

'Haven't you spoken to anyone at the office since you've been up here?'

'Nope! I don't believe in interfering. They'll have their own system and way of handling things; I have mine.'

'But you are the Managing Director of the company.

Surely you care?' Amelda exploded.

'I'll ring them tomorrow, maybe,' he said, standing up. 'Just to let them know the current situation.' He held out a hand and pulled her to her feet.

'So our holiday is over and it's back to London again,' she sighed.

'Are *you* coming back? I rather gathered that you wanted to finish with city life,' he said guardedly.

Amelda felt the hot colour rush to her cheeks. How could Michael be so blind. Couldn't he understand that she wanted to be wherever he was. It didn't matter whether it was in the quiet seclusion of the country or the mad bustle of London, just as long as they were together.

She would never be able to completely obliterate the memory of the terrifying explosion, or the trauma that followed, but the tranquillity of the last few weeks had put the incident into perspective. As long as they were together her fears were numbed.

Did he love her?

Michael's reluctance to ask the one question she longed to hear troubled her. She lay awake each night wondering what his true feelings for her really were. Even if he didn't experience the same fervour as she felt for him she was sure they could be happy together.

He seemed to take it for granted that she was content to continue as they were indefinitely, but she longed for a deeper commitment. She wanted to be able to face her family openly, not harbour feelings of guilt. She had deliberately refrained from taking Michael to Idwal Cottage because she was afraid of her grandfather's censure. Yet she couldn't spend the rest of her life hiding Michael away from her family.

Moving back to London was like stepping onto a different planet. The season was in full swing and Amelda found herself caught up in the whirl of lunching and dining out at smart restaurants, theatre going, bright lights, and disco-theques.

Michael was fêted by the rich and powerful as though he had returned from the dead. The women openly admired his leaner figure, his tanned, healthy physique.

His penthouse flat throbbed with activity as people dropped by to say 'hello' and have a drink. He was showered with invitations to parties at Annabel's, St Christopher's, Trader Vic's or at some other London 'in' place.

Even though she was now openly living with him, Amelda often found herself left out. Turning up for cocktails when she hadn't been invited, was one thing, but going along for the weekend to country-house parties took more nerve.

'What's the problem, honey?' Michael asked in baffled tones whenever she protested that the invitation didn't specifically include her. 'They all know we live together. Love me, love my dog, as you British say.'

His flippancy, as well as his sentiments, rankled. She had never thought of Michael as being a male chauvinist but now she wasn't too sure.

Probably she would have found it easier to accept if she had still been doing her job, Amelda decided. Working not only helped to keep her wits sharpened but dulled her more sensitive feelings. Being idle left her time to think.

'It wouldn't work, honey,' Michael told her when she said she was ready to return to the office. 'Everyone would know we were living together and it would be bad for staff morale.'

'But your friends all know . . .'

'That's something else again,' he pointed out. 'What I do in my own time is my own business.'

'Well, let me work as a freelance,' she begged. 'I'm a good researcher, you've said so yourself, so why let my talents lie dormant?'

'You might find yourself working for the opposition and it could be construed as industrial espionage,' he countered. 'Anyway, honey, I like things just as they are. It gives us more time to enjoy ourselves.'

At first, she had to agree that it was great fun. Michael took plenty of time off and they explored London with the same enthusiasm as they had wandered round North Wales. They had a wonderful time shopping. Michael showered her with new clothes and jewellery and spent lavishly on the penthouse, changing hangings and even furniture to please Amelda's taste.

As she looked round the elegantly furnished lounge, with its pale blue and gold décor that looked like a spread from *Homes and Gardens* she knew she should be in seventh heaven. But she wasn't. There was something lacking. She had felt happier at her grandfather's cottage in North Wales than she did in these opulent surroundings, she thought miserably.

As if sensing her discontent, Michael tried to provide more diversions. In late November they visited Hong Kong and the Far East. Michael suggested they should fly on to Bali and spend Christmas in the sun, but Amelda insisted on going back to England so that she could be at home with her own family for Christmas.

Wallasey was cold, wet and windy.

Amelda arrived at St Hilary's Hill in time to help with some of the preparations. As they put up the decorations, and trimmed the tree, she found herself reminiscing over each piece. It took her back to the family Christmasses of her childhood and made her wonder where the years had gone.

She and Nesta went to Liverpool for last-minute shopping. Gwilym took them both out to lunch and then insisted they went back to his office for a drink with his staff.

Amelda was impressed by the tremendous amount of

respect shown to him and she was suddenly conscious of just how much older he was than all the other men in the room.

Mum's in her fifties, too, she thought startled. No wonder she wants grandchildren. She felt edgy, wishing she knew what the future held.

Michael was spending Christmas in New York and she was missing him a great deal. He had given her a Christmas present before he left, but made her promise not to open it until Christmas Day, and she was suddenly curious as to what it might be.

'I'll be with you in thought when you open it, honey,' he had told her. 'It's something I know you want, and which I hope will prove how much I love you.'

Suddenly curious, she took it out of her suitcase. The small package was beautifully wrapped and very light in her hand. Her heart beat faster. It seemed too large to be an engagement ring, and yet . . . She felt it again, and decided it was definitely a small box. If it was a ring then it would have been nice to have Michael actually place it on her finger himself, but this was a very romantic way of doing things.

To resist the temptation of opening it, she took it downstairs and hung it on the Christmas tree. She smiled to herself as she thought of her father handing it to her when he distributed the presents.

Remembering Michael's promise that he would phone her on Christmas Day at four o'clock, so that she could tell him if she liked her present, made her more convinced than ever that it was an engagement ring.

She spent Christmas morning day-dreaming about what the ring would be like. Llewellyn arrived mid-morning, bringing his girl friend, Glenda ap Lloyd, to spend the day with them. She had not met Glenda before and felt slightly awed by the thin, serious girl. She had straight, brown hair framing her heart-shaped face and huge dark-rimmed glasses. The stark, white collar at the neck of the plain brown woollen dress made her appear very severe and prim.

'Glenda teaches at the same school as Llewellyn *and* she's a Plaid Cymru supporter,' Nesta whispered, as she came into the kitchen where Amelda was making coffee for the new arrivals. 'She is ever such a clever girl.'

'She looks formidable to me,' Amelda commented rather dubiously.

'She's terribly intelligent. She got a First at Oxford! She has the qualifications for a much better teaching post than where she is, but she stays there because of Llewellyn.'

'You mean it's *that* serious?' Amelda asked in surprise.

'I think so. They've been going around together for quite some time now.'

'No one told me!'

'Somehow, I thought you knew,' Nesta frowned.

Even though she didn't take very readily to Glenda, Amelda had to admit that her brother and his girl friend had a lot in common. Llewellyn had always been rather serious and scholarly so they were well suited. And he was engrossed in Plaid Cymru.

When her grandfather arrived with Wynne and Huw, it became obvious that they were all well aquainted. Rhys made no secret of the fact that he greatly admired the work Glenda did for Plaid Cymru and Amelda felt piqued that he hadn't told her about Llewellyn's girl friend when she had been staying at his cottage.

I'm losing touch with them all, she told herself as they sat down to their meal. Mum and Dad are not as I remembered them, and Aunt Wynne and Uncle Huw seem so old and cut off from the kind of life I lead that they are like strangers.

As she pulled a Christmas cracker with her grandfather, and listened to him reading the motto he had found inside, she thought enviously of the life he lived at Idwal Cottage.

He was probably the happiest of them all. He was answerable to no one. He was self-sufficient in every way, free to think and do as he liked, just as his mood of the moment decreed.

Whenever he felt lonely, Wynne and Huw were just a stone's throw away. He could meander at will through woods and cwms, climb mountains, walk along the seashore or wander round old castles and let himself drift back into the past. And when he was bored by that, he could take up the cudgels on behalf of Plaid Cymru and help in planning the future of Wales right through into the next century.

He might be getting old and grey haired, but he was still his own man, she thought admiringly.

They took so long over their Christmas dinner that Amelda grew concerned in case Michael phoned before she had opened her present.

'Dad, could I have one of mine first . . . that small one near the top?' she asked when Gwilym finally stood up and moved across to the Christmas tree and began to give out the presents.

'Now, Amelda, you must wait your turn,' he teased.

'Please, Dad. It's important. It's my present from Michael and he's phoning from New York at four o'clock to see if I like it!'

'Well . . .' he paused and compared his watch with the clock, 'since there is only five minutes to go, then I suppose we had better let you be first.'

She felt all thumbs as she took the package from her father and started to remove the wrappings.

'It seems a shame to open them at all when they are as pretty as that,' Wynne exclaimed, as Amelda tore away the ribbon ties and discarded the flower decorating the parcel.

'When they're as small as that it's probably not worth opening, anyway,' Rhys joked.

Amelda felt her cheeks burning as she finally reached the small jeweller's box. She looked round the table with shining eyes, aching to see what was inside and yet holding back the wonderful moment just as long as she could.

'Come on, open it up before the phone rings,' Llewellyn told her.

'All right!' She took a deep breath then flipped open the lid. For a second her disappointment was like a physical blow. There was no ring. Her fingers trembled as she lifted a gold key from its velvet bed. Tears blurred her eyes so much that she couldn't read the words on the tiny slip of paper rolled up alongside it.

Unable to speak she passed it over to Llewellyn, who read out: '"This is the key to Morfa Cottage, Betws-y-Coed. Michael."'

'What does that mean?' Gwilym asked, frowning.

'It sounds very much as if Michael Owen has aquired a cottage and has sent the key of it to Amelda as a Christmas present,' Llewellyn said crisply.

'He's done what?' Rhys roared.

'He's an American, isn't he?' Glenda asked, staring at Amelda from over the top of her glasses.

'It's bad enough the English taking over our cottages, but if the Americans are starting to do it as well then the prices will be pushed up sky high,' Llewellyn exploded, his face glowering.

'Is this some kind of joke, Amelda?' Gwilym asked, frowning at her.

'I'm sure it's not a joke,' Amelda whispered, looking down at the key still clutched tightly between her fingers. 'I think he meant it as a surprise . . . to please me,' she muttered, stunned as much by their reaction as by the present itself.

'Is there such a place as Morfa Cottage at Betws-y-Coed?' Nesta asked, bewildered.

152

'Of course there is,' Rhys exclaimed, his voice hoarse with anger. 'It was the home of the poet Geraint Glynne–Jones who died last year. There was talk of the place being turned into a museum, a kind of shrine for his works and for the works of other Welsh poets and writers, but there wasn't enough money to do it. Sad it was! Next thing, it was supposed to be put up for auction; but it was snapped up before the sale!'

'And now Michael has sent Amelda the key to it!' Wynne exclaimed.

'Well, at least we know who bought it. There's a scoop for the *Post*, Dad,' Llewellyn chortled.

'Don't jest about it, Llewellyn,' Glenda admonished. 'It's this sort of thing Plaid Cymru is against.'

'Yes, we've got to fight, every single one of us, or Wales will be overrun by damned foreigners,' Rhys exclaimed heatedly. He ran a hand through his thick grey hair until it stood on end. His slate-grey eyes were bright with fervour, even his greying beard seemed to become more pointed.

'Hold on, Granda,' Amelda exclaimed, her eyes darkening to dark purple with anger. 'I'm not a foreigner. I'm as Welsh as you or Llewellyn.'

'Yet you sneaked this foreigner into our midst and now he is buying a house that should by rights be going to a Welshman,' Glenda stated.

'What do you think I have been fighting for all these years?' Rhys exclaimed angrily. His voice rose to a crescendo, his beard stabbed the air as the blood rushed to his face.

'Hold on now, Da. We don't know the whole story yet. He may only be renting it,' Nesta said placatingly, laying a hand gently on her father's arm.

'You don't want to go getting yourself into such a state, Rhys. Not over an old cottage,' Wynne admonished.

'I won't stay here a minute longer,' Rhys stormed. He

stood up, pushing back his chair so forcibly that it crashed to the ground.

'Granda, please! We haven't opened any of the other presents yet. Don't spoil things for everyone,' Amelda pleaded.

'Spoil things!' He waved his fist threateningly. 'You expect me to sit here and watch you all gloat over your trinkets and baubles while Wales is being gobbled up by foreigners . . .'

His voice suddenly faded. His hands clutched at his chest and he doubled over as if in pain. Gwilym caught him as he slumped forward. He lowered him gently to the ground, loosened off his tie and undid the top button of his shirt.

'Phone for an ambulance one of you,' he rapped as he slipped his hand inside his father-in-law's shirt, feeling for his heartbeat.

17

'We have a new Managing Director and you know what they say about new brooms! He is just using the fact that I didn't turn in a story about your heart attack as an excuse. I've seen the writing on the wall for a while now,' Gwilym told his father-in-law. 'In recent months they've been pruning the place from top to bottom. To him I'm an old man!'

'At fifty-six! You're in your prime, Gwilym.'

'Not when your boss isn't yet forty and everyone else in the place is under thirty. It's the day of the younger man.'

'Young, bright and indiscriminate. Ready to betray their own mother if it brings them some kind of reward,' Rhys said scathingly.

'Well, yes. You know how it is!' Gwilym shrugged.

'Would they have sacked you, though, if you had given them the story? If you had told them that my heart attack was brought on because my grandaughter's American fancy-man had bought a cottage in North Wales.'

'Probably not this week, but they would have found some other reason and . . .'

'Then fight them! It's unfair dismissal. Take it to the European Courts.'

'And have our family's peccadillos dragged into the open? Make ourselves a laughing stock?' Gwilym exclaimed bitterly. 'No, Rhys, I'd sooner keep a low profile. I know that these days no one attaches very much importance to such things but I'm not all that proud of the fact that my daughter is Michael Owen's live-in lover.'

'No, nor of the fact that your son and your father-in-law both support Plaid Cymru,' Rhys growled.

'Yes, I suppose Llewellyn's name might be dragged through the mud as well,' Gwilym agreed heavily.

'And Glenda's! Though I don't suppose she would mind,' Rhys replied, his voice warm with approval. 'She'll make Llewellyn a good wife. Very supportive is Glenda and as sharp as a needle. Brilliant turn of phrase when she takes the platform.'

'Too politically minded, if you ask me,' Gwilym glowered. He found Glenda overpowering and far too serious. With her curtain of straight dark hair, and shrewd dark eyes behind the enormous spectacles, she was so intense that she unnerved him. And she had far too much influence over Llewellyn for his liking.

He didn't want Llewellyn to become as fanatical about Plaid Cymru as Rhys was. Politics were all very well, but not when they took precedence over your career. He had even overheard Glenda egging on Llewellyn to stand for Parliament. Llewellyn had dismissed the idea, but the seed had been sown and Gwilym judged it would only be a matter of time before Llewellyn capitulated.

When he had mentioned it to Nesta she had tried to laugh his fears away.

'Llewellyn loves teaching too much,' she assured him. 'Anyway, he knows that as a Plaid Cymru candidate he wouldn't stand much chance of getting in.'

'No, but it might jeopardise his chance of a headship. He has his heart set on running his own school.'

And this was just one more reason why Gwilym had held back the story of Rhys's heart attack. So many family issues would have had to be aired.

Only Nesta seemed to fully understand his predicament, Gwilym thought ponderously. At first she had been devastated by his news, but she had quickly rallied and attempted to find some sort of solution.

156

'Perhaps it is time for a change of direction,' she suggested.

'Journalism is my life. It is all I'm interested in doing,' Gwilym contended.

'But there are other forms of journalism besides holding down an editorial job.'

'Freelancing, you mean? Become a stringer who has to rely on the whims of the news editor as to whether or not your work is used. No thank you!'

'Freelance, yes, but not necessarily as a news reporter. What's wrong with feature writing or TV journalism?'

'Nothing at all wrong with them, except that they want the under-thirty brigade who can dash off to cover a story in any part of the country, or the world even, at the drop of a hat. Chaps who are fit as a fiddle and prepared to camp out for days at a time to watch the Royals at their antics or to get a live quote from a pop star.'

'You're exceptionally fit,' Nesta defended.

'Am I?' Gwilym grinned as he patted his slight paunch and pretended to gasp breathlessly.

'What about Public Relations, then? Perhaps Amelda's Michael would put in a word for you . . .'

'*No!*' His green eyes blazed. 'I always vowed I'd never interfere in my children's lives, but I never said I would condone the sort of lives they lead.' He sighed deeply. 'I don't know where we've gone wrong, but they are both turning out so different from what I expected. Llewellyn with his Plaid Cymru allegiance I can understand. That's your father's influence. But Amelda! Openly living with this American. It may be all right in London, but not in this part of the world. Why couldn't he have bought a cottage in Somerset or down in Cornwall . . . anywhere but in North Wales?'

'They both love the area,' Nesta said quietly. 'And can you blame them? There's something about the grandeur of the mountains that puts human problems into their right perspective. Perhaps we should sell up here and go to North Wales ourselves. The price we would get for this place would buy us a house there and leave some money over to live on.'

'It may well come to that.'

After almost a month of job hunting in the Liverpool and Manchester area, Gwilym found himself left with no alternative but to apply for jobs on some of the lesser-known provincial papers. He became increasingly depressed as another month went by without even the prospect of an interview. When Rhys phoned to say that the editor of the Clwydd Press, a small North Wales publishing company, was retiring he immediately applied in person. Three weeks later they sent for him to tell him he had the job.

'Managing Editor! That sounds very grand,' Nesta enthused. 'Does it mean we will have to sell up here and move to North Wales?'

'I thought that was where you wanted to be, back amongst your wonderful mountains!'

'Oh, Gwilym!' Nesta hugged him impetuously. 'I'm so pleased for you, for us both.' She paused, looking round their beautifully appointed home. 'It's going to be hell giving up all this, though,' she whispered.

'We'll find something you like just as much.'

'But this has been our home for most of our married life,' she said softly, her dark eyes misting. 'So much has happened here: love, laughter, tears, good news and bad . . .'

Gwilym drew her into the circle of his arms, tilting her face so that he could look down into her eyes. Gently his thumb outlined her brow, her cheek bones and her chin. Very slowly his mouth covered hers in a kiss so warm and tender that it sent her pulses racing.

'As long as we are together, I don't think it matters where we live, do you?' he whispered softly.

'Perhaps a fresh start is what we need,' she agreed smiling. 'At least it will stop us getting in a rut.'

'We'll have to start house-hunting right away. I start my new job in a month.'

'We'll never sell this place and be ready to move in such a short time,' she exclaimed worriedly.

'I could commute, I suppose. Or stay with your father.'

'Do you think that would work?'

'I was joking, of course. I can't see the two of us living together amicably, now, can you?'

'Why don't you use Morfa Cottage as a base,' Amelda suggested when her mother phoned to tell her the news.

'Well, that's very kind of you, but . . .' Nesta hesitated, not knowing how to explain Gwilym's feelings about Michael Owen.

'Oh, dear!' Amelda's laugh broke the awkward silence. 'Is it still a sore point? Is Granda still ranting on about Michael buying a cottage in North Wales? I suppose he would have preferred the cottage to stand empty, and go to rack and ruin, rather than someone he considers a foreigner should buy it. Now if I had bought the cottage, and not Michael, he would probably have been over the moon with joy.'

'There's more to it than that, Amelda.'

'You mean Michael and me are being blamed for something else . . . Is it Granda's heart attack, or Dad losing his job . . . or both?'

'No, it's not that at all, Amelda. It's just unfortunate that those things followed as a result. The chances are that they would have happened anyway.'

'What is it, then?' A sharp querulous note had crept into Amelda's voice, and Nesta wished she had never got onto the subject at all. Having done so she decided it was perhaps better to clear the air once and for all. At least Amelda would know where she stood next time she came home to see them.

'It's to do with you living with Michael Owen. Your father doesn't approve.'

There was a long silence.

'Are you still there, Amelda?' Nesta asked sharply.

'Yes, Mum. I just don't know what to say to you.'

'Why don't you get married?' Nesta said gently. 'I'm sure that would set matters right. Your father and Granda would accept Michael then without question.'

'Don't you think I would if he asked me?' Amelda said in a small unsteady voice.

Nesta felt stunned.

'Oh, Amelda. I didn't know . . . I'm so sorry. But why?'

'Just forget it, Mum. I don't want to talk about it.'

The knowledge haunted Nesta. Several times she tried to tell Gwilym, but he was so immersed in his new job that she hadn't the heart to add to his worries. They had still not found a house that was suitable and so Gwilym was having to travel a round trip of over a hundred miles each day.

'Why don't you stay a couple of nights mid-week with Huw and Wynne?' Nesta suggested. 'It would give you more time to look round the area and see what is for sale. Once you saw anything you thought might be suitable, I could come and view it.'

They had already sold their house on St Hilary's Hill and Nesta was worried about what would happen if they didn't find something for themselves quite soon. She had visions of having to put their furniture into store and possibly moving in with her father. He was still in poor health and she was afraid to mention the matter to him in case it might upset him and bring on another heart attack.

Within the week, however, Gwilym had found what he considered to be the ideal house for them.

'It's a cottage called Tryfan and it's between Capel Curig and Betws-y-Coed,' he told her. 'I'm sure you'll love it. You can actually see your beloved Snowdon from the windows!'

Amelda was less than enthusiastic when she went with Nesta to look at the cottage.

'It's very picturesque, but it's so small after St Hilary's Hill!'

'Oh, I don't know,' Nesta defended. 'It has been modernised and extended. It's got two bedrooms, a separate lounge and dining room, and the kitchen is large enough to eat in when we are here on our own.'

'Oh, I agree, it's been very tastefully modernised.'

'So why don't you like it?' Nesta asked in bewilderment.

'I think it's enchanting, but it's so isolated! Whatever will you do with yourself all day?'

'I'll find plenty to do. The countryside around here is magnificent. I'll be able to walk for miles. If there's enough money left over from the sale of St Hilary's Hill we might even be able to afford a second car. That would be marvellous for popping over to see Wynne and Huw and my Da.'

'Well, yes,' Amelda admitted grudgingly, 'you will be nearer to them. The way they are both ageing you'll probably end up having to look after them. Aunty Wynne is getting fatter and fatter. She waddles along! It's a wonder she can climb onto a bus. One day she'll become wedged on the steps and they'll have to call out the fire brigade to cut her free.'

'Oh, Amelda, you shouldn't talk like that about her. It's not her fault she looks so bloated. She's had kidney trouble for years. If Huw wasn't so crippled with arthritis she would probably get him to do the shopping. Now I can help her more.'

'Well, just don't go overdoing it, Mum. I remember how you wore yourself out looking after Granda when he had his heart attack.'

161

'He is as fit as a fiddle again now and taking better care of himself,' Nesta smiled. 'He's even talking about getting himself a dog for a bit of company. It will be nice to be able to see him more often. And if I do manage to get a car of my own I shall enjoy taking him out and about. He'll like that.'

'I'm sure he will,' Amelda smiled thinly. 'But is acting chauffeur to Granda going to be enough for you, Mum? If you move away from Wallasey you will lose all your friends, and you'll miss the charity committee you serve on. You will be giving up your whole life, in fact. It seems an awful waste.'

'Really, Amelda, you are a fine one to talk,' Nesta rounded on her heatedly. 'What are you doing with your life? You talk about me! You could be doing so much after the education you had. You have talent, ability, looks, personality and, what is even more important, you have youth on your side. Yet here you are frittering them all away just for this Michael Owen! And you have the gall to reproach me.'

'There's no need to lose your temper, Mum,' Amelda told her coolly. 'Michael doesn't want me to work.'

'Why ever not? He doesn't want to marry you, he doesn't want you to go out to work, what does he want?'

The relationship between Amelda and Michael Owen troubled Nesta deeply. When she had met him she had been charmed by his smooth drawl and recognised that the handsome American had tremendous sex appeal, but she hadn't expected the affair to last or that it would have such a devastating affect on Amelda. She also knew it was a situation she had to accept.

Amelda was twenty-six, old enough to be independent and to know her own mind. Nevertheless, it grieved Nesta to see how she had changed from a happy, ambitious, career-girl into a woman utterly dependent on a man who was not her husband.

162

When Amelda had left university, Nesta had thought she was set for a brilliant career. And she still believed that Amelda could achieve great things if she stopped letting Michael Owen dominate her, and struck out for herself.

It grieved her much more than if it had been Llewellyn who had settled into a backwater. Ever since Amelda was born Nesta had hoped that she would achieve all the things that she herself had missed in her own life.

At first it had seemed that her dreams were coming true. Amelda had been so pretty, with her fair wavy hair and huge violet eyes that she had been the centre of attention. Even when she started school and grew leggy and coltish, she had been enchanting. She'd been so sweet natured that everyone had loved her. Her soft pansy-purple eyes could melt the hardest heart.

School work had come easy to Amelda. She had attained the necessary O and A Level results to take her on to university and Amelda's achievements there had been the fulfilment of her own dreams. And now she felt saddened and frustrated that Amelda was just marking time, doing nothing creative or productive, because of Michael Owen.

Once we've moved into Tryfan, she resolved, we'll have a house-warming and invite them both. It is time the rest of the family met him, she decided. She would mention it to Amelda when she came over to help with the move.

She had never suggested Amelda and Michael coming to stay because she knew Gwilym would object to them sleeping together under his roof. Now, with Morfa Cottage being only a few miles away from Tryfan there was no need for them to stay overnight, so it was no longer a problem.

When Amelda did arrive, however, her news temporarily put everything else out of Nesta's mind. She looked so upset that Nesta immediately thought something had gone wrong between her and Michael Owen.

'No, it's not that,' Amelda told her, choking back tears. She rummaged in her handbag and brought out a solicitor's letter which she passed to her mother. 'Read that!'

As Nesta opened it up her heart thudded with foreboding. She read it through twice before she fully understood it.

'Oh, Amelda!' Tears blurred her eyes. 'I didn't even know Alice was ill!'

'She sold her café a couple of months ago because she felt it was getting to be too much for her. She mentioned then that she hadn't been feeling too well lately. I invited her to come to Morfa Cottage for a holiday and she said she would once everything had gone through on the sale of her business. The solicitor rang me two days ago to say she had died suddenly. This letter is just a confirmation of what he told me on the phone . . . Alice has left me everything, Mum. The solicitor said it would be around £20,000.'

18

The move from St Hilary's Hill to North Wales went surprisingly smoothly. The furniture vans arrived on the Friday and by Sunday night everything was in place in Tryfan. Even the pictures were hung and Nesta's treasured collection of china dragons had been arranged to her satisfaction. As she stood at the cottage door, feeling the late April sunshine warm on her face, she felt as if she had lived there all her life.

Nesta revelled in her new surroundings. Wherever she looked there were memories. Ahead, she could see the Eyrie, the Snowdonia range that guarded the Vale of Ffestiniog where she had worked as a Land Army girl. To the left, the three peaks of the Moelwyns where her father and Wynne lived. Away to the south west was Moel Hebog with Beddgelert nestling at its foot, and the River Glaslyn racing down to Tremadoc Bay and the open sea.

She was never happier than when her father came to visit. Although he had made an excellent recovery he tired easily and had grown very tetchy. He was still full of fire and rhetoric, however, and Nesta was apprehensive when Amelda phoned to say that she and Michael would come to see her over the Spring Bank Holiday.

The day they were due to arrive, Nesta polished and dusted the cottage until everything gleamed in the May sunshine. Putting all her energies into cleaning helped to stop her worrying about how her father would react to Michael Owen. Gwilym had to go into the office to sign some papers so she persuaded him to take Rhys along as well.

As she heard a car draw up she nervously checked on

her appearance before opening the door. Michael was not at all like she remembered him. At their previous meeting he had been wearing a formal dark suit, white shirt and sharp tie. Now he was dressed casually in jeans and an open-necked checked shirt under a baggy red sweater. The moment he spoke, though, she remembered the charm of his attractive gravelly voice. As she looked into the keen, gleam of his calculating brown eyes she sensed he was as apprehensive about this meeting as she was.

She felt suddenly confident.

The mood of quiet gaiety lasted until Gwilym and Rhys arrived home for lunch. Then it was replaced by a sense of disquiet. Gwilym was rather distant and Nesta was acutely aware that he was studying everything Michael said and did in a cold, calculating way.

Rhys was more direct in his approach. As they shook hands, his dark eyes beneath their bushy brows had been shrewdly summing Michael up.

'I understand you've bought a cottage here in Wales,' he declared as they sat down to lunch.

'That's right. Morfa Cottage. You must come and see it,' Michael invited.

'There is no need for me to do that; I know it well. Home of the poet Geraint Glynne-Jones. It was very wrong to sell it . . . to a foreigner.'

'Surely that is better than leaving it to stand empty?' Michael said mildly, but Nesta saw that his jaw tightened.

'At one time there was talk that it would be turned into a museum of his works,' Amelda explained.

'It's quite a large cottage, I suppose one room could be used for that purpose, even now,' Michael said mildly.

'With you living in it?' Rhys protested.

'Why not? Some of your titled families open up their homes to the public, don't they?'

'They do in England, but this is Wales.'

'Am I right in believing that you have strong political opinions, Mr Evans?' Michael enquired challengingly.

'I support Plaid Cymru, the Welsh Nationalist Party, and we try to see that Wales is protected from the English, or any other foreigners who come here and try to impose their ways on us, if that is what you mean,' Rhys growled.

'Have you ever thought that by trying to erect a barricade around Wales you might be doing it a disservice?' Michael asked mildly. 'Keeping people out is not the way to educate them about your country.'

'Michael does have a point, Granda,' Amelda exclaimed enthusiastically. 'If more people knew how beautiful Wales was then they would be anxious to preserve it in every way.'

'And keener to buy up cottages that should by rights belong to Welsh people! If they needed them as homes it would be a different proposition,' Rhys declared adamantly. 'It's buying them just as holiday cottages that we object to.'

'Better that than they should fall into ruin.'

The argument remained the focal point throughout the meal. Rhys was inflexible that foreigners should be kept out of Wales, but Michael refused to accept his viewpoint.

Amelda felt like a spectator at a battle. Llewellyn and Glenda, who had arrived just as they were about to start lunch, remained neutral at first, but Amelda could see the angry gleam in Glenda's dark eyes, as she listened to the exchanges going on around her. She was not in the least surprised when Glenda made an acid remark about Americans having no real understanding of what was meant by national pride.

Michael's drawl became more pronounced, his frown more formidable, as he questioned the source of her knowledge.

'One of my friends at university came from the States,' she told him.

'There's always the odd-ball, the exception to every rule,' he replied smoothly.

'Nothing odd about her, I can assure you,' Glenda retorted, coldly. 'She had an excellent brain!'

'But no soul!' Michael sighed exaggeratedly. 'A common fault with the over-educated.'

Amelda could see that Llewellyn's temper was about to erupt and she made a desperate bid to save the situation.

'Has Mum told you that Alice Roberts has died and left me all her money?' she asked her brother.

'No!' He looked surprised. 'Did it amount to much?'

'Around £20,000.'

'Fantastic! What are you planning on doing with it?'

'She will probably fritter it away on fast cars, clothes and high living down in London,' Rhys pronounced cynically.

'No, you are quite wrong, Granda,' Amelda smiled. 'In fact, I'm thinking of starting a business.'

'You are what? You never mentioned any such idea to me, Amelda,' Michael frowned. 'I thought we'd agreed you wouldn't work. That was the main reason for buying Morfa Cottage . . .'

'That is where I'm going to have my business,' Amelda interrupted triumphantly. 'Listening to all of you ranting on about Wales gave me the idea. Morfa Cottage is much too large for just the two of us. I agree with Granda; since it was the home of such a famous poet, people should be allowed to visit it. So, I am going to turn it into a craft shop.'

There was a stunned silence.

'Well, say something!' Amelda demanded, her cheeks flushed.

As they all began talking at once, and she parried the shower of questions and arguments fired at her from all sides, her brain seethed with ideas. She felt more alive, more excited than she had for many months.

'You would never get planning permission . . .'

'You've no experience of running a business of any kind . . .'

'You couldn't cope single-handed . . .'

'If you want to make it pay then you'll have to cater for the holiday trade. That means seven days a week in season and staying open until seven or eight at night during August . . .'

'What on earth would you sell there?'

'It would cost the earth to stock it out properly, take practically all your money . . .'

'Honey, it's a completely crazy idea,' Michael protested, his eyes pinning hers angrily.

'No, it's not! I admit I haven't worked out all the details yet,' Amelda said breathlessly.

'Forget it, Amelda. It's foolhardy,' Michael reiterated authoritively.

'And you intend using the money Alice left you to set it up?' Nesta asked, bewildered.

'That's right. And you can help me run it, Mum . . . you and Granda,' she said earnestly. 'It will give us all a new interest in life,' she told them seriously. 'Dad, you can help me sort out the legal side. And you two,' she smiled at Llewellyn and Glenda, 'can advise me on what I should stock.'

Amelda's outburst successfully diverted the row that had been brewing, but the moment she was alone with Michael she found he was still totally opposed to her scheme.

'A very clever ruse to stop your family feuding, honey,' he complimented her blandly, pulling her into his arms and kissing the tip of her nose. 'When are you going to tell them you haven't any intention of going through with such an idea?'

169

'Oh, but I have!' She pulled away from his embrace. 'I meant every word of it.'

'You are joking?' his eyes challenged, a nerve twitched angrily in his cheek.

'No, I am not!' she affirmed vehemently.

'And what if I object?'

'Why should you?'

'I thought we had agreed you wouldn't work,' he said softly, drawing her back into his arms. 'You have so much to interest you. There's our apartment in London, entertaining my business associates, the theatre and all our trips abroad. Morfa Cottage is for when you need a complete change of scene.'

'It's not enough,' she told him, pulling away so that she could look into his face as she spoke. 'Being a "kept woman" isn't my style. I'm not trying to pressurise you, Michael,' she added quickly as she saw his eyes narrow. 'I just need a life that gives me some kind of fulfilment.'

'Do you mean marriage and children?'

'In time, yes.'

'I thought you enjoyed the London scene, the parties, eating out, entertaining . . .'

'I do, I do. And the fabulous clothes you buy me, being seen in all the right places, and all the rest of it, but it's not enough. It's all so shallow. Mum is quite right . . . I am wasting my university education . . . I need to work, to stretch myself.'

'And running a shop will do that?'

'No,' Amelda admitted, shutting her ears to the sarcasm in Michael's voice, 'I don't suppose it will be the ultimate challenge, but for the moment it's what I want to do. I don't want to become politically active like Granda or Llewellyn, but making Welsh craftwork better known will be my way of helping Wales. I think Alice would have approved of my scheme,' she added decisively.

Right up until the moment he returned to London,

Michael tried to persuade Amelda to change her mind, but she remained steadfast to her idea. Her grandfather was surprisingly supportive. He had lived in the area for so long that he knew local crafts people had a great need of such an outlet, and he was eager to show Amelda what they could produce. Potters, weavers, painters, leather workers, artists of every kind expressed a willingness to supply her with exclusive items.

The more excited Amelda became about the project the more disinterested Michael seemed to be. Whenever she tried to tell him what was going on, he changed the subject. He appeared to be bored by the whole idea, and she constantly found herself torn between his demands for her to be in London to accompany him to business functions, or act as hostess at his parties, and commitments made on her behalf by her grandfather.

Things finally came to a head the weekend she was due to open the craft shop. Grudgingly, Michael had agreed to spend the weekend at Morfa Cottage. Then, at the last minute, he cried off because of a polo meeting at Smith's Lawn.

'Postpone the opening and come and join me here in Windsor,' he told her over the phone.

'I can't possibly do that! There's far too much for me to do here!' she exclaimed aghast. 'Even Llewellyn promised to give up his weekend to help.'

'Leave him to it, then. You could probably do with a break. Anyway, we haven't seen each other for three weeks now . . . doesn't that mean anything to you?'

'Of course it does! That was why I was so looking forward to you coming here this weekend.'

'If I had done so you would have been working flat out, by the sound of it.'

'There would still have been time for us . . . there always is,' she told him softly.

'Then make time and come to Windsor. That's an order.'

He had put down the phone before she could reply, leaving her fuming with indignation. She began to see why her grandfather thought him arrogant and overbearing.

When Llewellyn arrived half an hour later, Amelda was upset and angry. He was surprisingly understanding.

'I'll be able to manage. You go to Windsor,' he offered.

'The first weekend the shop is open? No fear! Thanks, all the same, but it is my baby. I want to see it launched. And what would Granda say if I wasn't here?' she grinned.

'I think it does mean a great deal to him,' Llewellyn admitted. 'And to Mum. She talks about nothing else these days.'

'I know, they've both been tremendous. Without all Granda's contacts I would never have been able to get together such a wonderful collection of stock.' She looked round at the large selection of gifts and craft items displayed in the room which had once been the front parlour of the cottage. On the floor were enormous wicker baskets, each one spilling over with quality craft items of every description. Pottery, leather goods, pewter, carved wood, beautiful woollens; everything from inexpensive items like decorated slate coasters, tweed purses, woollen hats and gloves, to the super-luxury goods such as sheepskins, leather coats, hand-loomed tweeds, sculptured figurines, glasswork and framed water-colours, which were displayed around the walls.

'Come and look at these framed copies of the last poem Geraint Glynne-Jones wrote, Llewellyn,' she invited. 'It seemed like a fitting tribute and the idea certainly seemed to please Granda. I think he has almost forgiven Michael for buying the cottage, now that it has been put to such good use.'

'I wouldn't be too sure on that score,' Llewellyn told her grimly. 'Mr Owen is not his favourite person and I can well see why. OK, OK' he held up his hand as Amelda was about to defend Michael. 'I'm not going to

172

start an argument with you, but I think you could do better for yourself . . . we all do. Mum is worried about you. She doesn't like the fact that you are openly living with Michael Owen. She wants to see you married. I think she is anxious to have some grandchildren,' he grinned, softening his reproach.

'Then why don't you marry Glenda ap Lloyd and give Mum what she wants?' Amelda retorted sharply.

'Neither of us want to settle down yet. Glenda isn't ready to give up her career.'

'She doesn't have to. She can go on teaching after you are married.'

'It wouldn't work. Anyway, if we decided to start a family Glenda would have to stay home.'

'Not permanently. She'd qualify for maternity leave and then she could go back to work,' Amelda argued.

'And farm the baby out? No, thank you!' Llewellyn snapped.

'So, deep down you're a male chauvinist like all the rest of them, and expect your wife to be the one who gives up her career. You want her to be dependent on you.'

'You're in no position to talk. You gave up your career just to live with Michael Owen,' he retorted angrily.

'At least we are open about our relationship. You and Glenda are sleeping together, yet pretend you are not.'

Llewellyn turned away, refusing to be drawn into a row. His chiselled lips were set in a hard line and there was anger in his dark eyes.

'You really are a carbon copy of Granda, you know,' Amelda said tightly. She stared at her brother for a long moment. 'It's stubborn pride that keeps you from marrying Glenda. You can't bear to think she would be earning more than you, or that she might even get a headship before you did.'

'We were discussing your future not mine,' Llewellyn

reminded her. 'Why don't you marry Michael Owen and set me an example?'

'For the very simple reason that he hasn't asked me,' Amelda said quietly. 'I'd marry him tomorrow if he did.'

19

Amelda was so involved in her new venture that at first everything else paled and was pushed into the background, even her relationship with Michael Owen.

Nesta and Rhys were helping to run the shop, but keeping the books, ordering stock, and finding new lines was her responsibility and one which she took very seriously. She was determined that everything she stocked should be the very best of its kind and she was determined to build up a reputation for the unusual. She would travel miles to meet new crafts people and spent hours discussing their work and arranging terms.

Llewellyn was very supportive and often went with her, but Glenda refused to help in any way.

She had been scornful about Amelda's idea right from the start and even now, when it was becoming a flourishing business, she refuted the claim that it was helping local people.

'You're exploiting them,' she exclaimed scornfully, waving an arm at the wicker baskets piled high with merchandise.

'Oh, come on, Glenda, be fair. It provides a showcase for almost fifty different crafts workers,' Llewellyn remonstrated.

'It looks like a flea market! Commercialised junk! People rummaging around as if they think they're going to find some rare treasure.'

'All my suppliers are quite happy,' Amelda told her tartly. 'It gives them an outlet for their work and I pay fair prices.'

'In that case, why is Llewellyn always trying to do what he calls "special deals"? You are as bad as any capitalist retailer, screwing the manufacturer down to the last penny so that there are bigger profits in it for you.'

'That's not so,' Amelda told her heatedly. 'I have overheads to meet, and if I am to go on expanding then I have to keep the whole project viable. First and foremost it's got to be a commercial proposition.'

'And use free labour whenever you can. You're working your mother and Rhys into the ground, you take up most of Llewellyn's spare time, even your father gets dragged into it at the weekends. Well, you're not getting me involved so don't think you are. It's bad enough seeing Llewellyn neglect his other interests . . . and me.'

Michael Owen had much the same outlook on the venture. He resented the fact that Amelda had become completely absorbed in what she was doing and although he found time to visit her, she hadn't been up to London once since the shop had opened.

'You are coming up to London next weekend, I hope?' he told her as the entire family sat down to a meal on the Sunday evening after the shop was closed. 'I've managed to get tickets for the new Tom Stoppard play.'

'I'm sorry, Michael, it's impossible. It's the height of the holiday season and I must be here.'

'So what do I do with these tickets, honey?'

'I'm sure you'll find someone who will take them off your hands.'

'Or I could take someone else,' he drawled softly.

If he had thought that would sting Amelda into action he was wrong. She merely shrugged.

'I'll be in London next weekend if you want to sell one of them,' Glenda told him.

'Just one?'

'Llewellyn will be too busy helping Amelda to take advantage of such an opportunity. I'm planning a trip to London to do some shopping, and a spot of sightseeing.'

'Then why don't we do the show together?' Michael invited. 'We can have supper afterwards. Give me a ring when you get to town so that we can finalise the details.'

'I thought you didn't like London,' Llewellyn said, staring at Glenda in surprise. 'You told me you absolutely hated it when you went there with your parents.'

'Only because they imposed too many restrictions about where I could go and what I could do. I haven't been there for years. With the right company it might be quite enjoyable,' she added archly.

It became the first of many weekend visits.

By late September, when the tourist season eased off, Amelda felt drained. She was looking forward to closing for a month or so, and having a holiday. When she phoned Michael at the office to let him know she was on her way to London, she was shocked to learn that he was in America.

She couldn't understand why he hadn't been in touch to let her know that he was going away. She knew Glenda had been in London the previous weekend and wondered if she had seen Michael and whether perhaps he had mentioned anything to her.

'Oh, yes! Michael did give me a message for you, but it went right out of my head,' Glenda told her blandly. 'He was called away suddenly on Sunday evening, just as I was leaving for my train.'

'For a business meeting?'

'Oh, no!' Glenda paused dramatically. 'His wife had been rushed into hospital. He's gone over to the States to see her.'

'His wife?'

The words echoed over and over inside Amelda's head as she stared open-mouthed at Glenda. For a moment they had no real meaning because they didn't relate to the man she knew. Then as her own gaze locked with Glenda's, and she saw the gleam of triumph directed towards her from behind the heavy-rimmed glasses, the full impact of what Glenda had said hit her.

She fought back the memories that crowded her mind: the tenderness and passion of Michael's lovemaking; the sumptuous apartment she had shared with him; their mutual interests and friends.

The 'highs' and 'lows' of their long affair were like a colourful banner unfolding in her head. The tumultuous happenings that bonded them together had entwined and entangled the strands of their emotions into a colourful tapestry. The path down which she had been tripping so happily had, without warning, become a quagmire.

'His wife!'

'Yes. Didn't you know he was married?' Glenda's voice was a mixture of concern and gloating, and seemed to be coming from a long way off.

'No!'

Amelda sank down onto a chair as the colour drained from her face. Her violet eyes widened like two great bruises. Llewellyn coming into the room to see if Glenda was ready to go home stared at her in alarm.

'What's wrong, Amelda, aren't you well?'

'I think I have upset her,' Glenda confessed contritely. 'I just happened to tell her that Michael had gone back to the States because his wife is not well. I didn't realise that Amelda didn't know he was married.'

'So how is it you know?'

'Michael told me . . . last weekend . . . in London.'

'I thought you were visiting a friend,' Llewellyn said, frowning heavily.

'I did. But I also saw Michael. We all went to the theatre together on Saturday night to see Alan Ayckbourn's play *The Norman Conquest*. When we got back to his place afterwards there was a message to say his wife had been taken ill. He flew out on Sunday morning.'

'Without a word to Amelda?' Llewellyn asked

brusquely.

'Well, he did ask me to let her know he'd gone to the States.'

'And to tell her why?'

'I'm not sure . . .' Glenda chewed her lower lip uncertainly. 'I can't remember. I wasn't taking too much notice at the time. We'd had such a splendid evening and I had had rather a lot to drink . . .'

Llewellyn turned away with a look of disgust on his dark handsome face. He had been so engrossed in helping Amelda that he hadn't stopped to wonder about Glenda's frequent weekend visits to see a friend in London. What blind fools he and Amelda had both been, he thought bitterly. While they had been concentrating on the Morfa gift shop, Glenda and Michael had been living it up in London. Hoodwinking him about how she spent her weekends was one thing, but he took umbrage that she should be deceiving Amelda as well.

Remembering how angry and resentful Glenda had been when she had first heard that Michael had bought a cottage in Wales, Llewellyn wondered how the change of heart had come about.

Whatever the reason, he decided, it could be sorted out later. For the moment it was enough that Amelda was in hock and needed help.

Looking back, remembering how steadfastly Michael had refused to marry Amelda, they should have realised that Michael was probably married. Yet he was quite sure that Amelda had never for one moment suspected the truth.

Amelda was still subdued and listless when Michael returned ten days later. The estrangement between them loomed like a stone wall. His explanation that he had been living apart from his wife for a number of years, even before he had come to work in London, failed to convince her.

179

'Why didn't you tell me in the first place?' she argued in a dull flat voice.

'I never thought it necessary,' he shrugged.

'Why didn't you get a divorce if you had no intention of ever living together again?'

'She was against that on religious grounds.'

'If she meant so little to you,' Amelda persisted, 'then why did you go rushing back when you heard that she was ill?'

'Conscience, I suppose,' Michael said, looking acutely embarrassed. 'Perhaps if you had been in London with me, sharing my life instead of being embroiled with your gift shop, I wouldn't have reacted as I did.'

He tried desperately to make amends, but Amelda had backed herself into an emotional corner and nothing Michael said or did seemed to overcome her sense of deep bewilderment. It was as if her overpowering love for Michael had been reduced to ashes and she was engulfed by gloom.

Michael felt so utterly rejected that in the end he returned to London, hoping that perhaps separation would help to heal her battered spirits.

Amelda felt too numb to analyse her feelings for Michael. She became even more deeply involved in the gift shop, masking her grief in a frenzy of work. She had intended to close down completely until spring, but since there was still a good number of tourists around each weekend, she decided that she would open up on Fridays, Saturdays and Sundays. The rest of each week she spent sorting out the stock and visiting small out-of-the-way workshops and ordering new lines.

Llewellyn was unable to accompany her on these trips now that the new school term had begun, but Rhys was always pleased to be invited along. Now in his late seventies, he was crippled with arthritis and unable to walk very far so he thoroughly enjoyed the opportunity of visiting

180

the small woollen mills, potteries and individual craft workers by car. And Amelda welcomed his company.

Remembering his initial distrust of Michael, she had been reluctant to tell her grandfather that he was already married. When she finally did so she found him far more understanding than she had dared hope.

Her parents showed much greater rancour. It had been hard enough for them to accept the fact that she had moved in with Michael. Now, discovering the reason why he had always shied away from marrying Amelda, it angered them both.

Nesta grieved about it deeply. She had always wanted the best for Amelda, and that included a happy marriage and children. In Nesta's opinion, Amelda had squandered her youth on a man who was not worthy of her.

Gwilym was also worried about the situation. He felt Amelda had wasted a first-class education and he held Michael Owen responsible. The uncertainty about the future of their relationship troubled him. There were dark shadows under Amelda's amethyst eyes, and she barely smiled or laughed. It was as if she was in another world, her eyes bleak with despair. And there was no way he could reach her or help her.

The reconciliation between Michael and Amelda took a long time.

Right through the autumn she refused to see him, saying she needed time to think things through. Twice Michael had come to spend the weekend at Morfa Cottage and on both occasions Amelda eluded him by going off on a buying trip on her own.

'Why don't you ask Michael to sell Morfa Cottage to you, so that you have security as well as a purpose in life?' Rhys suggested, unable to watch her growing more and more dejected. 'I have money put by and you can have that as the deposit,' he told her. 'You can get a mortgage for the rest.'

Michael refused to sell.

'It's the only link I have with you these days, honey,' he told her sadly. 'If I pull out, then I feel it will be the end of things between us.'

'Perhaps that would be for the best,' she whispered brokenly.

'How can you say that, Amelda?' he blustered. 'Don't you feel anything for me any more?'

'It's because of my feelings for you that I want to be free,' she told him bitterly. 'I can't bear sharing you, Michael.'

'I'll get a divorce! My wife is coming to London in June for the Silver Jubilee celebrations. I'll talk to her then.'

'You mean she's staying with you?' Pain bruised her eyes.

'Not at the flat! We're completely finished, I've already told you . . .'

'Then why did she send for you when she was taken into hospital?'

'She didn't. Her family sent for me. They knew we were living apart, but they had no idea it was a permanent arrangement.'

'But they know now.'

'I suppose they do, but what does it matter? They're 3,000 miles away in America, I'm here and this is where I intend to stay . . . with you.'

'I won't come back to London, Michael.'

'Then can I come here . . . to live?' His brown gaze locked with hers, compelling her to give him the answer he wanted. As his hands reached out to take hers, Amelda felt her senses reeling.

Great waves of longing swept over her as she remembered the months of loneliness and soul-searching she had endured. Her nerves felt raw, she began to tremble with the strain, and when Michael finally gathered her into his arms she went without a struggle, nestling against his

182

broad chest like a bruised animal finding sanctuary.

He held her close for a long time, his head resting on the crown of her soft golden head. His deep, gravelly voice had a soothing effect as he murmured tender endearments. When she finally lifted her face to his her eyes were still misted with tears, but a hopeful smile played around the corners of her mouth.

'I do love you Michael,' she breathed softly.

Very tenderly his mouth came down over hers, warm and comforting. As his lips became more demanding and possessive, she felt the old excitement stirring through every fibre of her being.

That night they slept in each other's arms, the months of separation forgotten as they indulged their love for each other.

Next day, when it was time for Michael to return to London, Amelda couldn't bear to say goodbye.

'Come back with me, honey,' he pleaded as they clung passionately to each other.

'No! Not until you are completely mine,' Amelda whispered, tears drowning her eyes.

'But once I'm free?'

'Then I'll come anywhere you want me to,' she agreed impetuously.

'And until then?'

'It might be better if we didn't see each other,' she told him, as with sensitive fingers she lightly traced his lips, the smooth cheeks, redolent with after-shave, and his round chin.

'Not even here?' He trapped her hand, burying his lips in the palm of it.

'Just go. We'll decide about that later,' she choked, as fresh tears spilled down her cheeks.

20

'Whew! I think this has been the most hectic week since I opened,' Amelda exclaimed, as she locked the door behind the last customer. 'Thank goodness there won't be another Silver Jubilee in a hurry. This heat doesn't make it any easier, either,' she gasped, undoing another button at the neck of her sleeveless, cotton dress. Exhausted, she collapsed onto the settee, by the open window, kicking off her open-toed sandals, and flexing her aching feet.

'Trade has certainly been brisk,' Michael agreed, as he handed her a glass of ice-cold lager. 'I think we've earned these,' he said, joining her on the settee.

'I don't know how I would have coped without your help,' she told him with a grateful smile.

'You would have managed. Llewellyn's been here for most of the day, and your mother stayed until after the lunchtime rush was over.'

'Yes, both of them were tremendous,' she agreed. 'It's when more than one coachload of people arrive at the same time that it becomes so chaotic. And today, it seemed to be worse than ever because nearly everyone seemed to want Jubilee souvenirs.'

She took a long drink, then rested her head against Michael's shoulder. 'Glenda will probably be furious with Llewellyn,' she said reflectively. 'She wanted him to go up to London with her to see the procession.'

Michael frowned but didn't answer. The very mention of Glenda's name was still a sore point. With hindsight, he knew he had acted badly. During their bitter-sweet reconciliation, Amelda had magnanimously accepted his promise that his friendship with Glenda was over, but

184

the memory still rankled.

Glenda had been less generous. Her dark eyes had smouldered angrily when he had told her that their brief fling was at an end. She had argued, taunted, and then finally used tears and entreaties to try and cajole him into changing his mind.

It was the main reason that he had opted not to stay in London for the festivities, but to visit Amelda, even though she had warned him that she would be working most of the time.

'Be fun to see you in action,' he had told her. What he had really meant was that he would be safer there because he knew Glenda intended being in town and had already suggested that they should see the procession together.

'Your office overlooks the route,' she had argued, 'so it would be the perfect viewing point. I thought we could have a hamper and champagne . . .'

'No!'

He had not intended to be so abrupt. Enraged, Glenda had slammed down her receiver with a crash that had almost deafened him. When he had had time to get his breath back he had felt overwhelmingly relieved by his action. Amelda was worth twenty of her.

On reflection, he found it hard to understand why he had been attracted to Glenda in the first place. She was so moody and self-centred. The deep brown eyes, behind the heavy glasses, half hidden by the curtain of dark hair, were cold and calculating, not fiery and passionate as he had at first believed. She was brilliantly clever, but her wit was acerbic and often wounding. He knew he was no match for her.

He lowered his head, until his face rested on the top of Amelda's soft golden hair and he could smell the clean, sweet sharpness of her perfume. He ran his hands over the light golden tan of her smooth, bare arms and felt desire stirring as she moved closer against him.

The knock on the door startled them both.

'Visitors?' Amelda groaned, freeing herself from his embrace and reaching for her shoes. 'Who on earth can it be?'

'A late customer? Ignore it and they may go away.'

'It could be family or friends,' she groaned. 'I'll have to answer it. They'll know we are here because all the windows are open.'

'Hurry up and get rid of them, whoever they are,' Michael whispered conspiratorially.

'Take our glasses out to the kitchen and I'll see what I can do,' she giggled.

Amelda didn't know whether to be pleased or piqued when she saw who her callers were.

'I thought you had gone to London for the Silver Jubilee celebrations, Glenda,' she said in surprise.

'I came home earlier than I planned and I've brought a friend back with me,' Glenda smiled. 'Knowing your fondness for Americans, Llewellyn and I couldn't wait for you to meet her.'

'Oh?'

'This is Diana.'

As Amelda held out her hand in greeting she was aware that the stranger was very tall, with shoulder-length auburn hair, and so slim that she was almost angular. Her lemon linen suit was beautifully cut. It fitted her so perfectly, and her make-up was so flawless, that Amelda wondered if she was a model.

'Isn't it a small world?' Glenda laughed. 'Diana is over here for the Silver Jubilee and is staying with a couple of girls I knew at college. She was just dying to see North Wales so I brought her back with me for a few days.'

'Well, won't you come in?' Amelda invited.

'You are quite sure we are not interrupting your evening? Glenda has told me a lot about you. Your cottage is certainly enchanting.'

186

Amelda smiled politely as she ushered them through into the living room. She was relieved to see that Michael had whisked away their glasses and from the clatter coming from the direction of the kitchen she judged he must be washing them up, and their lunchtime dishes.

She felt annoyed that Llewellyn hadn't persuaded Glenda to leave visiting with her friend until the next day. Before he had left she had told him that she and Michael were planning to watch the procession on television and then have an early night.

It was the first time she had come face to face with Glenda since she had found out that she had been meeting Michael in London, and she felt vaguely uneasy that Glenda had come to the cottage at all. Surely Llewellyn must have told her that Michael was there?

To quell her feeling of disquiet, Amelda turned her attention to the American girl, sitting on the settee beside Glenda. She was older than she had seemed at first glance. A myriad of tiny lines encircled her cold, light grey eyes and were repeated at the corners of her thin lips.

'Did you enjoy the procession?'

'Absolutely stunning. So much atmosphere! The crowds cheering and your queen looking so opulent in that magnificent horse-drawn coach. And that wonderfully handsome Prince of Edinburgh in his gorgeous uniform,' Diana drawled.

'I suppose you watched it on TV, Amelda?' Glenda said.

'No, far too busy! we were planning on watching the rerun after the News tonight . . .'

'We?' Diana looked round in surprise. 'You don't live here on your own, then?'

'No . . . not all the time. I have a friend who comes to stay . . . usually at weekends.'

'And he's here now?' Diana's grey eyes narrowed.

Before Amelda could reply Michael came through from

187

the kitchen. He had heard Glenda's voice when Amelda had opened the door, and had taken as long as he could with washing up and putting the dishes away, hoping that perhaps she was only making a fleeting visit and he would not have to meet her.

As he came into the living room his jaw fell as he stared across towards the settee.

'What are *you* doing here?' he gasped, in a tight strangled voice.

For a moment Amelda thought he was speaking to Glenda. Then her heart began to thud with an inexplicable fear as she saw he was looking at Diana.

'This is a friend of Glenda's . . .' she began then stopped as she saw anger and something else she couldn't fathom in Michael's eyes.

'Oh, don't bother introducing us,' Diana said with heavy sarcasm. 'He knows who it is all right!'

'Did you plan this?' Michael asked, his tone savage as he looked directly at Amelda.

'What do you mean?' she asked bewildered.

'Someone must have told Diana I would be here and who else knew except you?'

'I don't understand . . .' Amelda's amethyst eyes darkened in astonishment.

'Amelda didn't arrange anything,' Glenda snapped. 'I brought Diana here.'

'You would, you interfering bitch.' He gave her a vicious glare. 'And what do you hope to gain by this little trick?'

'What's going on?' Llewellyn asked bemused. 'I take it you two know each other already,' he said looking from Diana to Michael and back again.

'We sure ought to, since he is my husband,' Diana drawled, cuttingly.

There was a moment of silence, so loud that everything paled into insignificance. Amelda tried to concentrate on the ticking of the pendulum clock on the wall behind her. This is a dream, she told herself. Any minute now I shall wake up. I've been working too hard. It's not really happening.

She looked beseechingly at Michael, silently willing him to say it wasn't true. As his eyes met hers and she saw the abject misery in their brown depths, it was like a sharp knife being thrust into her heart.

As he reached out a hand to touch her, to draw her to his side, she felt outraged. With an anguished cry she ran from the room. Upstairs she locked herself in the bedroom, refusing to come out when first Michael, then Llewellyn, knocked on the door and pleaded with her.

Dry-eyed, her throat aching as she struggled to keep back her tears, she stood resting her forehead against the windowpane, staring out at the distant mountains, wondering how she was ever going to face the world again. She tried to close her ears to the sounds coming from downstairs. The anger in their raised voices seemed to permeate the entire cottage.

I should have known the moment I saw Glenda on the doorstep that it meant trouble, she thought bitterly.

She heard the front door opening and then being violently slammed and the next moment she saw Llewellyn striding down the path, his face white with anger, his thick dark hair awry as though he had been running his hands through it in despair.

At the moment, it seemed as if the only person she could rely on was walking out on her and she drummed on the window hoping he would hear. From the set of his shoulders she sensed his anger, and knew he was incensed by the deception. When he climbed into his car without turning round, she found she was gritting her teeth with frustration.

She sighed and turned away, her own sadness a solid pain inside her chest. She wanted to go downstairs and

189

find out what was happening but pride wouldn't let her. She cared so deeply for Michael. When he had flirted with Glenda she had been angry and jealous, and it had taken a great effort to forgive and forget, but this new situation was far more dangerous.

Discovering that Michael was already married had been a trauma, but his wife had been a mere background shadow. He had been living in England for so long that she had accepted without question when he said there was no real attachment between them.

Now, she didn't know what to believe.

Llewellyn felt incensed as he strode down the path to his car. He still couldn't believe that Glenda would stoop so low in her desire for revenge as to take Michael Owen's wife to Morfa Cottage. She had behaved despicably.

It was the end of their relationship. He would never be able to trust her again.

He thought back to the days when they had first known each other and how they had worked side by side for Plaid Cymru. It was only in the last few months, since she had met Michael Owen, that things had changed, he thought bitterly.

He was so immersed in his own black thoughts that he hardly noticed where he was driving until he found himself outside his grandfather's cottage.

Shep, Rhys's black and white sheepdog, had heard the car and was at the door before Llewellyn had time to kill the engine.

'Not celebrating then, Llewellyn?' Rhys greeted him with a wry smile, as Llewellyn warded off Shep's over-enthusiastic welcome. 'I thought you'd be at one of these street parties or out flag-waving somewhere.'

Llewellyn tried to rise to the occasion, and return his banter, but Rhys regarded him shrewdly and Llewellyn knew it was impossible to deceive his grandfather.

'Better come on in and tell me what's up, hadn't you, boyo?' Rhys said. 'The kettle is on I was just going to brew up.'

As they sat together in the book-lined living room of the cottage, Llewellyn poured out the whole story of what had happened.

'Very unpleasant,' Rhys agreed, shaking his white head from side to side, his long gnarled fingers stroking his grey beard thoughtfully.

'I just can't understand why Glenda's changed so much,' Llewellyn repeated wearily.

'Can't you? Well I can! Just you think about it . . . and when it all started.'

'Things began to go sour when Amelda brought Michael Owen home and introduced him to Glenda,' Llewellyn said wearily.

'No!' Rhys shook his head. 'It started when you seemed likely to be the next Parliamentary candidate for Plaid Cymru.'

'Nonsense! Glenda is more for it than I am. And anyway, I haven't been chosen yet.'

'Glenda is as keen as you are, for *her* to be one of the leading figures in Plaid Cymru. She is jealous because there was talk that they would select you and not her for the next vacancy. She took damn good care not to let you see it, but it was there. Women are strange creatures, you should have learned that by now.'

'But what's that got to do with her bringing Diana onto the scene?'

'It's a way of getting back at you. She can't find a way to hurt you directly so she attacks through Amelda, knowing how much you care about your sister.'

'Are you saying that this is the reason she made a play for Michael Owen?'

'She knew how much you disliked him buying a property here in Wales, so she knew how deeply offended you

191

would be if she transferred her affections to him. She was out to make you jealous, don't you see that?'

'Well, she succeeded. I made no secret of *that* fact!'

'But that wasn't enough. Glenda is hard. She wanted to punish you even further.'

'I thought you liked her. You always seemed to approve of how she worked for Plaid Cymru.'

'She was a marvellous worker, but it didn't take me long to realise that she was only doing it to gain your attention. She didn't have her heart and soul behind it all. Not like Amelda.'

'Amelda has done hardly anything to support Plaid Cymru!' Llewellyn said in surprise.

'Not in actual canvassing or attending meetings, but she supports it in her heart and in her actions. Take this gift shop, for example.'

'What do you mean?'

'When Amelda first decided to turn the cottage into a shop she was trying to appease me because she knew I was so angry because a foreigner had bought the cottage. Once she started to meet the local crafts people then she had the urge to do something that would benefit Wales. After that, there was no stopping her. You know yourself how hard she has worked.'

'And what happens now? Morfa Cottage belongs to Michael Owen. If he decides to sell it Amelda will be homeless and the shop and all the work she has put into it will be lost.'

'Not as long as I have breath left in my body,' Rhys vowed. 'I'll help her fight for it. I've already told her she can have my savings if she can persuade him to sell the place to her. Raising the money for that and keeping the shop going, is the least of our worries.'

'I suppose I should go back and let Amelda know she has my support. She was so cut up about what was happening that she shut herself in the bedroom. When

I left Michael Owen was still having a heated argument with his wife. And Glenda was there, looking like the ringmaster at a prize fight,' he added bitterly.

'Don't rush things,' Rhys advised. He rose and went across to one of the bookcases and rummaged around behind a row of books and brought out a bottle of whisky. 'We'll have a quiet drink. Leave Amelda to deal with the situation in her own way. Go and talk to her tomorrow when she's had time to cool down.'

21

Llewellyn and Rhys sat talking late into the night. Through the open window, the mountains all around became dark silhouettes as the sun sank. The evening air cooled as they refilled their glasses and put the world to rights.

They gossiped about the family, about Gwilym's new job, Nesta's delight at being back in North Wales, of Llewellyn's career and plans for the future and then, finally, about Plaid Cymru, the topic so dear to the hearts of both of them.

'I'm proud of both you and Amelda,' Rhys told him garrulously, when just after midnight Llewellyn insisted that he must be going. 'I wish I could count on a few more years to work alongside you both.'

'You'll always be an inspiration to us,' Llewellyn told him warmly. 'If I can do only half as much for Wales as you have then I'll be happy.'

'Keep the foreigners out, especially the English,' Rhys rasped, as he walked to the door with Llewellyn. 'There's too many of them here already. You have only to look out there at all the bonfires and fireworks there are tonight to see that.'

'There will be Welsh as well as English celebrating,' Llewellyn reminded him. 'People love the excuse for a party.'

As he drove home the spasmodic spatter of fireworks, followed by bursts of vivid colour that lit the night sky like exploding stars, and the dull glow of bonfires past their prime but still burning, echoed Llewellyn's own turbulent feelings.

His anger bubbled up anew at the thought of Glenda's deception in passing Diana off as a friend. He felt ashamed that he hadn't given Amelda more moral support. He should have stayed by her side, not left her to face the music on her own.

The talk with his grandfather had made him realise how constricted he had allowed his own life to become. By letting Glenda dominate him as she had, he was going through life in blinkers. He recalled the number of times he had particularly wanted to do something, or go somewhere, and Glenda had persuaded him to change his mind. Last year he had missed out on the occasion when Alan Llwyd had attained both the Crown and the Chair at the Royal National Eisteddfod. He had been so looking forward to going to Cardigan for the ceremony, but Glenda had kept telling him that it was a waste of time since he didn't speak Welsh.

This year it was being staged in Wrexham and no matter what happened, he resolved, he would be there. He might even take Amelda. She might not have the tongue, any more than he had, but he was sure she would enjoy the music and the atmosphere.

It was as if the scales were being ripped away from his eyes and he was seeing Glenda in her true colours, he thought morosely. Clever but callous, scheming and devious and so set on revenge that she would crucify even his sister to gain her ends.

He would never forget the look of triumph on her face when Amelda realised who Diana really was. He wondered how the evening had ended.

As he drove down the hill, towards Morfa Cottage, he saw a great red blaze of fire flickering through gaps in the trees and was surprised that they should have decided to have a party. Then, as the road straightened out, he could see the cottage starkly outlined and realised that it wasn't a celebration bonfire but Morfa Cottage itself that was lighting up the night sky.

Terror brought bile rising into his throat.

He parked some way from the cottage, afraid that the flames were so fierce they would reach the car if he went any closer. In the distance he could hear the clanging of a fire engine bell and the klaxon siren of an ambulance.

The heat was already forcing back the tiny knot of people and as he reached them Glenda turned and saw him and flung herself into his arms, weeping hysterically.

'Has everyone got out?' he demanded, holding her tightly by the arms and almost shaking her in his anguish.

'No, no, there's still . . .' Sobs choked her words as she collapsed against him.

'Who is it that is still in there?' he demanded fiercely, his hand under her chin, jerking her head back so that he could look into her face.

'There's still one young woman in there,' a man's voice answered.

'We saw her at the window, clamouring for help,' a woman exclaimed in shocked tones. 'One of the men tried to get to her, but the flames were monstrous. No chance at all.'

Sick with apprehension, Llewellyn watched as the fire engine pulled up. Hoses were reeled out, and a turntable ladder was placed in position against one of the upstairs windows. As the jets played on the burning fabric of the cottage several firemen attempted to enter it.

As the minutes ticked by, even the firemen on the turntable were beaten back by the heat and flames. Llewellyn felt sick with despair. He should never have stormed off as he did. What could have happened between them all for things to end like this? When he looked round for Glenda he saw she had already been taken into one of the ambulances.

'She doesn't appear to have been hurt but she's badly

196

shocked so they've sedated her. They'll take her to hospital,' one of the firemen told him.

'Was she able to tell you anything? I tried to question her but . . .'

'She was too shocked to be of any real help. She kept repeating something that sounded like "she's trapped in there", but we already knew there was someone else in there. Other people had already reported seeing a woman at one of the windows . . .'

'I . . . I think it could be my sister . . .' Llewellyn stuttered, his lean face looking haggard.

'We're doing our best. We hope to have her out soon,' the fire officer assured him as he moved away towards the blazing inferno.

When firemen eventually brought the woman out it was obvious that she was dead. Before they placed the stretcher into the waiting ambulance, the fire officer asked Llewellyn if he would identify the body.

Llewellyn nodded. His stomach churned as he forced himself to look down at the charred figure on the stretcher.

For a moment he was too dumbfounded to speak. He had steeled himself to see a halo of fair hair, Amelda's pretty, gentle face, even the amethyst eyes wide with shock or terror.

But it wasn't Amelda.

'Can you tell me who she is?'

'Mrs Diana Owen.' He struggled to keep the relief out of his voice as he stared transfixed at the singed auburn hair, the thin angular face, the crumpled lemon suit. 'She's an American over here on vacation.'

'I see. And the woman already taken to hospital?'

'Glenda ap Lloyd. She brought Diana Owen to the cottage earlier today.'

'You seem to know a lot of the facts,' the officer frowned. 'Was there anyone else likely to be in the cottage with them? You did mention your sister . . .'

197

The feeling of elation that had swept through Llewellyn the moment he realised the body wasn't Amelda slowly ebbed away. Amelda and Michael Owen might still be trapped in there. He looked across at the blazing inferno. No one could survive that heat. A new wave of despair swept through him as he turned to answer the fire officer.

'When I left the cottage earlier this evening my sister Amelda Vaughan and a man, Michael Owen, were also there,' he muttered dully.

'And you think they might still be inside?'

Llewellyn shrugged hopelessly. 'I don't know. Glenda ap Lloyd would be able to tell you . . . but you said she has been sedated.'

The fire officer issued fresh instructions to his crew. It seemed to Llewellyn that hours passed before the fire was finally reduced to a smouldering mass of masonry. No trace of any other bodies had been found.

News of the fire had spread. A crowd had gathered, police, newspaper reporters and photographers were all there.

'Are you sure you're fit to drive, sir?' a policeman asked, as Llewellyn walked over to his car and slid in behind the wheel.

'I'm fine. I'm only going about three miles, to Tryfan, to let my parents know what has happened.'

'We are very anxious to trace your sister and . . .' he consulted his notebook, 'this Michael Owen. What relation was he to the deceased?'

'He was Diana Owen's husband.'

'I see!' His shrewd eyes crinkled as he waited expectantly. When he realised that Llewellyn wasn't going to tell him anything more he snapped his notebook shut and stuffed it back into his top pocket.

'We would like to talk to you again, sir, and to your sister. Perhaps we could contact you at Tryfan later in the day.' He frowned. 'Do you think there is a chance your sister might have already gone there? Perhaps we should go along with you and find out.'

For a moment Llewellyn looked at him blankly. The possibility had never crossed his mind. With a deprecating shrug he turned on the ignition.

'If she is there then I will phone you right away,' he promised.

'Not to worry, sir. We'll make our own routine check.'

Once he was out of their sight, Llewellyn put his foot hard down on the accelerator and drove at breakneck speed towards Tryfan. At all costs he must get there before the police did, he thought anxiously. Amelda had been through enough. He wanted to shield her from any more shocks. Telling her what had happened to her home and business, as well as about Diana, was going to be traumatic any way, he thought sadly.

Tryfan was in complete darkness.

Llewellyn hammered on the front door for some minutes before he managed to rouse Nesta. She came down barefooted, her dressing-gown clutched together, followed by Gwilym in only his pyjamas.

At first, from his smoke-blackened, dishevelled appearance they thought that Llewellyn had been involved in some kind of accident. When they learned the truth they were completely taken aback.

'Amelda is upstairs in bed. She arrived here about ten o'clock saying she didn't feel well. She looked pretty awful, as though she had been crying. She never mentioned that anyone was at Morfa Cottage, so we assumed that she and Michael had quarrelled and that he had gone back to London and she didn't want to be on her own.'

'Blasted American! He's brought nothing but trouble to this family,' Gwilym stormed, his voice savage.

'You can't really blame him,' Nesta protested. 'He didn't set the place on fire!'

199

'How do you know he didn't? And where is he now?' Gwilym snapped.

'Do you think he drove Amelda over here?'

'I've no idea. She just arrived on the doorstep on her own. I never even thought to ask her how she'd got here.'

'Just what has been going on?' Gwilym looked directly at his son. 'Amelda wouldn't walk out on her guests. And, anyway, if Glenda was there when the fire broke out why weren't you?'

'Later, Dad. Later.' Llewellyn ran his hand through his hair. 'The police will be here at any moment to question Amelda. I really think we ought to waken her. Tell her to get dressed . . . and perhaps you two should as well. Is there any hot water? I could do with a wash or a shower.'

'I'll get you a towel . . . and one of your father's shirts,' Nesta told him. 'That one smells like a burnt offering. Don't be long. I'll call Amelda and then I'll make some coffee.'

Over strong coffee laced with brandy, Llewellyn told them the whole story. He knew his mother was growing more and more upset as all her worst fears about the relationship between Amelda and Michael came to light. He couldn't bear the anguish on Amelda's face, but he felt that everything had to be brought out into the open. As he related Glenda's part in what had happened, he felt himself becoming increasingly incensed at the duplicity of both Michael Owen and Glenda.

'I think we ought to phone Rhys as soon as it's daylight and put him in the picture before he hears about it from anyone else,' Gwilym told Nesta.

'I'll ring Wynne. It might be better if she told him, just in case it brings on one of his turns,' she agreed.

'And let him know I am OK,' Llewellyn reminded her. 'I was at his place until after midnight. He might think that

I went back to Morfa Cottage and that I was there when the fire started.'

'Shouldn't we try and get in touch with Michael?' Amelda asked hesitantly.

She still couldn't believe what was happening. She had been in a deep sleep when Nesta had roused her and it had taken her several minutes to realise where she was, let alone take in what her mother was trying to tell her. It all seemed to be part of the nightmare that had started when Glenda had brought Diana Owen to Morfa Cottage.

She knew she had behaved childishly, running off as she had, but she had felt outraged. The shock of coming face to face with Michael's wife had been so humiliating.

'The police are already looking for him,' Llewellyn assured her.

'Was his Porsche at the cottage? If not, he may have gone back to London,' Amelda suggested.

She wished now she had let Michael talk to her, then perhaps none of this would have happened. She knew he had been as shocked as she was by his wife turning up out of the blue. At the time, though, she couldn't even bear to look at him, she had felt so betrayed.

They let the number ring out for a long time but there was no reply.

'He's still probably on the road between here and London,' Gwilym said, looking at his watch.

'OK. We'll try again in about an hour or so,' Llewellyn yawned. 'I could certainly do with some sleep.'

'There's a bed made up in the spare room,' Nesta offered.

'No!' Llewellyn kissed the top of his mother's head. 'It's out of the question at the moment. The police, the reporters and all the rest of the world will be here at any moment.'

'Do you want me to phone the hospital and see how Glenda is?' Gwilym offered.

201

'No.' Llewellyn shook his head. 'Not for the moment. I'll do it later.'

Even as he spoke, Llewellyn knew deep in his heart that he no longer had any feelings for Glenda and that he would rather not see her again. He would never be able to forgive her for the part she had played in the débâcle. Seeing how white and stunned Amelda looked, the pain and worry on his mother's face, and listening to his father's constrained concern, Llewellyn felt an overwhelming bitterness towards Glenda. He wanted to apologise to them all.

Before he could speak, a thunderous knocking on the front door announced the arrival of the police. The long nightmare of questioning and cross-questioning was about to begin.

22

It seemed to Amelda as if the police would never complete their investigations. Life appeared to be one endless session of questions and answers. What she hated most was the way they seemed to doubt every word she said and cross-questioned and checked-out almost every statement she made.

'I wasn't there when the fire started,' she repeated over and over again, but still their questioning went on.

She knew she wasn't the only one being put under this dreadful strain. Llewellyn, her mother and father, even her grandfather, complained bitterly about the never ending questioning since, like her, none of them had actually been at the cottage when the fire had broken out.

'It has been even worse for Michael,' she told them indignantly. 'They took him in for questioning and kept him there for two days. He said the police took it in turns. It was almost as if they thought that if they managed to wear him down he would confess to arson, or whatever it is they suspect him of having done.'

'But he wasn't at the cottage either when the fire started,' Llewellyn pointed out.

'There are no witnesses to prove that. He keeps telling them he left just a few minutes after I did, but there is no one to corroborate his statement.'

'Surely Glenda could?'

'She's suffering from loss of memory.'

'In that case, why don't they suspect her of starting the fire?' Llewellyn said.

'Because apparently they don't consider that she had any motive.'

'And what reason do they think Michael could have possibly had?' Llewellyn exclaimed exasperatedly. 'He would hardly set fire to his own home!'

'Precisely! And why should I have done it? I've lost my home and business,' Amelda reminded him.

'Well, I still don't know why they should question me!' Llewellyn protested.

'I think I do,' Gwilym stated. 'I overheard one of the sergeants talking to the Inspector who questioned me say that you might have done it because Michael Owen was an American and you were against foreigners buying up local cottages.'

'In other words, they are laying the blame on Plaid Cymru,' Llewellyn said heatedly.

'It looks that way.'

'It's a wonder they haven't accused Granda of doing it,' Amelda added caustically.

'The police have been to see him,' Llewellyn reminded her. 'That's possibly another reason why they regard me with suspicion. He told them I went to see him that night. They probably think it all part of a grand plot,' he added morosely, his dark eyes burning with anger.

'Oh, Llewellyn, don't!' Amelda placed a hand over her eyes in despair. 'I wish they'd leave him out of this. He's so old and frail these days. If he gets upset his heart trouble could easily flare up again.' She ran a hand through her hair, pushing it back from her forehead. 'I feel it's all my fault. If I hadn't lost my temper and stormed out when I discovered who Diana was then none of this might have happened.'

'That's ridiculous! How were you to know Glenda was going to play such a despicable trick on us all, producing Diana Owen like a rabbit out of a hat? It's something I'll never be able to forgive.'

'I still blame myself for having walked out like I did.'

'Nonsense! You could just as easily say I should have

realised who Diana was when Glenda brought her back from London and said she was staying for a few days. If I had, then I would never have brought them to your place that night so none of this would have happened.'

'Why argue? It's all in the past and nothing any one of us says or does now can change what has happened,' Nesta sighed.

'One person could solve everything if only she would admit to what went on after Amelda and I had both left.'

'You mean Glenda, of course,' Nesta sighed. 'Do you think perhaps you should go and see her again, Llewellyn? If you talked to her, and gradually led her back over what happened that evening, then she might recall something that would help.'

'I doubt it. I don't think she has had a memory lapse. I think she is simply refusing to say anything in case she implicates herself. For all we know she might have been the one to start it . . . accidentally, I mean,' Llewellyn added hastily as he saw the shocked look on Amelda's face.

'We ought to do something to help Michael,' Amelda insisted. 'Somehow we've got to find a way of proving to the police that he wasn't there when the fire started. Now that they've released him on bail it may be easier. Perhaps if he was the one to talk to Glenda she might respond,' she added, biting her lower lip to keep her emotions in check.

Llewellyn held out little hope that this would do any good, but he didn't attempt to persuade Amelda not to go through with the idea.

'Michael thinks that Glenda is more likely to respond if he goes to see her on his own,' Amelda told Llewellyn later in the week.

They waited anxiously for the outcome of his visit. When Amelda collected Michael she could tell from the excited look on his face that Glenda had said something that had given him new hope.

'Well?' she asked as they pulled away from the hospital. 'Was it any good? Did she tell you anything?'

'I think she has said enough to clear my name.'

'Then let's go straight to the police and tell them.'

'Wait! I think you should hear what she said first.'

Amelda pulled in off the road and cut the engine.

'You were quite right. Glenda isn't suffering from loss of memory,' Michael said hesitantly. 'That's just a pretence because she doesn't want to incriminate Llewellyn.'

'I don't understand?' Amelda frowned.

'Glenda claims it was Llewellyn who started the fire.'

'That's nonsense!' Amelda's violet eyes darkened angrily. 'He left Morfa Cottage before I did! You know that for a fact. You were there when he left.'

'Oh, yes, I know when Llewellyn left, but that doesn't make any difference.'

'Are you trying to say that he came back later and started the fire? Did you see him?'

'He didn't come back while I was there . . .'

'What time did you leave, then?'

'About an hour after you did.'

'So you left round about ten o'clock.'

'Yes, something like that.'

'Then what Glenda has told you is all nonsense. Llewellyn was with my Granda at ten o'clock . . . the police have a signed statement from both Llewellyn and my Granda. You can check it out.'

'That doesn't mean it's true.'

'What are you saying? Are you implying that there was some sort of collusion between the two of them?' she demanded, her eyes blazing with anger.

'That would seem to be the case. It's the on-going story isn't it. Planning and plotting by Plaid Cymru supporters to get rid of anyone they consider to be a foreigner. It's not the first cottage that has been burnt down . . .'

206

'Michael! You don't know what you're saying! You are accusing my grandfather and my brother of deliberately setting fire to Morfa Cottage. And, what is more, doing it when they thought we were all in the cottage. You must be mad! As far as Llewellyn knew I was still in there. Do you think he would set fire to the place with his own sister inside?'

'But did he think you were in there . . . or did he know that you had already left and that you were safe and sound with your parents?'

'Stop it!' Amelda clapped her hands over her ears. 'I'm not going to listen to any more of this. Llewellyn is with my grandfather now. We'll go there, right this minute, and you can face them both with your accusations.'

Despite Amelda warm embrace and affectionate kiss, Rhys frowned ferociously when he saw that Michael Owen was with her.

'We've come to see Llewellyn,' Amelda stated.

'He's out,' her grandfather told her curtly. He peered at her fiercely. 'What do you want with him? Is it something to do with the fire?'

'No . . . no we haven't any fresh news,' Amelda said quickly.

'It was about the fire I wanted to see Llewellyn,' Michael drawled. 'I think he started it deliberately!' he added blandly.

The silence was hypnotic. Amelda tried desperately to speak, but her mind was a complete blank and words would not come. Her grandfather's face contorted into a mask of hatred, his steel-grey eyes hardened and his mouth clenched into a hard uncompromising line. A vein high on his forehead pulsed. The sinews in his thin neck stood out like knotted ropes as his hands clenched into fists.

'Why should he do that?' he demanded harshly.

'Because he hates foreigners coming into Wales. He has always disliked me. On the night of the fire, things

207

happened which you know nothing about,' Michael told him dismissively.

'If you mean your wife appeared on the scene then I do know about it,' Rhys told him scornfully. 'Adulterer . . . liar . . . cheat . . .' His voice rose, the pulse became more rapid, his eyes blazed.

'Granda, stop it . . . you mustn't upset yourself like this,' Amelda protested.

She placed her hand on his arm, pleading desperately, but he shook her away without taking his eyes from Michael Owen. His glare was so fierce that Michael gave ground. He took a pace backwards, holding up a hand in an attempt to placate the older man.

'You dare to come and accuse my grandson . . .'

'Yes, I do!' Michael Owen made one last blustering stand. 'If one half of the rumours I have heard about you are true, then he was probably acting under your instructions.'

'Michael!'

'Keep out of this, Amelda,' he snarled. 'This has nothing to do with you.'

'It most certainly has! You don't think I am going to stand by and allow you to accuse my grandfather of being responsible for what happened? He was nowhere near Morfa Cottage when the fire broke out.'

'Nor was Llewellyn,' Rhys snapped. 'He was here with me.'

'That doesn't prove a thing. Timed fuses, delayed action explosions, you people know all about those sort of things and how to plant them,' Michael declared angrily 'It wouldn't be the first cottage Plaid Cymru supporter had set on fire, now, would it?' he added scornfully.

'You are ignorant as well as bigoted,' Rhys told him scathingly. 'Plaid Cymru believes Wales should be for the Welsh, but firing cottages is something we abhor. Get that straight.'

'I'd need proof before I'd believe a word you said,' Michael sneered.

'Perhaps the arsonist, if arson was the cause of the fire, was nearer home than you think,' Rhys told him shrewdly.

'What do you mean by that?'

'Have you stopped to think what your own wife's feelings might be? What brought her over here in the first place? Was it because she suspected you were living with another woman? Now there's someone who might have a reason for revenge!'

'Granda! How can you say such things?'

'You seem to forget my wife was burned to death in that fire,' Michael reminded him. 'Would she let the place burn down around her if she was the one who started it?'

'Who knows what a woman in her tormented state of mind might do?' Rhys Evans said cryptically.

'Look, let's leave,' Amelda intervened, as Michael looked distressed and began to mop his brow with his handkerchief, and loosen his tie and the neck of his shirt. 'Llewellyn's not here. We can always come back later.'

Both men ignored her. They stood like stags at bay, each of them psyched up for a row and determined to best the other. Rhys looked grey, his lips were tinged with blue around the edges and Amelda's heart pumped with fear in case their confrontation brought on a stroke. She edged towards the phone, wondering if she could make a call to her mother, but her grandfather spotted her from the corner of his eye and wheeled round to demand what she was doing.

'I . . . I was just going to phone Mum and see if Llewellyn was there,' she said lamely.

'He's not. He's taken Shep for a walk.'

'So you do know where he is! Have you any idea when he will be back?'

Rhys didn't answer her. His attention was focused on Michael Owen.

'Get out!' he thundered, breathing heavily. 'I never want to see you ever again. Before you go, though, retract your accusations. I want a full apology.'

'I am certainly not going to do either,' Michael told him in a scornful drawl. 'You couldn't stand the thought of me owning one of your precious cottages. A cottage you and he wanted to see preserved as a shrine to some dead poet that no one outside Wales has ever heard of. It's pathetic.'

'Michael! I think we should go,' Amelda exclaimed uneasily, grabbing his arm and pushing him towards the door.

'It's too late,' Rhys barked, barring their way. 'Before you leave this house, Michael Owen, you will withdraw your accusation. Neither I nor Llewellyn set fire to Morfa Cottage.'

'Your word carries no weight, not with me or anyone else,' Michael drawled scornfully. 'The police haven't finished with you yet. Let's see what their investigations reveal.'

Rhys's face became contorted with rage. Raising his arm threateningly he lunged towards Michael who quickly sidestepped. As Rhys stumbled forward, he lost his balance and fell with a thunderous crash, his head striking against the edge of the table.

With an anguished cry, Amelda dropped to her knees beside her grandfather as blood gushed from a gash on his head. For one awful moment, as she tried to stem the flow, Amelda thought he had stopped breathing.

'Phone for an ambulance, Michael!' she implored.

'I didn't touch him! It was his own fault . . . he . . . he just fell,' Michael protested.

'Never mind how it happened, we must get him to hospital. Look how much blood he is losing.'

23

Tears streamed unchecked down Amelda's cheeks as she sat by her grandfather's bedside, his limp hand cradled in her own.

His fall had resulted in a massive heart attack from which he had not regained consciousness. He had been taken straight to the intensive care unit, but despite doctors and nurses doing everything possible he was growing weaker all the time.

Amelda ached with self-reproach. If only she hadn't taken Michael to her grandfather's cottage in the first place, then none of this would have happened.

Her thoughts spun backwards, if she had never gone to work in London and become involved with Michael Owen, then there might have been no tragedy, no fire, no recriminations, no anguish.

Nurses and doctors came and went, silently monitoring her grandfather's progress. Her mother and father arrived and sat with her at the bedside, but she couldn't bring herself to talk to them. Llewellyn tried to persuade her to get some rest, promising he would stay with Rhys until she returned, but she shook her head, refusing to abandon her vigil and so finally he left.

All through the long night, Amelda went on sitting there, holding her grandfather's hand. It was as if by doing so she hoped to give him strength and bring him back from the edges of darkness. By morning his breathing was so shallow that it was difficult to know if he was still alive. Her gaze alternated between his ashen grey face and the monitors and dials by the side of his bed.

She knew it was over even before it registered on the

screen. The hand that had been lying so limply in hers suddenly tensed, his eyelids flickered, but he was too weak to open them fully. Then a long sigh shuddered through him and his hand went slack. When she looked up the flickering dials had stilled.

Amelda had no more tears left.

Utterly distressed, she rang for a nurse. Then, stunned by shock, she walked out of the hospital. The blazing sunshine dazzled her, yet she shivered despite its heat. She sat down on a low wall edging a flower-bed because her legs felt weak and her brain too numb to think what to do next.

She was still sitting there, gazing into space, almost overcome by heat, when her parents arrived half an hour later. Nesta sat down beside her, slipping an arm round her waist, pulling Amelda's head down onto her shoulder, and crooning words of comfort as though she was still a small child.

Amelda made no resistance when, ten minutes later, the hospital formalities completed, Gwilym took her arm and led her back to the car. When they reached Tryfan, he settled her in a deckchair in a shady spot in the garden. Nesta made her a cup of hot sweet tea, and sat with her while she drank it.

Amelda remained in a dazed state for the next few days.

'She ought to be told the result of the enquiries that have been going on about Morfa Cottage,' Llewellyn said. 'It might help her to come to grips with things.'

'It certainly might stop her blaming herself,' Nesta agreed. 'Will you tell her? Or would you rather your father and I did?' she added hastily as she saw the pained look that came into Llewellyn's dark eyes.

'She is more likely to believe it is the truth if I tell her,' Llewellyn said grimly. 'Leave it until later. I'll wait for the right moment.'

Finding the right opening was not easy. Amelda didn't want to talk. She lay in the deckchair, her eyes half-closed, oblivious even to the sound of birdsong, or the sheep high up on the nearby mountain calling to each other. As the light breeze stirred the leaves of the apple tree under which Gwilym had placed her chair she gave herself up to reliving the past.

It was as if her grandfather's death was a watershed. A turning point from which she must make a fresh start. But before she could do that, she needed to analyse all that had happened before. Only then could she decide which path he must follow from now on.

Always her thoughts went back to Michael. He was the pivot on which her life seemed to turn.

At first she reproached herself for taking the course she had done. Until she left university her life had followed a completely conventional pattern. She had enjoyed her childhood, and the warmth of her homelife. There had always been harmony at home, between her parents as well as between her and Llewellyn. She had been exceptionally close to her mother; it was as if they were linked by some special bond.

University had been a fascinating experience. She had never got involved with any of the fast set. She had avoided drugs, and never went to wild parties although there had been plenty of opportunity to do so. She had worked hard at her studies and she knew her family had been proud of her achievements.

It was after she had left university that the world had begun to spin. Moving to London and sharing a flat with Cindy and Penny had probably been the first mistake. At university it hadn't mattered that they had come from such different backgrounds because they were all restricted by the same set of rules. In London, responsible only to themselves and each other, she had found it was so much easier to swim with the tide than strike out on her own.

Perhaps if she had listened to Llewellyn and become a teacher like him she would have settled back into the lifestyle she had grown up in. The glamour of London, the ease with which she had landed such a well-paying job, had all influenced her into believing that breaking away from the family was the right thing to do.

And then there had been Michael.

He undoubtedly had been the biggest influence of all. Perhaps it was because he was so much older, because Cindy and Penny had thought him so devastating, that she had been flattered when he had singled her out for attention.

She had enjoyed being escorted by someone so suave and attractive. His deep gravelly voice, and air of confidence, his well-cut clothes and his good looks had all combined to make him irresistible. She had lost her heart as well as her head.

And Michael had taken advantage of the fact.

Looking back, she suspected that Michael had realised long before she did that she had fallen head over heels in love with him. And it hadn't taken him long to avail himself of the fact.

She closed her eyes, remembering the first time they had made love. A shiver went through her, despite the heat from the sun blazing down on her. It was as if she could hear his deep honeyed voice in her ear, feel the strength of his hands as they gently caressed her flesh.

His kisses had devastated her. Before Michael, her experience was limited. The few boyfriends she had known at college had been amorous in a bashful way, or clumsy in their eagerness. Michael had not been like that. His lips had hovered over hers like a butterfly debating where to settle. At first they had been warm and gentle, delicately exploring. Then, as the glow between them both built up, his mouth had become hungry and demanding. The first time his tongue invaded her mouth

214

she had felt excited, shocked and alarmed. Then she grew to like it, and became as challenging and as expert as he was himself.

After that, it seemed natural that they should explore each other's bodies with the same fervour. Michael had been adept at rousing her feelings, playing her along gently, step by step, until she reached a peak of passion that demanded complete satisfaction.

She would never forget the very first time they had made love. He had been very tender. She had lain absolutely still, conscious of the rippling movements of the muscles of his powerful back as with desperate urgency his body covered hers.

She could still hear his gasp of pleasure as she surrendered, and the husky emotion in his voice as he whispered in astonishment, 'It really is your first time!'

The first time but certainly not the last.

Love-making became like a drug. Their appetites were insatiable. It was a drug that neither of them could live without.

They made love whenever they met, wherever it might be. His car, the flat, the office, in the most unusual and unlikely places. It became a game. Sometimes there were no preliminaries, just a snatched moment that excited and thrilled. It was like stealing sweets.

Once or twice, during their more relaxed encounters, she had questioned him about his family. She had never mentioned the word 'wife' because she just hadn't considered that it was a possibility. His anecdotes were mostly about his childhood, when he had lived on a ranch with his parents. As soon as he realised that farming was not his scene, he had told her, he had headed for New York, and the business world. Since then he had devoted all his energies to making his mark.

'Coming to London was the very pinnacle of success, as far as I was concerned,' he avowed in his warm, gravelly, drawl. 'Meeting you was the cherry on the top.'

Living with Michael in his sumptuous flat, Amelda felt that she, too, had achieved the ultimate. So much opulence, as well as the exciting lifestyle she was enjoying, put everything else out of her head. To drive Michael's Porsche, to be able to use his charge card for clothes, to find herself being wined and dined every night, banished her feelings of guilt and dampened down any apprehension about what she was doing with her own life.

She wondered just how long the illusion of fulfilment, the belief that she and Michael inhabited a private Shangri-la, might have lasted if the IRA had not bombed the London Hilton. As the ceiling of their room had caved in, and masonry and dust had showered down on them, the thought uppermost in her mind had been that she wished she had taken her parents into her confidence, since they would be shocked when they read in the newspapers the truth about her lifestyle in London.

Yet, even then, Michael had mattered most in her life. And for a brief interlude, while Michael had been recuperating, and she had stayed with her grandfather so that she could visit him each day, they had recaptured their special magic.

It wasn't until after they returned to London, and Michael refused to let her carry on working, that the worm of discontent had begun to gnaw. With so much free time, a lot of it spent on her own, she began to realise how she had wasted her education, and she longed to be doing something positive.

She even began to envy her grandfather his interest in Plaid Cymru. When she and Llewellyn had still been at school he had cajoled them into helping with his struggle to achieve things that he thought were right for the future of Wales. She remembered the meetings, the heckling, the arguments and debates. She recalled the riots when she and Llewellyn, along with other Plaid Cymru supporters, had fought so hard to have Welsh taught in schools. Life had seemed to have a very real purpose in those days and she found herself longing to be doing something as forceful again. Making use of the legacy Alice Roberts had left her to start a gift shop had seemed to provide the perfect answer.

Building up the Morfa gift shop had not only given her a sense of purpose but had re-established her closeness with both her mother and grandfather. It had even made Rhys less resentful about Michael buying Morfa Cottage. He had been overjoyed when he learned that it was to be put to such a good purpose, and that it would provide an outlet for the work of local people.

She would never forget how his steel-grey eyes would light up when they went along to a craft studio or pottery and found something suitable for the shop. The only line he refused to show any interest in was the selection of slate items she stocked.

'You'll never get him to like slate,' her mother sighed. 'In his eyes, the slate quarries have scarred the countryside. He's thought that way ever since he was a boy. It was the tradition that all the men from his family went to work in the slate quarries, but he refused to join them.'

'Is that why he ran away to sea?'

'That's right. He was as stubborn then as he is now,' Nesta laughed. 'Only don't tell him I said so!'

Amelda now felt a deep sadness as she thought about her grandfather. He had been a man of strong principles rather than stubborn, she thought affectionately. A man whose word had always been his bond.

And now he was gone.

No matter what anyone else might think or say, in her heart Amelda felt that it was her fault that her grandfather had had his heart attack. Just as she also felt responsible that Michael's wife, Diana, had died in such tragic circumstances.

She would have liked to draw a veil across the fact that Diana was Michael's wife. What she had found hardest of all to accept was the discovery that it had been Diana, not Michael, who owned the company where she worked. Despite the burning sunshine, she shivered with self-contempt that it had been Diana's money they had been spending so freely, Diana's money that had bought Morfa Cottage!

As she struggled to pull herself up from the cold, dark depths of despair she could think only of Diana Owen's charred remains. If she hadn't stormed out when she had learned who Diana was then none of it might have happened, she thought miserably.

In the days that followed, while the rest of the family made arrangements for Rhys to be buried, Amelda wallowed in her feelings of self-recrimination. Nesta despaired when she lost all interest in food, in her appearance, even in what was going on around her.

Despite his promise to tell Amelda, that from what they had uncovered the police were pretty certain that the fire had been started by Diana, Llewellyn kept putting it off.

'One of us should tell her,' Nesta protested. 'She's coming to the funeral tomorrow, and you never know, someone might mention it to her.'

'Yes, you are right,' Llewellyn agreed. 'I'll tell her right away.'

Amelda listened without being convinced.

'Why on earth would Diana do such a thing?' she asked, staring at him blankly.

'Diana found out that Glenda was having an affair with Michael,' Llewellyn told her abruptly.

Amelda frowned, bewildered. With an effort she dredged from the depths of her memory every detail of the relationship between Glenda and Michael. Glances, innuendos, all the minute details that she had pushed to the back of her mind, refusing to recognise them for what

218

they were. She remembered the day that Glenda had told her that Michael was married. At the time she had been too hurt, too distressed to recognise that Glenda had been deliberately trying to break up her relationship with Michael so that she could have him.

Had it been jealousy or rage that had driven her to such extreme action, and why over Glenda? Then slowly it dawned on Amelda that Diana couldn't have known she had left the cottage, either.

'As far as Diana knew, I was still in the cottage . . . upstairs in my bedroom. She must have meant to kill me as well as Glenda!' Amelda shuddered violently at the thought. 'Will all of this have to come out at the inquest Llewellyn?' she asked, a trace of shame on her face.

'More than likely.' He squeezed her hand. 'Try not to worry about it. We'll all be there with you.'

From the look in her brother's dark eyes, Amelda knew that the disclosure about Glenda had been traumatic for him too. Even their parents would have to face the gossip and speculation, she thought unhappily as she tried to hold back her tears.

'If only Granda was still alive,' she murmured heart-brokenly. 'He would have been such a tower of strength for us all.'

24

They buried Rhys in the shadow of Moel Hebog. The sky was overcast as if it, too, was mourning the passing of one of its much loved sons.

Amelda, standing beside her parents and Llewellyn while the coffin was lowered into the ground, was conscious of an overwhelming sense of loss. He had been so wise, and so understanding, the one person she had always felt she could turn to when she was in any kind of trouble. And now he was gone. Never again would she be able to listen to his deep melodious voice retelling local legends and anecdotes, advising or counselling her on what she should do.

For Amelda it was the ending of an era.

As she looked over at the crowd clustered on the other side of the grave, people from all walks of life who had come to pay their last respects to a man who had been their friend, and who for most of his life had championed the cause of local people, she was startled to see Michael Owen.

In his Saville Row suit, Gucci shoes and pure silk tie, Michael looked more as if he was on his way to attend a business meeting than a funeral. For a long moment she thought it must be some kind of hallucination because he had been in her thoughts so persistently.

When Amelda moved away from the graveside, flanked by her family, Michael approached and spoke to her. The feel of his hand gripping her arm came as a shock. She had the overwhelming urge to pull away. Instead, she forced herself to meet his eyes. From the agony in their brown depths, she sensed he was suffering too. She was filled with a sudden urge to alleviate his discomfort, but couldn't bring herself to speak. She felt too bruised, too deeply wounded, to have the strength to reach out and comfort him.

'Amelda,' he said hoarsely, 'I am sorry about your grandfather . . . I know I am in part to blame for what happened.'

Amelda tried to speak, but although her lips moved no sound came. She touched his arm to acknowledge what he had said, her eyes so full of tears that they looked like rain-drenched purple pansies against the pallor of her cheeks.

His hand squeezed hers understandingly, and it set every fibre in her body trembling. Quickly she pulled away. She wasn't ready yet for any closeness between them. There were so many questions still unanswered, making it difficult for her to meet his gaze.

A thunderclap pealed out, followed by a spatter of fat raindrops. The dark clouds seemed to press down all around them. The thunder sent involuntary shivers chasing down her spine. She looked up gratefully at Llewellyn as he placed a hand protectively on her shoulder.

'I will be coming to North Wales again in a week or ten days,' Michael told them stiffly. 'Perhaps we could meet then . . . and talk. There are a great many things to be settled. Shall I phone you?'

'Yes, do that,' Llewellyn nodded brusquely.

As Michael walked away, Amelda had an overwhelming urge to call him back and ask him if Morfa Cottage had been owned by Diana and, if so, what would happen to it now. She wanted so much to keep it going as a permanent tribute to her grandfather. Finding an outlet for the work done by local crafts people would be her way of perpetuating the aims he had struggled to attain. Without Morfa Cottage it would be more difficult to do that. Then Llewellyn spoke to her, distracting her attention, and the moment was lost.

She returned to Tryfan with her parents, leaving Llewellyn in deep, earnest conversation with Plaid Cymru supporters who had come to pay their last respects to Rhys.

When Llewellyn returned to Tryfan later that evening he seemed to have gained a new stature. He had been asked to take a more decisive role in the affairs of the party.

'They want me to stand for Parliament,' Llewellyn told them. 'Granda's idea, really. They had approached him to suggest a candidate for the next election, and he put my name forward.'

'Without mentioning it to you?' Nesta said, bemused.

'Well, I knew I stood a chance, but it has only just been agreed.'

'Give it some very careful thought,' Gwilym warned. 'It could interfere with your career.'

'I know that. There is another problem too. Glenda's father is standing as Tory for the same constituency.'

'Well, that's awkward! You'll have to talk to her about it.'

'No.' Llewellyn's jaw set determinedly. 'I've already agreed to stand.'

'You're putting Glenda into something of a quandary, aren't you?' Nesta said worriedly. 'Her father will expect her to support him.'

'Will he? He must know she is a member of Plaid Cymru.'

'It's bound to cause trouble between the two of you,' Gwilym persisted. 'Don't do anything rash. Give it more thought. You should have told the party that you needed time to think it over.'

'But I don't!' Llewellyn was adamant. 'If Granda put my name forward then I have to accept, it's as simple as that.'

As Gwilym had forseen, Glenda protested violently

222

about Llewellyn putting up against her father. The row between them was so bitter and protracted that soon friends, as well as family, began taking sides.

'Can't we cool all this election fever?' Gwilym protested. 'It's becoming like a battlefield. It's even spreading to my office. My secretary went to school with Glenda and she had the effrontery to suggest Llewellyn should either stand down or fight in a different constituency.'

'And what did you tell her?' Llewellyn asked, his dark eyes brilliant and hard, his handsome face flushed.

'That it was none of my business. Implying it was none of hers either.'

'It would be a sensible compromise,' Nesta murmured.

'Then let him change constituencies,' Llewellyn said forcefully. 'He thinks that because it has always been a Conservative stronghold that it will be a walkover. What he doesn't seem to realise is that most of the younger people, who will be voting for the first time, know what is right for Wales. Plaid Cymru will win, you wait and see.'

'You mean you think you've got a safe seat?' Nesta asked frowning.

'Not so safe that I won't need to work hard for it,' Llewellyn admitted, 'but I intend to win. I must! I'm doing it for Granda.'

Llewellyn's enthusiasm inspired Amelda into action. She visited Morfa Cottage, and was surprised at how little structural damage had been done. Her hopes of getting the business under way again quite quickly soared. Even so, she couldn't bring herself to meet Michael. She was still not ready to resume a relationship of any kind with him.

As the days passed she became more and more worried and anxious about what she should do. Llewellyn was so busy with his political career that she didn't feel it was right to distract him with her problems. Nor did she want to implicate her father. In the end, she sought the help of a solicitor.

He listened to her explanation of the situation in such an impersonal manner, and without any kind of censure, that she felt surprisingly little embarrassment, even when she checked over the bald facts that he had listed.

A week later he phoned to explain that the deeds of Morfa Cottage were in her name. Since she was the legal owner she could recommence trading just as soon as the insurance claim had been met and the repairs, which had already been put in hand by Michael Owen, were completed.

The news stunned her.

Tears which she had held back since the funeral drenched her pillow as she remembered the bitter, senseless argument that had raged between her grandfather and Michael Owen over the ownership of Morfa Cottage.

Had Rhys known that legally it belonged to her, there would have been no row between him and Michael, and he might never have suffered a stroke. He might even be alive and well right now, she thought sadly. Now, more than ever, she needed to dedicate the shop to his memory.

There was still the inquest into Diana's death to be faced and the horde of press and public gathered to hear the truth.

Because she already knew she was the legal owner of the cottage she was less shocked when this information was made public than she would otherwise have been.

Amelda was uncomfortably aware of how distressed her parents were when intimate revelations about her life with Michael Owen were paraded.

The bare facts, stated so coldly, made it all appear so sordid. A young girl falling for her wealthy boss. Their casual liaison. The trusting wife, who had staked her own personal fortune so that her husband could expand his business, coming over from America to pay a visit.

When she is introduced to Glenda ap Lloyd through mutual friends, and accepts Glenda's invitation to visit North Wales, her shock at finding her husband already there with his mistress, ensconced in the love-nest he has bought for her, made stirring evidence. It was made to sound as though Diana had been so full of jealousy and despair when she realised the truth about the relationship between her husband and Amelda that she had not been responsible for her actions.

Glenda was cleared of all responsibility for what had happened. She was even praised for the courageous way she had summoned help on the night of the fire.

So much of the evidence was biased that Amelda found herself reading the reports as though it was something that had happened to someone else. In many ways this helped.

Like Amelda, Nesta had found the inquest traumatic. The way the truth had been twisted sickened her. Gwilym, with his vast experience of newspaper reporting, merely shrugged off the veiled innuendos and blatant mistruths. It saddened him that it was his own family at the centre of such banner-headlines but he tried to keep it in perspective.

'It's a nine day wonder,' he told them. 'There's never much hard news in August so the papers have latched onto this. In a week or so, it will be the Trade Union Congress hitting the headlines, or some motorway accident.'

The strain of living through it all took its toll. Each of them sought refuge in their own particular diversion. For Amelda it was planning the reopening of the gift shop, while Llewellyn became preoccupied by Plaid Cymru.

'He gets more and more like my Da by the day,' Nesta confided to Amelda. 'He's even growing a beard now! When they take pictures of him people will think it's Rhys Evans reincarnated.'

Amelda smiled understandingly. She knew it was Llewellyn's way of paying tribute to the man they had loved so dearly and now missed so deeply.

She was finding that visiting crafts people who had known and admired her grandfather was distressing. Their praise of him was gratifying, but it made her acutely aware that he was gone for ever. It also made her more than ever determined to support the local people he had loved and served for so much of his life.

As summer waned, her storerooms became full up with new stock and she began to worry. Her money was almost exhausted and unless she did some trade soon she would have to stop buying. That would mean letting her suppliers down. Yet it was much too late in the season to open up the shop.

When she mentioned her problem to Llewellyn he suggested she should try mail order.

'Advertise in some of the national newspapers and see what sort of response you get,' he suggested. 'With Christmas not all that far away you might find people will welcome the opportunity to buy gifts that are a bit different.'

The response was overwhelming.

All through October and November the orders poured in. She employed two local women to help with the packing and despatching and worked herself from early morning until late in the evening, invoicing and paying accounts.

By Christmas, even before the doors had officially opened, Morfa Cottage Gift Shop was not only back on its feet but showing a profit. Those who supplied her and who had had little hope of repeat orders until early spring, found their order books full and were delighted by Amelda's prowess.

Christmas was a quiet, family gathering. There was still friction between Llewellyn and Glenda so he didn't bring

226

her to Tryfan. Gwilym went to fetch Huw and Wynne on Christmas morning. They had both grown old and frail. Losing Rhys had blighted their lives too.

'We've brought you an extra Christmas present, Amelda,' Wynne told her when they arrived. She turned to call her husband. 'Come on in, now, Huw and bring Amelda's present, she's just dying to see what it is.'

'Here you are, then, Amelda.' He stood aside to allow Shep, her grandfather's black and white sheepdog, to walk past him into the room. Shep stood sniffing at the unfamiliar surroundings, then with a low growl he walked over and placed his great shaggy head against Amelda's leg, looking up at her trustingly through the white fringe that covered his eyes.

'Shep!' Amelda bent down to pat him. 'What does this mean?'

'It means that we are too old to look after him properly, even though we liked having him after our old dog died. So we thought Rhys would have wanted him to come to you,' Huw told her. 'He's missing Rhys. He's not getting any exercise for one thing. I can't walk like Rhys could. He used to take him off up the mountain and let him run to his heart's content. Now, the most he gets is a walk to the end of the lane.'

'We thought he would be company for you. You're here on your own such a lot,' Wynne added.

'But I do go away from time to time . . . and stay overnight,' Amelda reminded them.

'When that happens Shep can come and stay with us,' Nesta told her quickly. 'We can share him, just like my Da shared him with Huw and Wynne. As soon as they mentioned to me about you having Shep I thought it was a good idea. I've never liked the thought of you being in Morfa Cottage at night all on your own. I'll feel so much happier knowing you have Shep there.'

They had just finished their meal when they heard a car

stop outside, followed by a knock on the front door. As Gwilym rose to answer it, Nesta and Amelda exchanged puzzled looks.

'Someone to see you, Amelda,' he said in a tight hard voice as he came back into the room.

'Michael!'

The colour drained from Amelda's face as she walked out into the hallway and saw who was standing there. He looked fit and well and elegantly turned out in warm casual clothes. He was wearing a beige sheepskin jacket, over a red cashmere sweater and grey trousers.

Slowly she moved towards him. She hadn't seen him since the inquest, and during the past months she had tried desperately to shut him out of her thoughts, but always there had been the deep-seated longing to see him again. There had been countless sleepless nights when no matter how much she tossed and turned she could still see his face and feel his presence and wish he was there beside her.

So often she had been on the point of phoning him. Only pride had stopped her. If he truly loved her, really wanted to be with her, then he would call her, she told herself.

'Oh, Michael!'

His arms went round her, his lips hovered, then locked with hers in a kiss of exquisite tenderness that filled her with a momentary dizziness.

'Amelda, honey, let me look at you,' he whispered. His brown eyes locked on hers, then slowly took in every detail of her appearance, from the way she had done her hair, catching back the froth of fair curls with a jewelled velvet bow, to the black patent courtshoes.

'You look wonderful, honey,' he smiled, as he ran a finger lightly over the embroidered neckline of her velvet dress that was the same colour violet as her eyes.

'Oh, Michael! I nearly didn't bother to dress up,' she

confessed. 'Nothing has seemed worth while without you.'

He gathered her back into his arms, whispering her name over and over again. The long separation was forgotten, recriminations wiped out. They both knew that in spite of all that had happened they still needed each other as desperately as ever.

'Come!' She held out her hand, her face radiant, 'the rest of the family are in the sitting room.'

'One minute, Amelda. Before we face them there is something I want to ask you. I'm returning to the States early in the New Year . . . will you come with me?'

25

By Easter, when the tourist season began in earnest, Amelda's mail order business was well and truly established. Working late into the evening helped to stop her thinking about Michael Owen.

Most nights she was so tired when she finally went to bed that she fell asleep the moment her head touched the pillow. When she didn't, then the dilemma as to whether she had done the right thing in refusing to go to America with Michael haunted her.

She still loved him deeply and she had the feeling that the threads of their two lives were too closely interwoven to have been broken completely. Some day they would meet again.

For the rest of that year all her energies went into the gift shop. Any time she might have over, she spent with Nesta and Gwilym at Tryfan, exercising Shep or helping Llewellyn in his work for Plaid Cymru.

His personal life was still in shreds too. There was still a rift between him and Glenda. They had gone their separate ways after Glenda's relationship with Michael Owen had been revealed. Outside his family, however, people thought it was politics that had caused the severance.

They still saw each other but their relationship was tenuous, and Amelda judged it was held together by their many common interests rather than by their feelings for each other.

Like her, Llewellyn had licked his wounds in private, put on a brave face and devoted his energies to other things.

And it seemed to pay off. Just as the gift shop thrived

once Amelda devoted all her energies to it, so Llewellyn's prospects seemed to brighten.

Not only had his name been put forward to be one of the Plaid Cymru candidates at the next general election, but he had also been nominated for a headship.

'I don't know what to do, really,' he confided in Amelda. 'It seems to be all or nothing. I can't do both and I don't know which one I ought to withdraw from, that of MP or headmaster.'

'If you don't win a seat, where are you then . . . just an ordinary teacher. Stay in the running for both and take the decision when you have to,' she advised. 'If you are appointed headmaster then take it, even if it is only for a few months. It might help in your future career whether you eventually return to teaching or end up as Prime Minister.'

'Not much chance of that! Plaid Cymru never manages to get more than two or three seats at the most,' he grinned.

To Amelda's relief, Llewellyn allowed his name to go forward for the headship. Her excitement almost equalled his when she heard he had been short-listed.

On the day of his final interview she couldn't wait to hear the result. Leaving Dee Williams, her new assistant, to run the shop, she drove to Wrexham where the interviews were being held so that she could be the first to congratulate him.

As she saw him emerge from the education offices her heart sank. He looked so dejected that she knew without asking that he had not got the appointment.

When she learned the reason her disappointment turned to anger.

'I've always intended to learn Welsh,' Llewellyn told her morosely as they sat in a nearby café drinking tea. 'I thought that since I was so involved with Plaid Cymru I ought to be able to speak the language, but I never

231

seriously thought that it might jeopardise my chances of promotion.'

'You can still learn,' Amelda told him brightly. 'I would like to be able to speak Welsh so we'll both go to night school. There's bound to be other openings. You'll get your headship yet.'

'I don't think I could face night school. I wouldn't mind private tuition . . .'

'Then come to dinner on Saturday night. I might have found just the right person to teach you,' she told him.

For the rest of the week Amelda was on tenterhooks. It was a long time since she had given a dinner party and although she knew that her guests would be nowhere near as critical, or discerning, as Michael's friends had been, she still wanted to surprise them with her culinary skills.

Shep sniffed the air appreciatively as she basted the joint. His faithful eyes beneath the shaggy white fringe looked puzzled when he brought over his lead and she took it from him and hung it back on its hook.

'Sorry,' she told him, patting his rough coat. 'No time for walks today. An extra long one tomorrow, if I can fit it in,' she promised, as she began preparing the vegetables.

At first, Amelda had found having to exercise Shep each day was something of an imposition. Gradually, however, she discovered that she was looking forward to their daily walk almost as much as Shep.

To begin with, she took him round the lanes and fields in the vicinity of Morfa Cottage. Then, as her pleasure in walking increased, she ventured further afield. Often she would drive some distance, park her car and set out on their walk from there.

The first time that they drove back to Moelwyn, near the cottages which had been his home for so many years, Shep's enthusiasm was infectious. Once on familiar territory he bounded away, leading her over the foot of the mountains, until they finally ended up in what seemed to be the outlying fields of a hill farm, where his intrusion set the hens squawking in fright.

'Can I help you? You are trespassing, you know.'

Amelda swung round to find a man of about her own age towering over her. He was dressed in brown corduroy jodhpurs and a check flannel shirt open at the neck, the sleeves rolled halfway up his immense brawny arms. As he lowered the pitchfork he was carrying over one shoulder, and rested it on the ground, his clear blue eyes were questioning.

'I'm sorry . . .'

She stopped, aware that Shep was bounding all over him, barking in a highly excited state.

'Shep! Down boy! Heel!' she called, but both the dog and the man completely ignored her. They were greeting each other like long lost friends. When the man finally stopped patting Shep and looked up, his fierce look had become a friendly grin.

'You must be Rhys Evans' granddaughter, Amelda. I heard you'd taken on old Shep.' He held out his hand. 'I'm Roderic Morris. I farm here at Moelfre. Perhaps Rhys mentioned my name to you? He was a wonderful man, a lifelong friend of my family. Come on in and meet my mother. She will be so pleased you have called. Father died three years ago, but Rhys still used to come up to see my mother. And to counsel me about farming.' He grinned. 'Great on theory, was Rhys Evans.'

Mrs Morris made a great fuss of Amelda.

'Oh, there's nice it is to see a woman's face around the place,' she confided, as she poured tea for them both and held out a plate of freshly made bakestones towards Amelda.

She was a small, bird-like woman in her late fifties with black button eyes in a small gnarled face. It was hard to believe that she could be Roderic's mother, they were so

233

unalike. He seemed to fill the stone-flagged kitchen, he was so tall and broad. His sun-bleached brown hair was almost brushing against the ceiling, and his wide, powerful shoulders blocked the doorway as he stood for a few minutes talking to them before going back out to attend to jobs on the farm.

'I'll take old Shep with me,' he told Amelda. 'I'm going to bring down some ewes from one of the pens a couple of fields away. He'll enjoy the challenge. Just sing out when you're ready to leave and I'll return him.'

It was the first of many such trips. Amelda found herself looking forward to visiting the farm and seeing Roderic almost as much as Shep did. Each time there would be the same warm welcome, the ritual of Roderic taking Shep off for some exercise on the farm while she and Mrs Morris chatted over a cup of tea.

As they grew to know each other better, Amelda sometimes went along with Shep and Roderic, scrambling up the rough mountain tracks in search of lambs that had strayed, or, as winter approached, helping to carry out feed for sheep that had been brought down to the lower slopes for the winter.

She found the ever-changing beauty of the surrounding countryside a constant source of delight. Her friendship with Roderic deepened. She was impressed by his gentleness when he handled sick animals, by his strength as he carried out the many heavy tasks around the farm and, most of all, his consideration for his mother and his eagerness to please her.

In time, Amelda also discovered there was another side to Roderic Morris. Although not as fanatical as Llewellyn, he firmly believed that Wales should be given much more say in its own affairs.

'It's all right these politicians down in London saying what we should and should not do, but it's the people who live here who know the truth about the land and

234

what needs doing. Many of the hill farmers are having such a hard time making a living that it's easy for these consortiums from London to persuade them to sell out to them. And the minute they do that these scoundrels plant the land with Sitka. It will be the ruination of Wales as we know it, mark my words.'

'You should come to the Plaid Cymru meetings,' Amelda told him. 'My brother Llewellyn needs as much support as possible if he is to get into Parliament at the next election.'

'I'll be there when the time comes,' Roderic promised. 'And so will most of the farming community. We may not spend as much time as people like your brother talking about what needs doing, but we know which way to vote.'

'I'd like you to meet Llewellyn. Why don't you come to Morfa Cottage for dinner next weekend,' Amelda had suggested shyly.

The dinner party was a great success. The food was excellent, and Llewellyn and Roderic took to each other immediately. At the last minute Amelda had invited Dee Williams, the girl who worked for her in the gift shop, to come along as well and they made a harmonious foursome.

Amelda was pleasantly surprised at how well Llewellyn and Dee got on. Amelda liked her tremendously and found her of enormous help at the shop. She was not only willing but quick to learn, as well as neat and methodical in everything she did. She had an excellent manner with customers and seemed to take a special pride in selling goods which had been made locally.

It was the first time Amelda had seen Dee dressed up and she was impressed by how pretty she looked. At the shop, Dee usually wore a neat blouse and skirt, but tonight she was wearing a soft wool dress in palest blue, the bodice decorated with black and silver Swiss embroidery that shimmered as she moved. The clinging fabric accentuated her curves and the translucent colour enhanced her tawny complexion. The muted blue eye-shadow softened her serious dark eyes under their wide brows. At work, she usually wore her straight dark hair caught back in a slide at the nape of her neck, but now it was loose, sleekly framing her small round face.

When, towards the end of the evening, Amelda broached the subject of learning Welsh.

'Then we have a perfect solution,' Roderic laughed. 'Dee can teach Llewellyn and I will teach you, Amelda, and we'll see who is fluent first.'

Two weeks later Llewellyn realised that he had left it too late to learn Welsh. His face was grey and drawn as he burst into Morfa Cottage just before mid-day.

'What's wrong?' Amelda asked in alarm as he stood there, running his hands through his hair in a distracted way.

'I've lost my job. The authorities say that because I don't speak Welsh they have no alternative but to terminate my contract.'

'They can't do that, surely?' Amelda exclaimed aghast.

'Under the new ruling, all teachers must be bi-lingual. The ironic thing is that I have been one of those supporting the campaign for Welsh to be taught in schools.'

'I didn't know it was one of the conditions in your contract that you also had to be able to speak Welsh, though,' Amelda exclaimed in astonishment.

'Oh, no, it wasn't one of the requirements when I applied for the job. It's a new ruling that has been brought in since.'

'And they took the trouble to check your contract! Why?'

'Apparently someone complained that I wasn't Welsh-speaking and they have been forced to take action. They have promised me a good reference so I shouldn't have any difficulty in getting a job in a school over the Border in England,' he added bitterly.

'Who on earth told them?' Amelda's violet eyes darkened angrily.

'I don't know!' Llewellyn shrugged helplessly. 'It could have been anyone.'

'It's pretty vindictive and it does seem to have been done deliberately.'

'Possibly.' He shrugged hopelessly.

'Surely it must go in your favour that you actively campaigned for children in Welsh schools to be taught in their own language as well as English?' Amelda persisted. 'I remember you helping Glenda when she was canvassing for Cymdeithas yr Iaith Gymraeg, the Welsh Language Society.'

'Yes, she used to laugh because I was so enthusiastic yet I couldn't speak a word of Welsh myself. She promised to try and teach me, but we were so busy campaigning that there was never time. She was forever quoting Saunders Lewis, who maintained that the language is the touchstone of Welsh nationality, the feature of Wales that most clearly distinguishes that nation from England. Glenda even used to say that linguistic apartheid might well become the structure of Welsh society. She tended to regard anyone who didn't speak Welsh as a second-class citizen . . .'

'That's your answer,' Amelda exclaimed, banging her fist on the counter. 'Glenda must be the one who informed on you and told the educational authorities that you didn't speak Welsh.'

'Rubbish! Of course she wouldn't.'

'No? Go and ask her . . . if you dare.'

Llewellyn's disbelief turned to anger when he discovered that Amelda was right.

'Well, at least you don't have to worry any more about your loyalty to Glenda in contesting for the same seat as her father,' Amelda smiled grimly.

'No, that's true!'

The preparation for the forthcoming election seemed to dominate Llewellyn's life from then on. Amelda was indignant, though, when she discovered that as well as asking her to help, he had even roped Dee in to do some canvassing.

'If Llewellyn hadn't asked me then I should probably have volunteered,' Dee smiled shyly. 'We've been seeing quite a lot of each other since your dinner party. Why don't you ask Roderic to give a hand as well?'

'I hadn't thought of it, but I suppose I could,' Amelda agreed. 'He did say he heartily supported what Llewellyn was trying to do so it would give him an opportunity to prove it.'

26

Amelda found herself more and more involved in Llewellyn's election campaign.

'Since I can't stop you spending your spare time, and even some of your working day, helping my brother I may as well join you,' she laughingly told Dee Williams.

'I really do try not to let party work encroach on business hours. I have told Llewellyn not to come here during the day,' Dee said contritely. 'You know, Amelda, I am surprised he is so keen to go on fighting when one of the things listed on the party manifesto is that children should be taught Welsh in school. It certainly shows tremendous character, being able to put what is right for Wales above his own personal interests,' Dee said thoughtfully. 'I'm sure I couldn't champion something that had ruined my career.'

'I know. He can be just as stubborn as my grandfather was,' Amelda smiled. 'Mind you, since most of the teachers and farmers say they support Plaid Cymru, you wouldn't think there would be any need for all this campaigning,' Amelda commented, moving a large box of leaflets out of her way as she spoke.

'Sorry!' Dee apologised, moving the box from the counter to a shelf at the back of the shop. 'Llewellyn asked me to collect those from the printer.'

'I see, and what are we supposed to do with them? Go out and deliver them or hand them out to our customers?'

'He said he would pop in later to pick them up. If he doesn't, then I said I would take them home with me and he can collect them this evening.'

'Oh?'

The teasing tone of Amelda's voice brought a flush to Dee's cheeks.

'Don't pretend you didn't know we were seeing each other,' she challenged, a half-smile on her lips.

Amelda's violet eyes gleamed with mirth as she smiled back at the girl who in the last few months had proved not only an excellent assistant but had become a very close friend.

'Of course I know and I'm delighted,' she said warmly. 'Llewellyn deserves someone like you. Even mother has noticed that since you two have been such good friends he has lost the chip he's had on his shoulder ever since he was turned down for that headship.'

'It's nice of you to say so,' Dee told her colouring up. 'Don't be too hasty, though. I dread to think what he is going to be like when his teaching contract actually ends.'

'With your support, he'll get over it. Anyway, by then Llewellyn will be too busy campaigning to realise what is happening. Let's hope he gets elected, then all this bally-hoo over not being able to speak Welsh will fade into the background. No one at Westminster is likely to worry.'

'He deserves to get in, but it's going to be a hard battle. Iorwerth ap Lloyd, the sitting member, had a tremendous Tory majority last time.'

'Yes, but he's an old man compared with Llewellyn. And you must admit he's not half as good-looking. Those things seem to matter almost as much as their aims and promises when it comes to collecting votes.'

'You'd better not let Llewellyn hear you say that! He will argue that the real struggle is between those who have power but lack ideals and those, like him, who have ideals and need the power to promote them.'

'And I say it is looks, personality, empathy and the power of the *hireath* that wins votes. If only my Granda was still alive . . .' Amelda's violet eyes darkened. 'He was such a fine speaker. His voice had that special resonance. He could captivate and charm his audience, then thunder at them so that they shook in their shoes. He could stir them to fever pitch, make them determined to see Wales great again. When he was one of the speakers, people would queue for hours just to stand inside the hall!'

'Many people think that Llewellyn will be just as great one day,' Dee replied with quiet confidence.

Amelda didn't open the shop on election day. Dee was spending the day helping Llewellyn at the polling booth so Amelda offered to help ferry people from outlying parts of the constituency to their nearest voting point.

The day started with early morning mists that gradually cleared to give a cold but bright morning. By mid-day Amelda had made some twenty runs and was more than willing to take a break when she dropped in to see Roderic and he suggested a pub lunch.

'Llewellyn is going to win the seat, you know,' he told her. 'All the hill farmers I have spoken to are voting for him.'

'It's much too early in the day to be so confident,' she warned. Her eyes became a brilliant amethyst as she added fervently, 'I'm sure, though, that the best man will win . . . and we both know who that is!'

When they parted, Roderic promised to go with her to the party headquarters that evening to await the outcome of the count.

The first person they saw as they walked into the hall was Glenda. Amelda was startled by the way she seemed to have completely changed her image as well as her politics since she and Llewellyn had stopped seeing each other. Instead of her usual jeans and sweat-shirt, she was wearing a vivid blue and orange flowered dress with a large blue Tory rosette pinned high on one shoulder. She had also discarded her horn-rimmed glasses in favour of contact lenses and her lank brown hair had been permed into frizzy curls.

Glenda seemed to be enjoying herself immensely as she stood surrounded by a group of high-spirited Young Conservatives who were loudly voicing their opinions on what the result of the count would be. Occasionally, they would deliberately look in Llewellyn's direction, and make some pointed remark that would bring guffaws of laughter.

Amelda felt incensed by their behaviour and tried to persuade Llewellyn, who looked tense and drawn, to leave but he refused to do so.

'I'm staying right here until the poll closes. If I walk out now they'll certainly have the laugh on me,' he said indignantly, his lean frame taut, his mouth a hard line.

Amelda and Roderic agreed to stay there with Dee, but Nesta and Gwilym found the atmosphere unbearable and decided to go home, promising to return later to hear the result of the count.

Around ten o'clock, Roderic managed to persuade Llewellyn to slip out for a quick drink and a snack.

'I'll walk on with him just in case he changes his mind,' he told Amelda. 'You and Dee collect your coats and follow us.'

'This is the first meal I've had all day,' Llewellyn confessed as they sat in a pub just a short distance away and he tucked into a bowl of thick soup and some crusty bread.'

'No wonder you are a bag of nerves,' Amelda scolded. 'You had better have some sandwiches as well before we go back.'

'I'd just like to go home now and read the results in the *Post* tomorrow morning,' Llewellyn joked when they returned to the party headquarters where they found Nesta and Gwilym already waiting.

'And miss the chance to make that speech you've spent hours polishing up,' Dee teased.

When the results were finally announced, they were all overjoyed to hear that Llewellyn had been elected. He had ousted Glenda's father, Iorwerth ap Lloyd, who had held the seat for the Conservatives for more than twenty years, with a resounding majority.

Delighted with the results, they hugged each other, as cheers went up from the assembled crowd.

They listened to Llewellyn's acceptance speech with pride and waited patiently until he could free himself from the band of cheering helpers who had worked so hard on his behalf to attain victory and were now celebrating with champagne.

Too excited to feel tired, even though it was almost three in the morning and they had all been working nonstop since seven the previous morning, they all agreed to go back with Nesta and Gwilym for one final drink.

'I think we ought to fill up the glasses again and make this a double celebration,' Llewellyn said, after they had all toasted him as the new MP.

'Oh? What else do we have to celebrate, then?' Gwilym asked, raising his eyebrows enquiringly.

'Dee and I are getting married.' He placed an arm proudly round her shoulders, his face wreathed in smiles.

'You dark horse!' Amelda exclaimed as she hugged Dee. 'Why didn't you tell me?'

'I didn't know myself until a few minutes ago,' Dee told her, laughing. Her cheeks were flushed with happiness, her dark brown eyes, under their wide-swept brows, sparkling with delight. 'I'm almost as surprised as you are!'

As dawn spread a clear golden light over a hazy blue sky, Roderic drove Amelda back to Morfa Cottage. As they pulled up, Shep began barking wildly from inside the house.

'Poor old Shep, he must think we've deserted him,'

Amelda murmured, guiltily. 'Thanks for bringing me home, Roderic, it's certainly been a night to remember. Dee will make Llewellyn a wonderful wife. I'm sure they are going to be very happy.'

'I'm sure they will be,' Roderic agreed. 'Have you ever considered what a wonderful wife you would make, Amelda?' he added softly, drawing her into his arms.

His mouth covered hers before she could answer. His lips, hard yet tender, fanning her emotions into a flame of unbidden desire. Taken by surprise, she momentarily gave herself up to the sweetness of the moment, returning his kisses with equal ardour.

His hands slid down her back, drawing her even closer. She could feel the burning heat of his body, the beat of his heart, and she could sense the intensity of his feelings.

Alarmed, she drew back, fighting against the stricture of his embrace, struggling frantically to reach the car door.

Her action took Roderic by surprise. He released her instantly, his face hardening with shock at the ferocity of her actions.

'I'm sorry, Amelda. I thought you felt the same way as I did.'

'I do . . . I think so . . . it's just . . . I'm not ready yet.' Choked by tears, she spread her hands wildly. 'I made a bad mistake . . . I'm not over it yet.'

Grim-faced, Roderic turned away without replying. His knuckles shone white as his hands grasped the steering wheel. Without a word he let out the clutch, his wheels spinning wildly as he swung the car round and drove away.

Amelda stumbled indoors, blinded by tears. As Shep bounded at her, licking her face and hands, overjoyed at seeing her, she buried her face in his rough coat and wept.

'Oh, Shep, what have I done? Why did I hurt him like that? Why did I send him away?'

Even as the words burst from her, deep down she knew the answer. It was still Michael who held the key to her heart.

'I must be mad,' she told the dog as he lay panting at her feet, his patient eyes shining up at her through the long strands of hair that covered his face. 'Roderic is everything any woman could ever want. He's tall and rugged, good-looking, kind, gentle and understanding. Leastways,' she gave a twisted smile, 'he was until to-night. Now he is probably feeling as bitter and muddled as I am. I've done you a disservice too,' she smiled sadly, patting the shaggy coat affectionately. 'You would have loved it at Moefre: the sheep, so much freedom, and such a wonderful master.'

She stood up, pushing the dog away, her distress like a great weight around her shoulders. Every fibre of her being told her that she ought to have accepted Roderic, that he would make her a wonderful husband, but in her innermost being there was still the deep longing for Michael.

Weighed side by side there was no choice, she knew. Michael was twelve years older than her. He was from another country, was used to a completely different lifestyle. He could be selfish, bigoted, self-centred, money orientated and completely ruthless, especially when it came to business. In fact, he was as different in character from Roderic Morris, as he was in looks, she thought with some surprise.

She wished she could still turn to her Granda for advice. Instinctively, she knew that he would have been in favour of her marrying Roderic, not Michael. As a lifetime friend of the Morris family, he must have watched Roderic grow up, she thought with a shock. There was so much about her grandfather that still surprised her, she reflected.

The electioneering had made her keenly aware how

widely known, respected and popular her grandfather had been. So many people she had spoken to remembered Rhys Evans with deep affection.

She turned her thoughts back to the shop, remembering the promise she had made to herself that she would build it into a business her grandfather would be proud of, help the people of North Wales that he had known and loved, and she still intended doing that. It had been her main reason for not going to the States with Michael Owen.

Unable to see any solution to her dilemma, she locked up and went upstairs to bed.

She dozed fitfully, her sleep invaded by monstrous dreams. All her pent-up misgivings over Michael returned to haunt her. The guilt over Diana manifested itself. Shep seemed to sense that something was wrong and came to the side of the bed, laying his head on her chest and whining sadly.

'Come on,' she told him, throwing back the covers. 'Since I'm not going to sleep I may as well take you for a walk. It will help to make up for being shut indoors all day yesterday.'

She slipped into jeans and a white polo-necked sweater and picked up her red anorak. As soon as she opened the front door, Shep made straight for the car, barking excitedly.

'No!'. Amelda bent down and patted his rough coat. 'Moelfre is out of bounds for the moment. I will have to make my peace with Roderic before we go there again.'

Making Roderic understand that although she had rebuffed his offer of marriage she desperately wanted to retain his friendship, wasn't going to be easy. She knew she had hurt him badly and wished she had handled the situation more tactfully.

'Why, oh why, did such a wonderful day have to end with a broken friendship?' she asked herself forlornly.

It was such a beautiful crisp spring morning, with the

246

dawn chorus in full voice, and the air fragrant with lilac. As the early morning sun, its great glittering face pierced by the nearest mountain top, sent golden warmth spilling down into the valley where she stood, her heart lifted and the old sense of magic returned.

27

For Amelda, the taxi ride with Nesta, Gwilym and Dee from Paddington station to the Houses of Parliament was like stepping back in time. The myriad tower blocks knifing the skyline, the constant roar of traffic, the ponderous great red buses, weaving taxis, stunning window displays, jostling crowds of every colour and nationality, set her adrenalin flowing.

London brought back vivid memories of the glamour and excitement she had enjoyed when she had worked there. She loved the peace and tranquillity of North Wales. The special magic of the towering mountains would never fail to stir her, but suddenly she was filled with doubts as to whether or not she was ready yet to spend the rest of her life there.

London had so much to offer.

As they took their seats in the public gallery, Amelda managed to single out Llewellyn from the throng of new MPs. He stood so straight and proud that it brought a lump to her throat. At least he was doing something useful with his life and education, she thought enviously. Perhaps that was what she ought to do, put up for Parliament.

Quickly she dismissed the idea. It wasn't something one did on a whim. It needed a great deal of preparation and ground work. You had to win the trust of the electors as well as the confidence of the party. It had taken Llewellyn years of hard work and she didn't feel equal to such dedication.

Memories plagued her so that she gave only part of her attention to the proceedings. Glancing sideways she saw that Dee was completely absorbed by the ceremony and wondered how Dee would enjoy being part of the social scene in London once she and Llewellyn were married.

Envy built up until it was a deep ache inside her and she felt a compelling urge to be back once more at the hub of things.

And why not? She had no family ties, she told herself. It would take effort. She would have to find a job and somewhere to live, but the challenge might be just what she needed. Since the fire, and her grandfather's death, she had been living in a kind of limbo, behaving as if she was middle-aged. The years were rushing by. She would be thirty soon.

Telling Roderic would be the hard part. There had been a coolness between them since election night and he might think she was doing it to avoid giving him the answer he was still waiting to receive.

Remembering made her feel uncomfortable. She knew her family thought her absolutely crazy to have such a handsome man in love with her and not to accept his proposal. She smiled as she recalled Dee's description of Roderic as a 'Gorgeous hunk' and knew exactly what she had meant. With his broad powerful shoulders, slim muscular hips and long, strong legs, he had the physique of Adonis.

And his looks matched. His thick sun-bleached brown hair flopped over his brow so that he was constantly pushing it back from his strong-boned face, with its well-shaped nose, strongly defined chin and high cheek bones. The steadfastness of his clear blue eyes, and the generous mouth that could curve so readily into a friendly smile, lessened the severity of his features. His deep voice could be so reassuring.

Yet it was this solid reliability that made her hesitate. He was the exact opposite of Michael Owen who had shown her that life could be exciting. Here in London, it was as if Michael was by her side, whispering that she should turn back the clock, and enjoy life to the full again, before she settled down.

The others were so entranced by the pageantry of what they had just witnessed that only Nesta noticed how withdrawn and silent Amelda was when they met up with Llewellyn for lunch.

'Feeling homesick for London?'

'Yes! Well . . . just a little. Being here brings back so many memories.'

'Perhaps you should stay on for a few days . . . get it all out of your system, darling,' Nesta said softly, patting Amelda's hand.

'I might just do that,' Amelda smiled, grateful that her mother was so understanding.

She gazed round the lavish dining room with its mirrored walls, ornate ceiling sparkling with chandeliers, whiteclothed tables glistening with silver and cut glass, the discreet waiters, and remembered the many times she had eaten there with Michael.

The reflection in the mirrored wall facing her made Amelda swing round in her chair in disbelief. The man who constantly filled her thoughts was sitting at a table on the far side of the room with three other people. Amelda blinked quickly, wondering if she was dreaming, but there was no mistake. It was Michael Owen.

She felt paralysed.

Conversation bubbled around her but she was impervious to what was being said. Furtively, she looked into the mirror again, just to reassure herself that she wasn't dreaming. This time, as if drawn by an invisible signal, Michael looked up and she felt vibrant shock waves as his gaze locked with hers and she saw his brown eyes narrow in disbelief.

Galvanised into action, Amelda whispered to her mother that she would be back in a few minutes and left by a door at the farthest end of the room from where Michael was sitting.

In the powder room, she splashed water on her burning face and tried to regain her composure. Her thoughts and feelings were in turmoil as she admitted to the truth. It wasn't London she was missing, it was Michael!

Her head ached so much that she went out into the street for some fresh air. The pavements were hot under the thin soles of her shoes as she walked aimlessly, trying to sort out the muddle inside her head. She felt aghast as she realised that their separation hadn't dimmed her feelings one iota.

She couldn't understand why he hadn't let her know that he was back in London. Unless he didn't want to see her again! She dismissed that as impossible after what they had meant to each other. There must be some other reason. Perhaps he had flown in just for a business meeting.

When she rejoined her family, she found herself bombarded by a chorus of messages and questions.

'Where have you been? We were just going to send out a search party!' Gwilym frowned.

'Michael Owen is here. He spotted you and came over but he couldn't wait any longer as he had an appointment in the City.'

'He's the American you used to work for, isn't he? Very dishy!' said Dee.

'Fancy running into him here!'

The voices babbled on, filled with curiosity and surprise. Amelda smiled non-committally as she took the card Gwilym handed to her. Her heart thudded when she saw the telephone number scrawled on it. It meant that Michael had kept on the apartment when he went back to the States.

With casual deliberation, Amelda tore it up and dropped the pieces into an ashtray. She ached to be with Michael. Just to talk to him again, to look into his dark brown eyes, to hear his throaty American drawl, all filled her with deep longing. Yet she wasn't sure she could face it. To reopen the wound that had barely healed would be courting trouble.

When the others were ready to leave Amelda held back as they took their noisy farewells.

'Llewellyn, could I stay at your flat . . . just for one or two nights?' she asked hastily.

'Yes . . . I suppose you could. You'd have to sleep on the sofa.'

'Thanks!' Quietly she told her mother of her decision and asked her to explain to the others.

'See you in a few days then!' Nesta agreed, kissing her goodbye. 'You are sure, now, that you are doing the right thing, Amelda?' she murmured anxiously.

The moment she was on her own, Amelda phoned Michael. When he answered, his unmistakable drawl brought a tightness to her throat so that her own voice was just a strained whisper.

'Amelda, honey! Where are you?'

'Still in London . . . but only for a couple of days.'

'I must see you. Are you free now?'

'Yes!'

'Jump into a taxi and come round to my apartment . . . you do remember the address?'

'Michael!'

'Yes . . . yes, of course. Silly of me, honey. I'm so excited at the thought of seeing you. Come on over right away. I'll be waiting.'

He's waiting! Michael's waiting for me, she told herself over and over as the taxi nosed its way through the late afternoon traffic towards Knightsbridge. She gazed out blindly. The familiar landmarks, The Ritz, Hyde Park Corner, Harrods, hit her brain like time signals, but it was the sight of the massive luxury block of flats, where Michael had his penthouse suite, that cut through the mists of her mind. Momentary panic assailed her as she thought of what she was doing.

'Never try to turn the clock back,' her grandfather's cautionary admonishment burned in her brain, but she defiantly pushed it to one side. This was different, this wasn't turning the clock back, it was going to be the start of something new.

I should have gone to the States with Michael when he asked me, she thought as she paid off the taxi. Perhaps it was still not too late to put matters right.

As she entered the carpeted foyer, the doorman raised his hand to his cap in a friendly salute as he recognised her. He opened the lift door, and without asking pressed the top floor button as she stepped inside.

She kept her mind blank as the lift carried her up to the eighth floor in a smooth silent glide. Then she stepped out into Michael's waiting arms.

His kiss transported her back into the magic world she had known when they had lived together. The intervening time, with all its traumas and unhappiness, was temporarily obliterated as she nestled into the familiar comfort of his arms.

The flat was exactly as she remembered it. She wandered round, touching the familiar drapes, furniture, ornaments, that she had shopped for, feeling as if she had at last come home.

Michael guided her towards the bedroom they had once shared. She stood motionless inside the door for a second, trying to work out what was different about it, then Michael's arms were around her again, his mouth covering hers and all other thoughts were erased.

As his hands caressed her, she kicked off her high-heeled shoes, then he removed her silk jacket, unzipped her dress and expertly eased it from her shoulders. His mouth never left hers for a second as he peeled off her bra and panties, and divested himself of his own clothes.

Still entwined in each other's arms, they sank back upon the bed.

The cool satin sheets received them like an embrace.

Their lovemaking surpassed her wildest dreams. Tenderly he caressed every inch of her body, rousing her passion to its ultimate crescendo then letting it ebb before once again tantalising her into such a frenzy that she strained against him, savouring the feel of his body pressing heavily on hers.

Raising himself slightly on one elbow, his mouth sought her breasts. Tears filled her eyes as the crown of his head pressed beneath her chin. Why did she need this particular man so much, she wondered. As he held each nipple in turn between his lips, his tongue flicking over it, teasing it to a hard point she felt ripples of desire wash over her. Her hands went round his waist, as she arched towards him.

Even though he knew she wanted him, was ready for him, Michael continued to tantalise her body. His lips, hot and burning, moved from her breasts down the length of her body, bringing increasing explosions of desire as they sought out the most tender and intimate spots.

Almost groaning with need, her hands twisted in his hair, dragging his face back to hers, his mouth to her own. The peak had been reached for them both. She cried out as he entered her, hard, demanding, almost brutal. He was breathing heavily, his face and body dripping sweat as he reached his climax.

Exhausted and spent, he still lay heavily across her so that she was almost suffocated. Placing both hands against his chest she tried to ease his weight to allow her to breathe.

With a groan he rolled from her and reached out to the bedside table for his watch, squinting at it, then exclaiming as if unable to believe what he was reading.

'It's all right, there's no rush. I'm staying the night a

254

Llewellyn's flat,' she told him with a little laugh.

'It might be OK for you, honey, but it's not for me,' he told her as he struggled into a sitting position and began to pull on his shirt. 'Get your things on . . . hurry.'

'But why?'

'Nancy will be back any minute!'

'Nancy? You mean . . .?'

As the full implication of Michael's words sank in, Amelda shivered with embarrassment. She felt humiliated. That was why the room seemed different. He had another woman living here. It was her perfume, her personal touches, that had made the bedroom seem unfamiliar. Shame and indignation floundered in Amelda at the thought that they had just made love in the bed he had been sharing with someone else.

'Michael, how could you?' The words ended in a sob.

'Oh, come on, honey. We've made love before,' he said defensively.

'That was different! We were living together.'

'We both wanted each other. You didn't exactly resist, now, did you? Be reasonable. You came here quite freely.'

Disgust and hatred flamed in her amethyst eyes as she looked at him. The love she had treasured like some precious flower withered and died. She felt sick with loathing.

Sobbing with anguish at her own foolhardiness she flung out of the flat without even a backward glance.

Tears coursing down her cheeks, she flagged down a taxi and collapsed inside it. She felt sickened, ashamed of her own part in the fiasco, filled with self-disgust and self-loathing.

She had never for one moment considered he might be living with anyone else when he had asked her to the flat. She had thought it meant that he cared as deeply as she did and that he was ready to take up their life together again.

Now, all she wanted was to get right away from London. The noise and bustle that earlier she had found exciting was now oppressive and unbearable. She left a note for Llewellyn, to let him know she had changed her mind about staying.

Huddled in a corner seat, she stared out unseeingly as the train took her back to North Wales. All she could remember was the panic that had been on Michael's face, and in his voice, when he had looked at his watch.

She felt utterly humiliated.

28

An early summer heatwave drained Amelda. More and more she left the running of the shop to Nesta and the two assistants they had recently taken on. This left her free to get out and about, collecting new stock from the outworkers and crafts people in the surrounding villages.

Even so, her heart wasn't really in it.

Frequently, she would park the car and wander aimlessly along one of the rugged, mountain footpaths. When the going over the rough scrub and shale became precarious, or she felt too exhausted to go any higher, she would just sit staring at the view, thinking back on the mess she had made of her life. Often, she drifted into a trance, her mind a blank, so that she felt neither the heat of the sun nor the wetness of the rain until she was soaked through.

It worried Nesta to see her like this. Each day she hoped Amelda would confide in her, but she knew better than to pry or try and force her to explain what was wrong. All she could do was to see that she changed her wet clothes when she came home, ensure that she had regular meals, and wait.

Roderic was less patient. He couldn't understand her withdrawal, although he sensed it had something to do with London. He had been worried when the rest of the family had come home without Amelda. Nesta's explanation that she was staying on for a couple of days' holiday had a false ring. When he had found out that, in fact, Amelda had returned later that same day he was even more mystified.

'She changed her mind,' Nesta said vaguely when he enquired next morning. 'She's still asleep. I'll ask her to phone you when she wakens.'

But Amelda hadn't phoned him. Two days later when he phoned again to ask if she would like to go to an Agricultural Show she had sounded so listless, so disinterested, that he had been baffled.

Now, almost a month later, she was just as lethargic.

She hadn't been up to the farm once to see him or his mother since her trip to London. He had seen her car parked nearby. Several times he had hung around waiting for her to return to it, but after an hour he had been forced to give up. There were so many jobs waiting to be done back at the farm, he couldn't delay his return any longer.

He phoned her several times to suggest that since the weather was so hot they should go swimming at Barmouth.

Amelda would agree and then, at the last minute phone to say she wasn't feeling up to it, or that she was inundated with orders which had to be packed and posted and she just couldn't leave her mother to do it all.

Finally, determined to see her and find out what was the matter, he drove over to Morfa Cottage one lunchtime without any prior warning.

He found Amelda dozing in a deck chair in the garden and, as he stood looking down at her, he was shocked by how wan and ill she looked. She had lost weight. The curves of her breasts were barely visible, under her pale blue cotton dress. Her legs and arms were thin. The roundness had gone from her face, her cheeks were concave beneath her cheekbones and there were dark shadows under her eyes.

'Amelda,' he said softly and waited quietly as her eyes

fluttered open and she looked up at him. He was shocked by the pain in their amethyst depths.

'Roderic!' She struggled to sit up, squinting at her watch, frowning when she saw it was barely twelve o'clock.

'Was I supposed to be having lunch with you?' she asked bewildered.

'No, but I will take you to lunch if you like,' he invited. 'I just happened to be passing and since I haven't seen you since you went up to London nearly a month ago I wondered if anything was wrong. I didn't expect to find you dozing at this time of the morning,' he added in surprise.

'No!' She smothered a yawn. 'I haven't been sleeping too well at nights lately. I think it must be the heat . . . I just sat down to drink my morning coffee and must have dropped off. Can I get you a drink?'

'I invited you out to lunch. We'll find a quiet pub and have a bar snack.'

'Your mother will be expecting you home,' Amelda protested.

'I'll phone her while you get ready. Don't be long.'

Amelda hesitated, then unable to think of any further excuse, shrugged resignedly.

As they drove towards the coast, the sea breeze made the heat seem less oppressive. The roads were busy with holiday traffic so Roderic stopped at a small village pub a few miles inland.

He ordered beers and a ham salad for both of them, then took their drinks out into the garden and found them seats in the shade.

'Now,' he said firmly as he placed the glasses on the table and sat down, 'tell me what is wrong.'

'Wrong? What do you mean?' she frowned.

'You've been avoiding me ever since you came back from London.'

'Not deliberately.'

'Well, it seems that way to me,' he challenged, holding her gaze, his blue eyes questioning.

'I haven't felt well.'

'You don't look well. You must have lost at least half a stone. Have you seen a doctor?'

'No!' Her breath caught audibly in her throat. 'I don't need a doctor. I am perfectly all right,' she added, irritably.

'Rubbish! You just admitted you haven't been feeling well.'

'I'm not ill,' she argued stubbornly. 'Just tired. We've been inundated with orders over the past few weeks and without Dee I've been under terrific pressure. The new girls need a lot of supervision. And I have had to do most of the packing in addition to chasing round after fresh stock.'

'You coped in the past and still had plenty of time and energy for other things.'

'Probably that's why I'm feeling so tired now,' she prevaricated. 'I must have been overdoing it and now it's catching up with me.'

'That's nonsense and you know it,' Roderic told her bluntly.

'Then maybe it's the heat,' she said, avoiding his eyes. 'The past few days have been sweltering and I'm never any good in the hot weather.'

'Frankly, Amelda, I don't believe you.' Roderic took a long drink of his beer and stared at her steadily. 'Are you deliberately avoiding me? Is it all off between us?'

'No . . . no, Roderic, that's the last thing I want. I'm sorry you should think that,' she stretched out her hand across the table and took his strong work-hardened hand in hers. 'It's nothing like that. I . . . I just feel out of sorts I know I am not very good company so I thought it was better to keep myself to myself until it passes over.'

260

Their salads arrived before he could answer. Amelda picked at hers, nibbling the crisp lettuce and finally eating a few pieces of tomato and cucumber, but ignoring the meat and potato salad.

'Aren't you going to try the ham? It's home-baked and very good,' Roderic urged.

'No.' She pushed her plate across the table. 'You eat it, I haven't touched it.'

'You're not on some sort of slimming jag, are you?' he frowned as he speared the meat with his fork and transferred it to his own plate.

'No, of course I am not. Are you suggesting I'm fat?' she asked with a ghost of a smile.

'Far from it! You're wasting away. Look, I must get back. The vet is calling at three o'clock,' he told her as he finished his drink. 'Are you coming back with me to see my mother?'

'No . . . not today. I can't.'

The panic in her voice startled him, but he said nothing. Something was wrong with Amelda and it bothered him. Usually she was so vivacious and quick-witted, but today she was utterly washed out and had hardly spoken all through their meal.

She sat shrivelled into her seat as he drove her home. She knew he was surprised and even a little hurt by her refusal to go and see his mother, but she couldn't bear the thought of facing Mrs Morris's sharp, birdlike eyes. She might even guess what was wrong. And if she did then she was sure to put the wrong interpretation on it and that would make the situation even worse.

'When am I seeing you again?' Roderic asked as he pulled up outside Morfa Cottage.

'I'm not sure.' She laid a hand placatingly on his arm, 'I'll phone you. OK?'

'If that's how you want it, I haven't much choice.' He kissed her chastely on the cheek. 'Will you think about seeing a doctor, Amelda?' he begged.

'Yes, all right. In a day or so,' she promised.

She felt so sick and headachey as she watched him drive away that she went straight into the garden and flopped down in the deckchair. She closed her eyes trying to shut out the world, but confused visions swam beneath her lids, so that her mind was filled with anger and guilt.

It grieved her that she had upset Roderic, but she had felt too weary to take any positive action to put matters right between them. He had been waiting for an explanation, but how could she even start to explain what was troubling her? She couldn't even comprehend herself how it had happened.

She reproached herself for scurrying away from Michael's flat in such a guilt-ridden fashion. If she had stood her ground, insisted on staying there until this Nancy person returned, then she might have forced Michael into explaining exactly what was going on. She still found it hard to accept that he was actually living with someone else in the flat that had been their home, which she had helped to furnish.

When he had told her he was going back to the States, she had thought he meant for good and had assumed that he was disposing of their flat. She had felt sad, then, that all their possessions and treasures should pass to someone else, but accepted it as inevitable. Now, knowing that he was sharing it with another woman filled her with jealous hatred.

Michael couldn't have forgotten how much they meant to each other, not in such a short space of time, she told herself over and over again. She didn't know how long he had been back in London, or how long he had been living with this Nancy. Perhaps, she reasoned, he had only just arrived there and intended getting in touch with her just as soon as he was settled.

In her heart she already knew the answer.

Almost a month had passed since they had met and made love and in all that time Michael hadn't even tried to contact her. He had taken advantage of her naïvety and she had let him, so she had only herself to blame.

In her heart she had known for a long time that Michael was devious.

She thought back to when she had first gone to work in London. If only she had listened to Cindy! She had been so ecstatically in love with Michael, so convinced that she had found her dream hero, that she had been impervious to Cindy's hints and innuendos. She had actually thought that she was jealous! Now, with hindsight, she realised that being more worldly than her, Cindy had only been trying to warn her that a man like Michael was bound to have a wife tucked away somewhere. Her mother had also suspected it, she remembered.

She could see it all now. While he had been in London, getting things established in England, he had deemed it good fun to have her as a live-in lover. And if Diana knew, or even suspected, she also knew that she had only to snap her fingers to bring him to heel, since her money funded his business.

Tears welled up as she recalled those wonderful ecstatic early days. She had been head over heels in love. She had hung on his every word. The love and warmth between them had been genuine, on his part as well as hers, she was sure of it.

When he had grown so possessive, insisting that she should give up work, she had believed him when he said it was because of his great regard for her. Instead of which, she thought bitterly, it had been so that no one in the office would suspect what was going on and tell his wife.

It was ironic, she thought, that Glenda should have been the one to do that. If Glenda hadn't realised who Diana was when she was introduced to her and, out of spite, brought her to Morfa Cottage things might have turned out so very differently.

I might be the one living with Michael, still blissfully happy and harbouring the dream that someday we would be married, she thought cynically.

She tried to close her mind to the trauma that had followed. She still found it terrifying to remember the horror of the fire, of knowing that she, as well as Diana, might have died in the inferno.

If only she hadn't gone to London to see Llewellyn take his seat in Parliament, she thought bitterly, she might never have seen Michael again. Her yearning for him might have remained dormant, or at least under control. Seeing him had stirred up not just memories but passion as well. Their lovemaking had been as tempestuous as ever.

It was only afterwards, when faced with the bitter truth that Michael was not the man she had imagined him to be, that she had been forced to accept reality.

And now, because of that night, she had a new problem.

Desperately worried, Amelda went indoors and found a calendar and carefully checked the dates. Her hands were trembling as she replaced it on the wall. There was no mistake, her fears were well founded. Perhaps Roderic was right and she ought to see a doctor.

Next morning, after another sleepless night that left her feeling sick with fear, she made up her mind.

Unwilling to confide in their local doctor, she thumbed through the Yellow Pages. Please don't let it be too late to put matters right, she prayed, as with shaking fingers she dialled a Chester number.

29

The days following her visit to see the doctor in Chester seemed endless to Amelda. She had expected to be told right away whether or not she was pregnant, but the doctor had explained that this was impossible at such an early stage. He hadn't even bothered to examine her physically, merely taken blood and urine samples and told her he would let her know as soon as he received the results of the laboratory tests.

She had felt so depressed that she had gone on a shopping spree. Afterwards she regretted being so impulsive since if she was pregnant then in a few months' time she wouldn't be able to wear any of the things she had bought. And by the time she could, they would all be out of fashion.

The carrier bags bearing the logo of two of the most exclusive boutiques in Chester, had, however, supported her story that she had gone to Chester shopping.

'I do wish you'd said you were going,' Nesta told her. 'I would have come with you. It's ages since I was in Chester and I do so love shopping there.'

She admired Amelda's purchases and insisted she should try them all on.

'No point in putting them away in your wardrobe,' she scolded. 'You won't get any fun out of them that way. Wear them and cheer yourself up. You've been looking rather peaky lately. It will do you good.'

Amelda had promised to do so, but when she got back to Morfa Cottage she had pushed her purchases to the back of the wardrobe, out of sight. Even looking at them before the results came through was tempting fate, she thought, superstitiously.

The days dragged by. Each morning Amelda made a point of going through the post before her mother arrived to help in the shop so that she could make sure there was no letter that either by its postmark, or return address, might be incriminating or call for an explanation.

After three days she could stand the suspense no longer and phoned the doctor's surgery to find out what was happening. The receptionist was polite and helpful but had no records whatsoever of her visit.

'I came as a private patient,' Amelda explained.

'Even so, there should be a record of your visit. I'll look into it and contact you again as soon as possible.'

Inwardly Nesta fumed at the delay and incompetence. She felt so tensed up that she found it impossible to concentrate on her work so she decided to take Shep for a walk. The fresh air might clear her head, she thought irritably.

As they went out of the door, she heard the phone ring and some sixth sense told her it was the doctor. She turned and ran back into the shop, but she was too late, her mother had already picked up the receiver.

Amelda froze.

From what she could hear of the conversation she knew she had been right. As she took the phone she suspected that the doctor had said enough to arouse her mother's suspicions.

'Well, what was all that about?' Nesta asked as Amelda replaced the receiver. A Doctor Tarrant from Chester . . . you didn't just go shopping on your day out, did you?'

'No!' Amelda admitted, blushing guiltily.

'Do you want to tell me?' Nesta asked gently, her dark eyes full of understanding.

'All right. Look, let's go into the sitting room. The girls can manage the shop. We're not all that busy at the moment.'

In a voice choked with tears, Amelda told her mother

266

everything that had happened in London and what she now feared as a result.

Nesta listened to her outpourings in silence then went into the kitchen and switched on the electric kettle.

'I think a good strong cup of tea is what we both need,' she said, firmly. 'You haven't mentioned any of this to your father, have you?'

'Of course not! I haven't told anyone, except you . . . not even Michael. I wouldn't even have told you if you hadn't taken that telephone call and guessed something was wrong.'

'Perhaps if you had confided in me and we had talked about it you wouldn't have got yourself into the state you have. You are probably worrying over nothing, anyway,' Nesta chided.

'I don't think so. I'm three weeks overdue . . .'

'Delayed shock.'

'Do you mean from the fire?' Amelda asked incredulously.

'No, I meant the shock of seeing Michael Owen again, and the way he treated you.'

'Oh, I don't know . . . Isn't that wishful thinking?'

'Well, we'll soon find out,' Nesta said briskly. 'You should know for certain within the next twenty-four hours.'

'And what if the test proves positive and I am pregnant?'

'We'll worry about that when we hear the result. If you are it's not the end of the world,' Nesta told her as she poured out tea for both of them.

'You mean you would stand by me whether I decide to go through with it or have an abortion?' Amelda asked incredulously.

'Of course I will,' Nesta assured her. 'Now, come on, drink your tea and stop worrying.'

'You won't mention any of this to Roderic, or anyone,

will you Mum?' Amelda pleaded as she put down her empty cup.

'Of course not. It has nothing to do with him. I won't even mention it to your Dad . . . unless you want me to tell him.'

'Not yet,' Amelda hedged, a tremor in her voice. 'Let's wait until we know the results.'

Confiding in her mother lifted some of the guilt from Amelda's mind, but she still agonised over what the outcome might be.

Although she was doing her best to treat the incident in a matter-of-fact way, Nesta also felt apprehensive. If Amelda was pregnant it would mean she would have to help her bring up her baby. She wondered how Gwilym would take such news. He was looking forward to taking an early retirement but this could change everything.

It was a daunting prospect.

Nesta stood looking at her reflection in the mirror. It's time I could claim to be a grandmother, she told herself. It would be an excuse for my greying hair and wrinkles.

It seemed a long time since she had first held Amelda in her arms, but she would never forget the overwhelming joy she had known when they had told her the baby was a girl.

Much as she adored Llewellyn, and was proud of the way he was making his mark in the world, it was Amelda she identified with and worried over.

Aware of her obsession, she had always tried hard not to interfere in Amelda's life. Nevertheless, she now felt a sense of guilt that she hadn't opposed her relationship with Michael Owen. She knew Gwilym didn't like him very much, and considered him to be brash and over-bearing, but she, too, had felt susceptible to Michael's masculine charm and understood why Amelda was attracted to him.

In her heart, though, she had known he wouldn't make a good husband for Amelda and she had been relieved that they hadn't rushed into marriage. She had hoped that given time Amelda would see for herself that he wasn't the right one. She had never for one minute thought there might be an outcome such as this.

If there was a baby, bringing it up single-handed would be a terrible strain on Amelda, no matter how much support they gave her. She remembered her own childhood. She had been happy enough until she was nine. Then everything had changed so dramatically when both her grandparents had died in a flu epidemic within days of each other, and no one could trace her father. She had been foisted off on first one set of relations and then another and had grown up feeling unloved and unwanted.

That, Nesta vowed, was something that must not happen to Amelda's child. She and Gwilym must ensure that the child had the security of a good homelife and plenty of love.

She wondered if Michael Owen would cause trouble if he ever found out that Amelda had borne his child. She pushed away the thought that he might hanker after a child of his own and seek custody of the baby. A man of his calibre was hardly likely to do anything that might jeopardise his own future, she told herself. And having the responsibility of a young child would certainly be an encumberance. He was much more likely simply to wash his hands of the whole affair.

A phone call from Llewellyn to say that he and Dee had fixed the date of their wedding, temporarily wiped Amelda's problems from Nesta's mind.

'We thought we'd get married the weekend after next,' he told her. 'Will that conflict with any plans you and Dad have made?'

'No, I don't think so . . . although it is going to be rather a rush,' she told him. 'Where is it to be? In London or here?'

'Up there of course! We both want our families to be in at the kill,' he laughed. 'As a matter of fact I am thinking of asking Roderic Morris to be best man. And Dee thought that Amelda might like to be her bridesmaid. Will you ask her?'

'Yes. Yes, of course.'

'You sound a bit doubtful.'

'Sorry. I was just thinking of all the other arrangements that will have to be made . . .'

'Yes, we know. We are coming home this weekend and we can thrash out all the details then. I just thought you might like to have an advance warning.'

'You're not giving yourself a great deal of time.'

'We'll manage. I've got a special licence and we will go and see the vicar this weekend. Don't start worrying, Mum. We know what we're doing. Everything will be fine. Just let Amelda know. She needn't bother to phone back. We'll see her at the weekend.'

Amelda greeted the news with a look of dismay.

'What on earth am I going to do?' she wailed. 'I can't possibly be a bridesmaid . . . not as things stand. Supposing the next test is positive?'

'What on earth difference does that make?' Nesta said sharply.

'Mum, I couldn't! It wouldn't be right, somehow,' Amelda protested. 'Just think how Llewellyn would feel when he found out afterwards.'

Nesta remained silent, but kept her fingers crossed. The results of Amelda's first tests had been inconclusive; with any luck the problem might take care of itself.

Gwilym accepted the news of Llewellyn's impending marriage with an enthusiasm that surprised Nesta. She knew he liked Dee, and that he got on with her much better than he had with Glenda.

270

'Dee and Llewellyn are well-suited,' he said approvingly. 'It's what he needs, someone who will help him in his career rather than a wife who is set on making a name for herself. I must admit, it worried me when she decided to move in with him when he took on that flat in London. I didn't say anything, of course, but I was afraid that they might decide not to bother with a wedding ceremony.'

'Would it have mattered?' Nesta asked in surprise.

'Yes, in a way. It's not so much for them, since no one even raises an eyebrow at two people who are not married living together these days. It's what happens when they decide to have children.'

'As long as the children have loving parents, and a secure home background, then surely that is all that matters?'

'No! They need that bit of paper that says they are legitimate,' Gwilym said firmly.

'You can't tell from today's birth certificate,' Nesta reminded him quickly.

'Well, that may be so, but in my opinion, a proper family background is going to become more important not less,' Gwilym insisted. 'There are too many one-parent families these days, and as a result far too many insecure children. Half of them don't know who their dads are, or if they do they never see them,' he said angrily. 'What sort of parents are they going to make when it comes to their turn? People learn by example, remember.'

Nesta bit her lip and said nothing, but her thoughts went immediately to Amelda and she uttered a silent plea that everything would be all right and that Gwilym might never know of the dilemma that faced them all.

Gwilym's outburst had come as a shock. After thirty years of marriage she thought she knew how he felt about most things, but it seemed he could still surprise her.

He had certainly altered his opinion on many things since he had lost his job on the *Post*, she reflected. It was as if his whole outlook had undergone a radical change since they had moved from Merseyside to North Wales, and he seemed to have a different set of values.

In some ways, she mused, he had grown more like her Da. Gradually, over the years, he had come to respect Rhys's wisdom and wealth of experience. After they had moved to Tryfan the two of them had become much closer and whenever they met would sit discussing topical issues for hours at a time.

Neither of them had approved of Michael Owen. To them he was typical of the power-crazed business tycoon that they both despised. The incident over Morfa Cottage had only served to underline their opinion.

She was secretly pleased that Llewellyn had asked Roderic Morris to be best man. She knew he was someone Gwilym would have welcomed as an addition to their family.

Right from their first meeting they had seemed to get on well. For one thing, they shared the same political outlook. They were not as fervent as Llewellyn, but they supported most of the things he and Plaid Cymru stood for, particularly as it affected farming and the Welsh countryside. When the friendship between Roderic and Amelda had deepened she knew that, like her, Gwilym hoped it might become permanent.

If only it was Amelda's wedding that they were planning and not Llewellyn's, she thought wistfully.

30

The bright summer morning had a fairytale quality to it. The day had dawned sunny, the azure blue sky speckled with the lightest of high clouds that criss-crossed the purple mountain peaks like party streamers. Summer dew sparkled like diamonds in the grass, and the scent of roses pervaded the air.

As the wedding party emerged from the flower-bedecked grey stone church after the service they found themselves facing a battery of press and TV cameras and a crowd so dense that it was impossible for them to get through to the cars waiting to take them to the reception.

The police struggled to clear a way, but people still pushed and jostled forward, anxious to wish the bridal couple good luck and smother them in rice and confetti.

'Your brother has become quite a celebrity since he became an MP,' Roderic laughed, helping Amelda into one of the cars and taking the seat beside her. 'I thought we were going to be smothered. I almost lost my topper in that scrum.'

By the time they reached the Glyndwr Hotel where the reception was to be held, a similar crowd had gathered and once more they had to run the gauntlet of confetti and rice.

During the reception, Amelda tried to push her own problems to one side and concentrate on what was happening around her.

Dee looked beautiful in her white silk dress. The heart-shaped neckline of the figure-hugging bodice was encrusted with seed pearls. The ankle-length skirt, plain in front, flowed from the hipline in gathered tiers.

During the service, Dee had seemed nervous, but now, with her pearl-trimmed veil caught back, and her dark hair framing her heart-shaped face, she looked radiant. Her brilliant brown eyes shone with love and happiness and her soft pink lips parted breathlessly, as she constantly exchanged looks with her new husband.

Llewellyn looked equally elated. His dark eyes glistened with pride each time he turned to look at his new bride and a constant smile tilted the corners of his wide firm mouth. He had trimmed his dark beard to the same style that Rhys had favoured and he looked almost like a younger version of their grandfather, Amelda thought as she watched him.

'Wouldn't it have been wonderful if Granda could have been here today, Llewellyn?' she whispered softly, taking his arm. 'He would have been so proud of you.'

A momentary flash of pain darkened Llewellyn's eyes as he squeezed her hand understandingly.

When, at the end of the meal, Roderic rose to his feet to toast the newly-weds, Amelda was conscious of how distinguished he looked in the formal morning suit. I'm more used to seeing him in corduroy breeches and an open-necked shirt, she thought with an inward smile. Either way, he radiated strength and reliability, she thought admiringly.

She relaxed, amused by Roderic's extremely witty speech. Suddenly, the full implication of what he was saying hit her. He had extended a token invitation to those present to come to his wedding 'just as soon as Amelda names the day'.

Although she joined in the laughter that followed, Amelda felt sick with apprehension. As soon as she possibly could, she escaped from the room and out into the hotel grounds, to escape from Roderic. She needed to be alone to think what she must say in order to avoid committing herself, or hurting his feelings.

In her bridesmaid's dress of lilac silk, she knew she looked conspicuous so she took refuge in a small summer-house at the far end of the gardens.

She was so deep in thought, that at first she didn't hear footsteps approaching. When she did it was too late to move away. They had stopped outside and she sensed someone was watching her. When she looked up her heart pounded at the sight of Michael Owen standing there?

'What are you doing here?'

'I just happened to be up this way finalising a business transaction so I thought I would come and say a final fare-well to North Wales. I seem to have picked a particularly significant occasion,' he commented, his eyes taking in her lilac silk dress and elaborate hair style.

'Are you going back to the States for good?'

'That's right, honey. It's what Nancy wants.'

Tears misted Amelda's eyes. She dug her nails into her palms to control her feeling of shame as she recalled the degrading end to their last meeting in his apartment in London.

'Is something wrong, honey?' Michael asked puzzled. 'You surely guessed it was all off between *us* last time you were in London,' he added insensitively.

Silently, Amelda dabbed at her eyes. She wanted to tell him that she thought she was pregnant, but the right words wouldn't come. He seemed like a stranger. He was talking to her as if they were just casual acquaintances, not two people who had been so deeply in love with each other that every moment apart had been painful.

'I must be off. It's a long drive.' He bent forward to kiss her cheek, taking one of her hands in his as he did so. 'I don't suppose we'll ever meet again, Amelda, but . . . thanks for some wonderful memories.'

'Wait! There's something I must tell you, Michael . . .' She choked on a sob, unable to go on.

275

'Well, be quick, honey.' He looked at his watch impatiently. 'It's pointless going over old ground again, you know,' he frowned. 'We've reached the parting of the ways . . . it's over between us. My mind is made up. And you know me, Amelda, that's always been the secret of my success. Once I make a decision I stand by it. Come on, now, honey. No scene, please.'

'This isn't a business decision, Michael . . . it's a human one. Something that affects both of us.'

His brow furrowed as he stared at her uncomprehendingly.

'Michael . . . I think I am pregnant!'

Never, as long as she lived, would she ever forget the look of horror in Michael's brown eyes as he repeated her words.

In her fantasy she had imagined that he would be overwhelmed with joy. He would sweep her into his arms and tell her he loved her, wanted her to have his child and that they must be married right away.

Instead, he drew back as if she had some contagious disease. His face blanched, his deep gravelly voice became harsh and defensive as he denied vigorously that it could possibly be his.

'It's never happened before so why should it happen now?' he muttered querulously, running his hand through his hair in a distraught way.

'Other times I took precautions to make sure it didn't happen,' she whispered.

'And why didn't you do so this time?' he blustered.

'I hadn't expected to meet you in London, let alone make love,' she replied simply.

'One single incident and you are pregnant. Nonsense!' he ridiculed. 'Have you seen a doctor?'

'Yes!' She drew in her breath sharply. 'The first set of

276

tests were inconclusive. I had to have them done over again. I'm still waiting for the results.'

'That probably means you are perfectly all right,' he argued defensively.

She shrugged helplessly.

'Well, if you are pregnant then what do you intend to do?'

'That depends on you.'

'It has nothing to do with me, Amelda. I'm not accepting responsibility for your carelessness. Anyway, how can you be sure it is mine?'

His reply was as wounding as a slap in the face.

'You'd better arrange for an abortion,' he went on when she remained silent. 'I'll put up the money for one,' he added as brusquely as if arranging a business deal.

At that she turned away, sick to the soul, embittered by his callous rejection. No word of love or consolation. Just a cold harsh offer of money so that she could have the baby aborted.

Even when he grabbed her by the shoulder, spinning her round to face him, she felt nothing. It was as if she was encased in an inpenetrable wall of ice that left her completely numb.

'Surely, you understand why I can't do anything more, Amelda?' he said aggressively. 'I have my future to consider. I've decided to start again in the States. Nancy is putting up the money for a new business venture after we are married.'

She shook his hand away. Her tears had dried on her cheeks, leaving her amethyst eyes looking like rain-drenched violets as she looked him full in the face, seeing him for what he was. An opportunist who used women for his own ends. Diana had provided working capital for his first business, now it was to be Nancy. Perhaps if she had been rich and powerful he would have stayed with her, baby or no baby.

Suddenly the mould was shattered. He was no longer the handsome American who had dominated her thoughts and her life for so long, the man she had given herself to, body and soul, heart and mind. As she faced him she saw a middle-aged, paunchy, egotistical stranger. His hard brown gaze was shifting uneasily as she stared at him, his sensuous mouth twitching nervously.

She was free, her love for him dead.

'You'll be all right,' he exclaimed with false assurance. He patted her shoulder awkwardly. 'Just get rid of the baby. I reckon I paid my debts to you when I bought Morfa Cottage in your name. You have a prime piece of property there, honey. You can build that gift shop up into a good business. Or you can sell out and start a new life . . . you're still young enough. You'll be all right, honey,' he told her confidently. 'You are one of life's survivors!'

He had stood there for a moment longer, waiting for her to speak. When she didn't, he turned on his heel and walked out of the summer house. And out of her life.

Fury enveloped Amelda as she saw him disappear through the garden back into the hotel. How had she ever thought herself to be in love with him? She had let a juvenile crush blight her entire life. Now that she saw Michael Owen for what he was, she despised herself for having been duped.

Shivering, even though the sun still shone, she slipped back into the hotel. The wedding party was still in full swing and she flung herself into the height of things, drinking glass after glass of champagne, determined to blank out completely what had just happened.

When Llewellyn and Dee were ready to leave for their honeymoon, she helped Dee from her white silk wedding dress into a trim yellow trouser suit. She looked so radiantly happy that Amelda's heart ached.

If only my own life was as well ordered as Dee's, she

thought enviously as she hugged her new sister-in-law.

'Are you all right, Amelda?' Llewellyn asked anxiously as she kissed him goodbye and wished him well. 'You look awfully flushed.'

'I've probably been drinking too much champagne,' Amelda giggled, biting her lip nervously, her eyes jewel-bright.

'Don't worry, I'll look after her,' Roderic assured him, placing an arm protectively around Amelda's shoulders.

'Right! And don't let it be too long before you make that a permanent arrangement,' Llewellyn grinned.

Amelda felt the colour rush to her face as she remembered Roderic's speech. At the time she had felt apprehensive that he should still be thinking about her in that way, knowing that she was still in love with someone else. Now, having come to her senses, she felt a momentary sadness as she realised what a wonderful husband he would have made.

Lost in thought, she looked up startled when Roderic asked if she was ready to leave.

'I was going home with Mum and Dad,' she told him.

'I'll take you. I thought we could go on somewhere.'

'I'll have to go home and change. I can hardly go anywhere dressed like this,' she said sharply.

'You look lovely.' His eyes took in the lilac silk dress that clung seductively. 'We could go dancing.'

'You once told me you didn't dance.'

'I'm not very fond of dancing. I've got two left feet,' he explained, his eyebrows lifting in surprise at her crisp tone.

'I don't think I want to do anything. I have a lot of sorting out and thinking to do,' she told him evasively as she settled into his car.

'Oh?' He kept his eyes on the road and both hands firmly on the wheel.

'I'm going away.'

279

'On holiday?' He looked at her sharply.

'No. For good.'

'Rather sudden, isn't it?'

'I feel unsettled. Time is rushing by and I'm doing nothing with my life,' she added pathetically.

'What do you want to do?'

'I don't know. That's the problem. I've settled down here and lost all ambition, all sense of purpose.'

'That's rubbish! You started a business from scratch and you have built it up into something very successful. Most people would have thrown the towel in after that fire, but you didn't. You not only managed to salvage the business but you have made it an even greater success than it was before. That's hardly being a failure, now, is it?'

'I still don't feel I'm being stretched. I want a challenge . . .'

'Marry me, then. I have asked you.' He pulled the car into the side of the road and killed the engine, then twisted around in his seat so that he was facing her. 'I love you, Amelda. I'll do everything possible to make you happy.'

'Oh, Roderic,' her lower lip trembled as he took both her hands in his. 'I don't think I'm ready for marriage . . . not yet. There are so many things I still have to sort out.'

'Like Michael Owen!'

She looked up startled, her amethyst eyes saucer-wide with shock.

'I saw you in the summer-house with him!' he stated. 'When you left the party, you were outside for such a long time that I thought you weren't feeling well, so I came looking for you to make sure you were all right,' he explained as he saw the anger flare in her eyes. 'When I saw you together I walked away. I presumed it was a prearranged rendezvous.'

'No! It wasn't like that at all. He wasn't invited to the wedding. He was in the area, finalising one or two things

280

before going back to America . . . he gatecrashed.'

'So he'd come to say goodbye.'

'Yes . . . I suppose you could say that.'

'Or are you thinking of going to America?'

'No! Most certainly not. Whatever made you think that?'

'I thought perhaps you intended to join Michael Owen there.'

'No,' she shook her head emphatically. 'He means nothing at all to me . . . not now. It was infatuation on my part, anyway. He was my first boss, he paid me special attention and I fell for him. It's a commonplace enough story,' she added bitterly.

'True. But most girls can laugh it off. You can't. You've been carrying a torch for Michael Owen ever since I've known you. Are you trying to tell me that the flame has at long last gone out?'

'I'm not trying to tell you anything.' Her chin went up defiantly. 'You are the one who is asking all the questions.'

'I want to know where I stand,' he said determinedly.

Amelda tried to speak, but emotion choked her. She suddenly realised she was treating him in just the same way as Michael Owen had treated her. She kept her face averted, unable to meet his challenging gaze.

'So will you marry me, Amelda?'

'I can't.' The whispered refusal came from deep within her. How could she ever marry Roderic when she felt so soiled? His love was strong and pure. If he knew the whole truth about her and Michael Owen he would never have asked her in the first place, she thought bitterly. The way she had behaved with Michael made her no better than a whore. She had been a kept woman, but was too innocent to realise it.

'I'm waiting.'

With a supreme effort she forced herself to look up.

281

Since it was obvious that he wasn't going to be dissuaded without a very good reason, she knew she would have to tell him everything, no matter how distressing it might be. And when he knew the complete truth there would be no question of him wanting to marry her, she thought unhappily.

In a choked, stumbling voice she spared none of the details. She apportioned blame to no one, even accepting that she had been equally responsible for the way Diana had been deceived. When she told him about how she had bumped into Michael in London and how, after they had made love, she discovered he was through with her and living with someone else, Amelda felt her face burn with shame.

In a voice barely above a whisper, she told Roderic she now thought she was pregnant.

Roderic heard her out in complete silence.

'Now you understand why I need to get right away from here, away from everyone I know.'

'Running away will solve nothing,' he told her quietly. 'In fact, you've already paid for your indiscretion . . . and learned your lesson about people like Michael Owen. Now, will you marry me?'

'Roderic!' She looked at him in shocked astonishment. 'I don't think you have been listening to what I have been saying.'

'I have. Every word of it.'

'And you still want to marry me . . . even though I may be carrying Michael's child?'

31

Llewellyn and Dee's wedding made the front page, in national as well as local newspapers. There were banner headlines that ranged from 'Youngest MP marries the Girl Next Door' to 'Hero of Plaid Cymru Takes a Bride'.

There was also coverage on BBC TV, TV WALES and ITV news programmes, with group shots, as well as those of the bride and groom, taken outside the village church.

Family background, and reference to Rhys and his work for Plaid Cymru, played a prominent part in all the reports. Many claimed that Llewellyn had taken up the mantle of the late Rhys Evans, and would carry the party forward to even greater strength. Others stated that Llewellyn was an MP to watch.

As she read them over next morning, Amelda wondered what her grandfather would have made of the occasion. He had hardly known Dee, but at one time he had held Glenda in high regard. Perhaps it had been for the best that he hadn't lived to see how Glenda had almost alienated them all, Amelda reflected.

A great many changes had taken place since that awful night, she thought sadly. In some ways it was almost as if a completely new era had dawned and it made her feel restless and unsure about her own future.

She folded up the papers and put them to one side to give to Llewellyn and Dee when they returned from their honeymoon. Then she sat toying with the letter that had arrived that morning from the doctor in Chester confirming that the pregnancy tests had proved negative.

Uppermost in her mind was the commitment she had

made to herself, and to her mother, that if she wasn't pregnant then she intended doing something positive with her life. Now she wondered how best she could redeem that promise.

She envied people like Dee who were so single-minded, who knew exactly where they were going because their ambitions were forged out of love for someone else. Yet, in a way, she had been like that once – willing to submerge her own aspirations in order to ensure that the man she loved should attain his ambitions.

For her it had proved to be a bitter experience, but then, Michael was so much more egotistical and ruthless than Llewellyn. Llewellyn was ambitious not so much for himself as for the ideals he represented. If he could promote the aims of Plaid Cymru that was satisfaction enough for him. He didn't need private kudos to achieve a sense of fulfilment. And yet, ironically, he had managed to attain personal glory far beyond Michael's wildest dreams.

'I must do something tangible,' she said aloud.

Llewellyn and Dee's wedding had been a watershed. Seeing Michael there, and learning from him the bitter truth about their relationship, that he had no intention of ever marrying her, had come as a shock. But the real devastation had been his rejection when she had told him she thought she was pregnant.

It had been of some consolation to discover later that evening that her fears were groundless. And the letter from the doctor in Chester had doubly confirmed it. Yet it did nothing to eliminate her feelings of guilt and shame. Or the knowledge that money and power mattered more to Michael than she did.

That was the hardest thing of all to bear.

The trauma had helped her to clarify her own feelings for Roderic, however. Her heart warmed as she remembered how after she had told him about her affair with Michael, and that she might even be carrying his child,

284

Roderic had still insisted he wanted to marry her.

'Trust me, Amelda, I'll look after you,' he had told her earnestly.

'But if there is a baby . . .' her voice had choked as she had put her fears into words.

'It is yours . . . that is all that matters,' he had answered gently. 'It doesn't matter who else was involved, I shall always regard it as yours and, because it is yours, then it will be ours,' he added tenderly.

If only she had had proof before the wedding that she wasn't pregnant, she would have been saved the agony and the humiliation both of confronting Michael and of confessing to Roderic. Yet, what more positive proof of Roderic's love could she have ever had, she thought, remembering his words.

'If you are going to sit around feeling guilty and sorry for yourself you'll end up neurotic,' Nesta lectured her, when Amelda told her all that had happened. 'You are not the first woman in the world to find out that she is mistaken about the man she had placed on a pedestal, or that he has left her.'

'That's not the point.'

'Oh, yes, it is. If you had been married to Michael Owen and he had decided to leave you, or divorce you, would you be feeling so guilty?'

'Probably not, but that would have been different.'

'Legally it might have been, but as far as the personal relationship between you is concerned it would be the same. And if you were divorced, and Roderic asked you to marry him, you wouldn't hesitate for a second.'

At the reminder of Roderic's proposal, Amelda felt herself weakening. It would be so easy just to say 'yes'. To let him take over all her responsibilities, to be able to relax, knowing he was there to protect her. He was such a giant of a man, his love would cushion her against all of life's knocks.

Resolutely she hardened her heart, refusing to be tempted. If it was love Roderic felt for her then it would stand the test of time. Her feelings towards him were deep and warm, but she wasn't completely sure whether it was love. The wounds Michael had inflicted were still far too raw. She couldn't face another relationship going wrong.

'If you are not going to marry Roderic then, for heaven's sake, do something useful with your life,' Nesta added heatedly.

'Now that Llewellyn's wedding is over I intend to get right away and make a fresh start,' Amelda told her. 'I've never experienced any real hardship! I think I need to escape from the cocoon of comfort and safe living I've known all my life.' She sighed dramatically. 'Perhaps I take after you. Granda always said you spent your life feeling guilty about things and always trying to atone for what you've done . . . and he was right. I've seen it happening.'

'Then you should know better than to fall into the same trap,' her mother told her sharply. 'And stop trying to evade the issue of what you intend to do by side-tracking me like this.'

'I'm not,' Amelda assured her. 'Perhaps I've inherited your Catholic conscience,' she smiled weakly. 'You know, the need to confess and then make some sort of redemption.'

'What rubbish! You've not even been brought up as a Catholic,' Nesta exclaimed, shocked.

'You were . . . you still behave like one . . . except that you don't go to Mass every Sunday.'

'That's quite enough!'

An embryo idea began to form at the back of Amelda's mind, but before she could act positively she had to decide what to do about Morfa Cottage and the gift shop. She couldn't just walk away and leave it. And she wasn't at all sure about selling it. She knew she was being sentimental, but there was her grandfather's memory to be considered.

Furthermore, there were a great many orders outstanding and she was committed to buy from local craft workers for at least the next six months. She didn't want to let them down since she knew most of them were depending on those sales for part of their livelihood.

She wondered if her mother would be willing to take over. Ever since Dee had left, Nesta had been helping out full-time so that in some ways it was already almost a partnership.

If only her father could be persuaded to help out, she thought wistfully. He would handle everything so competently that she would feel completely happy about leaving.

She tried to talk it through with her mother, to see how the idea appealed to her, but Nesta only shook her head, her mouth set stubbornly.

'Why don't you just marry Roderic and settle down here and run it yourself? All this talk about helping others is all very well, but you can do that in your spare time. There are charity committees you can serve on, right here on your own doorstep, so why go chasing all over the countryside, or down to London?' Her face hardened. 'You are not planning to see Michael Owen again, are you?'

'No, of course I'm not.' Amelda's voice was flat. She felt so tired, so weary, that she couldn't even work up any strong feelings about her mother's insinuations. 'I would have thought that even you could see that London isn't the right environment for me,' she added bitterly.

'Then marry Roderic and stay here,' Nesta repeated, in a pleading voice.

'I'm not certain if that is what I really want,' Amelda sighed, her amethyst eyes unreadable. 'I honestly think I need to get right away, perhaps work overseas for a year or two for War on Want or one of the other charities.'

'Amelda! That's a crazy idea. You've no training for anything like that! Give it some more thought . . . promise me,' Nesta begged.

'I've given it plenty of thought,' Amelda told her grimly, remembering the sleepless night she had spent, tossing and turning, trying to reach a decision.

'You're out of your mind,' Nesta exclaimed angrily. 'What makes you think you can do work of that sort? Why,' her dark eyes flamed, 'you can't even organise your own life . . .'

'I don't intend to work on the organising side, I want to do field work,' Amelda interrupted.

'Field work?' Nesta frowned, as if unable to follow her line of reasoning.

'I want to go where the real trouble is. Spend six months, or a year even, out in Africa, or wherever help is needed, doing whatever has to be done. Nursing the sick, cooking for the starving, helping to share out the food.'

'Are you crazy? You haven't any nursing experience . . .'

'Then I'll drive a truck or do whatever else I'm asked to do,' Amelda snapped, her amethyst eyes darkening.

'Those places are full of disease.'

'Oh, Mum! I'm sure they'll innoculate me against all known germs,' she quipped, exasperatedly.

'It's sheer madness,' Nesta argued. 'What's wrong with this family?' she added bitterly. 'You all seem to need Causes. It's bad enough that my Da and Llewellyn should devote their lives to Plaid Cymru but at least they stayed around where their families could keep an eye on them.'

Roderic was just as appalled by Amelda's decision as her mother had been.

Her sleepless nights had taken their toll and he was

288

shocked beyond measure at how tired her eyes looked and how drawn her face was.

'Oh, Amelda!' he groaned. 'Do you know what you are doing to me?' He placed his strong hands on her shoulders, drawing her close until she could feel the heat from his body.

His strength made her feel weak. As his muscular arms held her protectively, she felt wonderfully safe resting against his broad chest. Roderic might not have Michael's wit and charisma, but his forthright approach to life, his utter dependability, were qualities that mattered far more, she decided. As she felt her resolves weakening she struggled to regain control, determined not to give in.

'It's no good, Roderick, I've got to do it,' she insisted, pushing him away. 'It's the only way I can learn to live with myself again. I will come back,' she promised. 'Six months or a year . . . no longer.'

'And expect to find everything just the same as when you left?' he asked harshly, his square chin jutting.

Amelda bit her lip, refusing to be daunted. 'That's a chance I have to take,' she said in a small tight voice, squaring her shoulders and facing his direct, blue gaze unflinchingly.

'Do you think it's right to burden your mother with the shop?' Roderic went on ruthlessly.

'Not really,' she admitted.

'If she had refused to help . . . would you still have gone?'

'Yes . . . but perhaps not right away. I would have had to find a manager . . . or close the shop down.'

'Think again, Amelda. Just wait for a few weeks. Give yourself time to get over the shocks you've had,' he pleaded.

His arms went round her, holding her so tightly that she was powerless to free herself. His clear blue eyes raked her face hungrily, before his mouth claimed hers, bruising her lips, leaving her breathless from the impact of his deep burning kiss.

'I need you, Amelda,' he breathed hotly, his voice hoarse with emotion. 'I'm not interested in anything you may have done in the past, it's the future I care about . . . yours and mine.'

'No . . . no . . . I've got to do it, Roderic. I've got to get away, be by myself. Please try and understand.'

He didn't answer, but his eyes had an alien gleam in them and his hands dropped to his sides helplessly.

32

Once her mind was made up about what she wanted to do, Amelda worked indefatigably to put her plan into operation.

Months went by before she learned that an organisation based in Chester had a party of volunteer workers preparing to leave for East Africa just before Christmas. She was determined to join them.

After numerous phone calls and meetings, and assuring them that her passport was up to date, and that she had arranged for visas and vaccinations, she finally persuaded them to include her in their expedition.

'I'm not at all sure that I shall be able to run Morfa Gifts on my own,' Nesta protested, when she heard the news, making one last stand to try to persuade Amelda not to go.

'We've already agreed that I can't just shut the door and leave everything on "hold" until I get back because there are too many orders outstanding,' Amelda reminded her.

'Supposing when you get back you don't like the way I have been running things?'

'You'll manage perfectly,' Amelda assured her. 'And, as I said, if you find you have difficulty in coping you can always take on some additional staff to help out.'

'Don't worry about it, Amelda. There won't be any need to do that.'

Amelda looked at her father in surprise. He had been sitting in his armchair, engrossed in his newspaper, and she hadn't even been aware that he was listening to them.

'I've decided to take early retirement, so from next

month I will be able to help out at the shop full time. We'll manage between us. You go and do whatever it is you want to do and don't give it another thought. The business will still be here waiting for you when you get back.'

'Oh, Dad, that's absolutely wonderful!' Amelda smiled with relief. 'It certainly takes a load off my mind. Can you both come with me to arrange things at the bank?'

Later that week, after the three of them had signed all the relevant papers, Amelda insisted that she should take them out to lunch as a celebration.

'Come on, it may be our last chance for a year.'

'I thought you said you would be away for six months,' Nesta said sharply.

'Six months, a year,' she shrugged. 'Now that I know Morfa Gifts is in such capable hands there will be no . . .'

'Does Roderic know you might be away for as long as a year?' Nesta interrupted.

'Well . . .' The colour rushed to Amelda's face. 'He knows what I intend to do . . . where I'm going . . . we've talked it through. Don't worry, Mum, he understands.'

Her mother gave her a long, searching look and, although she said no more, Amelda could tell from the set of her mouth that she was displeased. She was not at all surprised when her mother brought the subject up again later.

'Amelda, is everything all right between you and Roderic?' she asked, sitting on the edge of the bed as Amelda packed the clothes she intended taking with her in a kitbag.

'Of course. Why do you ask?'

'He hasn't called round once since you told us what your plans were.'

'We have already talked it all over and said all there is

to say. It's not as though I'm going for ever. I'll be back home again in six months.'

'Or a year.'

Amelda looked up from her packing, her face flaming.

'Or, as you say, in a year. What difference does it make?'

'Quite a lot if you are the one sitting at home waiting,' Nesta answered tartly. 'Stop taking Roderic for granted. You don't even bother to tell him how long you will be away, but you expect him to wait patiently for you to come back. You are taking a big chance, Amelda. That is if you really do care for him. Roderic is a very handsome man, you know. Others might not be content to let him sit waiting. Stop behaving so irresponsibly. I don't want to see you make a mess of your life a second time.'

'What is that supposed to mean?' Amelda blazed, the colour draining from her face.

'All I am asking, Amelda, is that you should play fair. Michael Owen was old enough, and self-opinionated enough, to look after his own interests, as you found out to your cost. Roderic is different. He's much more vulnerable.'

'Rubbish! He can take care of himself,' Amelda muttered, sulkily.

'He loves you deeply. You can hear it in his voice, see it in every look he gives you,' Nesta went on implacably. Her dark eyes were pleading as they locked with Amelda's.

'I refuse to listen to any more of this,' Amelda snapped, snatching up her anorak and running from the house.

Outside, a freezing fog festooned the bare trees. Shivering, she sought the shelter of her car. The cold stung her hands and cheeks as she unlocked the door and slipped behind the wheel. The damp, grey mist shrouded Snowdonia. The Eyrie crouched like an old man sheltering hunched under a grey cloak. Soon, though, it would be spring . . . the snow would melt from the tops of the mountains, lambs would be born, flowers would carpet the fields and hedgerow, but she wouldn't be there to enjoy any of it. By the time she returned it would be high summer, the lambs would be full grown, the harvest ready to be gathered in.

She drove to the cemetery where her grandfather had been laid to rest. As she walked across the close-clipped grass between the graves she saw with pleasure that the headstone donated by Plaid Cymru, as a tribute to one of their staunchest supporters, had been erected. It took the form of a winged dragon mounted on a stone plinth. The inscription read:

RHYS EVANS 1901–1977

An idealist and a true Welshman
Upholder of Plaid Cymru and its aims

The simple words brought tears to her eyes. It said so little but conveyed such a powerful message to those who had known and loved him.

With a stab of nostalgia, she thought of him with deep affection. His proud bearing, his penetrating dark eyes and his grey pointed beard. She had respected his wisdom. He had been so fiercely determined. In his fight to keep Wales for the Welsh, he had been almost like one of the Crusaders of olden days, she thought reflectively.

She wished he had lived long enough to know that her affair with Michael Owen had ended. He had never liked Michael, or what he stood for. He would approve of Roderic, she thought with a smile. He had seen him grow up, shared knowledge and wisdom with him. Roderic even farmed the mountains Rhys had loved so intensely.

Yes, he would have approved of Roderic, a man after his own mould.

She remembered the tears in Alice Roberts' eyes when she had told her of Rhys's great love for his wife and how for over fifty years he had remained faithful to Eleanor's memory.

'Rhys must love you a great deal, Amelda,' she had murmured. 'You are so very much like Eleanor when they first met. She was dainty and sweet-natured and had the face of a porcelain doll with her lovely amethyst eyes. You take a look at yourself in the mirror, and you'll see what I mean.'

'I must go on this trip, Granda, just to prove to myself that I am of some use in the world. Atone for my sins, if you like,' she sighed. 'If Roderic still wants me when I get back, then, for the rest of my life, I shall try to be as true to him as you were to your Eleanor,' Amelda vowed out loud as she stood stroking the headstone.

'That's a tremendous pledge to make. He would be proud of you.'

Amelda swung round at the sound of Roderic's voice.

'You startled me!' she gulped, her heart beating faster as she looked up into his craggy face.

'Your mother said you had gone out. I thought I might find you here . . . saying goodbye to Rhys. I didn't want you to leave with a cloud of uncertainty hanging over us,' he added sternly, his light blue eyes opaque and unreadable.

'Oh, Roderic,' she sighed and shrugged her shoulders helplessly. 'I'm so confused. Now that it's almost time for me to go I'm not even sure I am doing the right thing after all.'

'It's your decision,' he said stonily, a muscle at the side of his face twitching.

'I . . . I'm going to miss you so very much,' she murmured uneasily, her amethyst eyes misting.

'Stop playing fast and loose with me, Amelda,' he exclaimed exasperatedly. His mouth tightened as he drew away from her, his hands clenched into fists. 'If you really care for me, then admit it. Otherwise, go right out of my life.'

He gathered her close and for a moment she was content to rest against the hard warmth of his body, feeling safe and secure within the enclosure of his muscular arms. Then, reluctantly, she pushed herself free of his embrace. Holding her head back proudly, looking him directly in the eyes.

'It's no good, I must go through with this trip, Roderic,' she said determinedly. 'To pull out now, after persuading them to let me go with them, would cause chaos.'

For a long moment he regarded her with a steel-blue gaze that penetrated to her heart.

'Please don't reproach me,' she whispered. 'I seem to spend my time letting people down.'

She stood with her back towards him, the tears streaming down her face. Why had she made such a mess of things? No one had ever meant so much to her as Roderic, she thought unhappily. Her mother had been right . . . she was ruining her life all over again.

She felt so utterly deflated that she offered no resistance when Roderic swung her round to face him, his fingers digging into her shoulders like rods of steel.

'Stop prevaricating, Amelda. I just want a straight answer . . . the truth this time. Are you going on this jaunt just to tantalise me or . . .'

'No! No! No! I love you Roderic!'

'Oh, Amelda! I'm desperately in love with you!' he told her fiercely, pulling her back into his arms, and kissing her hard. 'I want you on any terms. I wouldn't dream of stopping you from going on this trip, just as long as you promise to hurry back.'

'I will . . . I promise.' Her face became suffused with colour, her eyes soft and dreamy. 'I meant every word I said to Granda,' she whispered softly.

His lips hovered over her eyes and cheeks for a brief moment then united with hers in the deepest of tender kisses.

'I came to ask if you would like me to look after Shep while you are away,' he told her when at last they drew apart. 'I imagine he's going to miss you almost as much as I am. I don't suppose your mother will have much time for taking him out.'

'That would be marvellous! He would certainly be far happier on the farm than shut up at home,' she smiled gratefully.

'And having him with me would be a daily reminder of you,' he grinned as he kissed her lightly.

'So you really did mean it when you said you would be waiting for me when I got back,' she sighed happily.

'Yes, I'll be waiting,' he told her solemnly. 'Why don't we fix a date for our wedding right now?' he suggested. 'That way, I can go ahead and make all the arrangements so that we can be married the moment you get back.'